I0600795

VICTIMS
Part 1

By: Preston Lingle

This book is a work of fiction. Names, characters, places, and incidents are the product of the author's imagination or are used fictitiously. Any resemblance to actual events, locales, or personas, living or dead, is coincidental.

Copyright © 2017, 2021 by Preston Lingle

All rights reserved. This book or any portion thereof may not be reproduced or used in any manner whatsoever without the express written permission of the publisher except for the use of brief quotations in a book review.

Cover by: Lauren Poitras
Edited by: Annie Pickerd & Preston Lingle

Printed in the United States of America
10 9 8 7 6 5 4 3 2 1

ISBN-10: 0-9993427-0-3 ISBN-13: 978-0-9993427-0-1 (pbk.)
ISBN-10: 0-9993427-1-1 ISBN-13: 978-0-9993427-1-8 (hbk.)
ISBN-10: 0-9993427-2-X ISBN-13: 978-0-9993427-2-5 (ebook)

IngramSpark Publishing
14 Ingram Blvd
La Vergne, TN 37086
www.ingramspark.com

First Printing, 2017
Second Printing, 2020
Third Printing, 2021

To Grandpa Brinkley

Chapter 1

I was born in the summer of the year 2022, on June 16th. At least, that's what my father told me. He seemed to know the dates of everything; he made a makeshift calendar after the world fell into chaos. He fixated himself on what date it was and how much time had passed since the end of civilization, known as The Fallout. When he made a new calendar each year, he drew stars on dates he didn't want to forget— New Years, Valentine's, Easter, Christmas, wedding anniversary, etc. He only circled one day on every calendar: June 16th. He put an obscene number of circles on that day, and he always pushed his pen fiercely on the paper. My father was passionate about keeping-up on the dates when I was younger; it was his way of coping with the ruined world, I guess.

My mother, however, used me as her coping mechanism. Some of my earliest memories included my lying in her protective arms while she rocked back and forth in her armchair. She read me stories from a selection of fairy tales and made me laugh. She performed the voices of all the characters and sang me songs from a handful of nursery rhymes from in the book, lulling me to sleep with her beautiful sound. I would often attempt to grab the fairy tale book. I was too young to read, though, and she would laugh at my attempts. She taught me basic words at first, but I caught on quickly; I was a sharp kid and a fast learner.

I recall a conversation between her and my father: He asked where she found the books she read to me, and she told him they were from the library. A library was a mystical place where thousands of books were stored. I remember this captivated me when I was younger. A land that existed before the time of barricaded windows and locked doors.

When I was young, my father forbade my mother and me from leaving the house. He didn't want us exposed to the badness of the world and intended to keep us safe. Thus, he was the one who would leave every day to find food and water for us. While he was gone, my mother led me around the house and taught me how to do simple duties and navigate my environment. I recall her showing me kindness. We used my father as a test subject at night before dinner. She taught me about love and what it means to love another, and the preciousness of life.

My mother was instrumental in my upbringing until I was six years old. I didn't talk much, outside of my mother's teachings. One day, however, I remember waking up and not finding my mother downstairs in her armchair, where she waited for me every morning. She would wake early and patiently wait for me so that we could embark on an exciting new day. I hardly remember the features of her figure, but her face and smile I can never forget. That face was not in the chair that morning; it was my father instead. He stared into the fire in the fireplace, which he must have kept alive all night. I asked him, "Where's mommy?"

He replied in his uniquely gruff tone—sorrow in his throat: "She's gone."

For the next year, I stayed confined to the house. My father left during the day to find supplies, including food and water. I waited to "protect the house," he told me. I attempted reading through the old fairy tales my mother read me, but I could only remember a few words—the rest were foreign to me. I could only half-remember the rhymes she sang, too.

Another year had passed, and it as my seventh birthday. I recall sitting by the front door of my house, beating my hands against my thighs in a rhythmic fashion, waiting for my father to come back. He'd gone to search for food; he hadn't found anything in a while, and we started to go hungry. However, we did have plenty of water—my father gathered a lot on his last run out. I didn't know where he went during the day. Whenever I asked to help, he'd always reply in the same low, depressed tone, "No." He'd sigh and continue, "I got this..." then grab an empty sack and leave without another word. I sat by the door until he came back.

Every day was cold, especially without a fire roaring in the fireplace. My father didn't allow me to touch the fireplace while he was gone. Most days, I curled into a ball and shivered as I waited for him to return. I stretched my legs often. I blew into my hands to keep warm. Wind seldom blew through cracks in the door, but it would cut through my entire body, and I became colder.

I heard footsteps outside. I stood, backed away, and my father entered. I ran to him. He stopped, shook his head, and I noticed the empty sack.

"That's two days now," I whimpered.

"I know. I'm sorry." He walked into the house, and I stepped to the side.

Our house reflected the outside; dirty, dusty, and gray. Everything had gathered dust. A blackened tint plagued the walls and crumbs of decaying remnants of food laid upon the stained carpet. Wooden veneers battened the windows, preventing me from looking outside. Our house was set up with a dining table in the corner and beyond that our cramped kitchen. Thankfully, we had a gas stove and gas to run it, so we could efficiently cook food when he had to. My father was an avid match-collector in his past life and collected matchbooks from restaurants and various locations. We always had a small flame to ignite the gas.

To the left of the entrance was our living room. A TV lay wasted in the corner—useless, as it sat upon a banister where dust gathered around the TV and balustrade behind it. Our fireplace sat indented in the wall, with a worn-down couch facing the fireplace and a reclining faded blue armchair. The chair faced the dusty TV. It was the chair my mother used to read to me. Now, it was my father's chair.

My father entered the house, shut the door behind him, and walked over to the fireplace. He pulled two packs of matches and a piece of flint from the sack. I remember thinking he was a magician; he said the bag was empty, and yet he was pulling items from it. He entranced me. He also pulled dust out of the sack—lots of it. He spread the dust overtop the wood in the fireplace, like a blanket that could comfort the raw log. He ripped a match from one of the matchbooks, struck it aflame, then threw it into the fire. He watched the dust ignite and give birth to a more significant flame that encompassed the wood. He stared into it the whole time.

I was amazed by my father in my younger life—he always did amazing things. He'd go into the dangerous world and explore all it had left. Then, he'd bring home things I thought were extraordinary. He awed my seven-year-old mind. In a way, he was my hero. At the time, he was my world.

He stood before the fireplace—contently focused on the flickering flames of the burning wood. This was my father's nightly routine—light a fire, sit, and stare. I decided to sit on the floor in a crisscross position—relative to the warmth of the fire—in my father's shadow. He towered over me, and was built like a Neanderthal: thick skin, hair all over, and wore flannels with the same jeans for years.

He turned away from the fire and walked over to his chair. He exhaled a loud grunt as he sat. He looked at the flint and matchbook in his hand and made them dance in his palm. The inorganic materials put on a show for me. Seconds later, he stopped and put the items on top of a nearby end-table. He placed them on top of a book, black and very thick. At one time, the sides of the pages had a shining quality but weathered with age. I used to open it and look at the black scrawls on the pages, but the English were too archaic for me to understand. To me, they were only symbols put together in some seemingly organized manner. Dust smothered its cover. Even if I tried to clear it, I couldn't see its title. Resting beside the book was a dusty lamp that sat unused. A light bulb was still inside the lamp, but it wouldn't turn on.

The items laid flat on the book for a few moments before the flint slung back into my father's dirty fingers. The light from the fire reflected off the flint and into my eyes—I looked away. I saw my father look at himself in the flint's reflection. He turned his head and rubbed his hairy chin with his caveman-like hands.

"Get me the knife," he commanded after a short while. I looked up, shocked that he spoke while we were in the company of silence. We hardly ever talked to each other; my father generally preferred the quiet, especially while the fire roared.

With no questions asked, I quickly got up from the floor, and briskly walked into the kitchen. It received more upkeep than the rest of the house. My father enjoyed cooking—it was one of the small pleasures he had in life. He hadn't been in the kitchen for a few days, so the dust began to settle once more. The dining table had a cloth draped across it, and some burnt candles laid toppled on its surface. The kitchen also had an island between the sink and refrigerator, usually covered in canned goods and plates of food. Today, it was empty. The stainless steel sink was so clean that stale water could fall from a flask and easily slide down its flange. The refrigerator didn't keep anything cold—it just stood as extra storage. We kept water in it, held in various jars, bottles, etc. The cabinets in the kitchen held bowls, plates, cups, and other essentials.

Knives sat perched in a knife holder, who sat by the sink, directly underneath a cabinet. We had a verity of knives, but the knife my father wanted to be the big one: the butcher's knife. I drew it from its sheathe and gazed upon it. Its blade was the size of my head at the time. It was marvelous to look at—and clean, too. I carefully paced, knife in hand, toward my father. I offered him the knife, and he yanked it from my hand. I jumped away—the image of my father with the knife scared me. He brought the knife to his eyes and studied it from all angles. He matched the knife to his flint and struck it a few times until a large spark erupted. The light astonished me— my father's ability to conjure flames from the knife, and flint made me believe he was magical.

My father turned the knife away from him, with the blade pointed outward. It took me a moment to realize that he wanted me to return the knife to the kitchen. I approached with caution. I put my hand across the end of the blade and wrapped my fingers around it. I pulled on the knife to release it from my father's grip, but my hands slipped, and my fingers slid up the blade. I quickly went back and pulled again—this time successfully from my father's hands. I made my way to the kitchen and laid the knife in the sink. It had a streak of red on it, and I saw my index finger slit open, blood oozing from the perforation. I panicked while the red river ran down my hand. I rushed to the fridge and poured water on my hand over the sink. It wasn't a deep cut, so it washed away easily. I also cleaned the knife so there no blood would smear its sheen. I applied pressure to my wound with my shirt until the bleeding stopped. I dried the knife with my shirt, too, and re- turned the knife to its holder.

When I entered the living room again, I heard my father say, "What were you doing in there?"

"I was, uh," I stammered. I didn't want to reveal my cut. "Um...cleaning off the knife."

My father grunted and looked at my shirt. "What's the red spot?" he asked.

I completely forgot about the stain I created to stop my bleeding. "I, uh, hurt myself earlier when I waited for you to get back," I replied. "Sorry."

He gave me a stern look, then turned from me to the fire. A sense of relief washed over me, and I stood there for a few seconds in recuperation. I returned to the floor in my original crisscross position, my back leaned against the couch, facing the fire.

We sat in silence for the rest of the night—looking at the fire until it had almost died out. We could hardly see the wood which kept it alive.

"I'm going to bed," my father mumbled. He slowly rose from his armchair, and leisurely shuffled his way up the stairs where our bedrooms were.

"Goodnight!" I yelled. No reply.

I stayed in the living room until the fire ultimately died, and I could see nothing at all. As darkness enveloped the room, I crept around in a crouched position. I felt strangely safe when it was dark out; I felt hidden, like a ninja. Though, I bumped into every object I could—very un-ninja like. I was not the most graceful kid.

Soon, I heard noises from outside the windows. I froze. I never heard noises like this before—especially not at night. I heard what sounded like a woman screaming for her life; my blood ran cold, and my hair stood on end. The noise was then cut short. Some footsteps echoed through the windows. An orange ball of light floated and shined between the boards on the glass. It stopped in front of me, and I saw the faint outline of a face staring back at me. I sat still, paralyzed by fear. Despite my petrification, I looked upon the mystery creature with curiosity. I slowly became less scared and more inquisitive about the situation: Why were they outside at night? Who were they? What caused that blood-curdling scream, and why did it end so abruptly? Did they have food?

A couple of seconds later, the face left, and the ball of light followed. I was once again left in the dark. I rubbed my arms and shivered.

Chapter 2

I recall a day when I was eight years old when my life changed forever. It began as a regular day for me; I awoke to a coughing fit from the vast amount of dust in my room. I wiped my eyes until I could see again. I got out of bed and surveyed the room. Next to my bed was a nightstand with nothing on it or in it. Across from the nightstand was a dresser, which was also empty, with a small pile of clothes lying beside it. My room was rather desolate.

I walked over to that small pile of clothes and swapped the pajamas I was wearing with the clothes on the ground; a long-sleeve gray shirt and faded blue jeans—my signature attire. They were the warmest clothes I had, though the house was cold anyway unless the fire was on. I never slept by the fire, as it was dead before I was tired enough to sleep. My father only slept in his bedroom. I like to believe he slept there so he could pretend my mother sat next to him, watching him sleep.

I reached underneath the dresser and retrieved my pair of red tennis shoes. I was beginning to grow out of them, and they were uncomfortable to wear; I told my father about them weeks before, but he hadn't come home with any new shoes.

Upon exiting my room, I saw my father exiting his. I was never allowed into his room when I was younger. I believed his room was mystical and magical, like him. My mind imagined the room stuffed with warmth, food, and comfort; it would be clean and have running water—electricity, even! My father spoke about the mystical energy known as electricity before, which he described as a magic power that does all sorts of things. It turned on lights, it cooked food, it kept food cold, it pumped water, it heated a home. My father never found any of this energy after the world ended, but I liked to imagine he had some locked away in his mysterious room.

I caught a quick glimpse of his room while he exited: the room had a pinkish tint, and I saw a nightstand next to his bed. I thought I saw a picture-frame—he shut the door, promptly and loudly. I waved to my father, startled. He walked away.

I followed my father down the stairs and into the kitchen, where he poured himself a mug of water. He went into the living room and sat in his chair. I stood for a few seconds, then jumped to the floor, sitting in front of his mighty legs.

"What are we doing today?" I asked, displayed in an innocent voice.

"I'm going out," He replied as if he was already tired of my nagging.

"Where are we going?" I said, prying and trying to get something out of him.

"I don't know."

"What do you mean, 'I don't know'?"

"I don't know."

"You have to have somewhere you go a lot."

"I don't."

"So, you just walk around?"

"Yes."

"Ok, then," I said. I thought he was playing with me at first. To be honest, that was the most he had spoken to me in months. Most mornings, he walked out of the door before I was awake. He fell into a habit of leaving earlier and earlier each day—not drinking or eating anything. He'd come back just before sunset and go straight to bed. The past couple of months, he left his bag behind, too. It sat in the kitchen corner, wasting away. He did, however, make sure we had enough food and water all the time, unlike in years past. I wasn't sure how he did it—I never saw him restock our supplies—but somehow, we always had something to eat and drink. My father also stopped lighting fires as the years passed. We had the wood, the matches, and the other materials needed to start fires, but he never did. I didn't know how to start a fire since he never taught me—there was never a roaring fire in the house like there used to be.

In any case, I remained seated on the space in front of him, stupidly staring up to him. A few minutes passed until my father emptied his mug and placed it on the countertop. I scurried away as he rose from his perished throne. I glanced over my shoulder and noticed his figure pass in my peripheral vision. Then, I heard his creaking footsteps toward the door. He exited; I didn't detect the usual, "SLAM!" of the door this time, though.

I began my daily routine. I ran upstairs and attempted to open my father's bedroom door. Locked again, as usual. Next, I'd fix my bed and pat the bedsheets in the vain attempt to get some dust off it. It usually ended up with me coughing a lot, and I'd stop trying.

Then, I'd walk downstairs and open the closet in the hallway next to the stairs. The only things in that closet were a couple of old jackets and a small metal baseball bat, which leaned against the wall to prop itself up. I would then walk around and look at all the empty shelves our house contained. I always wondered what used to be up there. Perhaps pictures of my young mother and father before the world ended? The only image I'd ever seen/knew about in the house was in a kitchen drawer. The drawer mainly contained several towels of different faded colors: light blue, green, pink, orange, etc. At the bottom, underneath all the rags, was a picture frame. This picture was also part of my daily routine.

In a white apron and chef's hat, the picture was that of my father standing inside of a building. He was pointing with a big butcher's knife, the same one we had in our house, at a sign that read, "Amit's Kitchen". My father was so young in this picture. He had shorter hair, paler skin, clean-shaven; his eyes were open, as opposed to the sort of half-open trance they'd taken then. The oddest thing about the picture was his smile. My father was smiling. I hadn't seen the man smile before. Ever. His happiness in this picture made it valuable to me. Beneath the pictures were medals and patches; tiny stars dotted the spot. The decorations were cold to the touch and pointed on their ends. I couldn't decipher the faded letters engraved into the metal, but I still felt a sense of pride from holding them. Then, I'd stow the picture and patches untouched until they graced my presence the next time. I never saw any pictures with my mother in them.

After leaving the kitchen, I organized the dinner table, straightened out the tablecloth, pushed in the chairs to be equidistant from each other, and set the plates and utensils at precisely the right place. I was the only one who ever ate from that table, since, to my knowledge, I was the only person in the house to eat anything. I mostly cleaned up my mess from the day prior.

Once I cleared the table, I'd go through the house and attempt to plug in every electronic item to an outlet. My father told me before that the objects in our house used to draw electricity from the outlets. Every day I would plug in the lamp, TV, and fridge, but they never turned on. I always tried anyway, hoping their lights would turn on one day.

After I unplugged the fridge from its socket, I walked into the living room in defeat to sit on the couch. Right before I sat down, I felt a cold wind against my skin. I shivered. I walked over to the closet at the other end of the house, opened it, and grabbed a thick jacket from in there. I decided to take one of the ones my father never wore since they were more substantial.

The jacket was dark and dusty and made of dark, brownish-green denim.

Dust glazed a tiny tint of gray onto it. It was too big for me at the time, but I threw the jacket on nonetheless and felt its warmth; it was warmer than any coat I had ever worn. As I began to feel my fingers once more, I wondered where the odd chill originated. Upon that thought, I immediately checked the door.

The door was slightly cracked open, allowing the cold air from outside to enter the house. My father hadn't fully closed the door when he left. Intrigued, I looked out and exited the home, carefully closing the door behind me.

I never left the house before that moment. I don't know what compelled me to leave the safe containment that the house provided. My eyes strained as I coughed heavily into my jacket. After a few minutes, my eyes didn't hurt so much, and the coughing died down. It was this moment as well that I found out our house had a porch. To my right was a swing that hung from the top of the porch, and next to it an empty pot. I walked down the porch and off the stairs, periodically coughing into my jacket. Our lawn had dead grass all along the surface—no sign of life anywhere on it, similar to our neighborhood. Ruined homes dotted the street, grounded, with a dark gray atmosphere. It wasn't as cold as it was inside the house, surprisingly. Maybe it was the addition of the jacket onto my attire that was warming me up, but even when I wore the jacket inside, the house seemed much colder than the outside air. The most biting aspect of the outside was the bone-chilling wind that cut through my entire body as it passed by. Although the jacket seemed not to be affected by the wind, it was a shield from the wind and fragile air of the world.

The outside was still so surreal to me and became increasingly more perplexing the longer I stood there. Our home provided me with a world that I knew—a world that was mine, albeit the dust and chaotic mess of its contents. I knew what to expect in the house. Any place else, and I didn't know what sorts of monsters would exist.

My father told my mother and me never to go outside: "The end of the world changes people," I remember him saying. I never really questioned him before. Anything he'd say

I'd just mindlessly follow, and I believed everything he said as the truth and nothing more. The image of the monster who gazed upon me that one night was another excellent deterrent for me to stay inside.

Without thinking, I took a few steps away from the porch and was eventually looking back upon the house from a distance. I don't know what compelled me to walk away from my little haven that day. Maybe it was out of curiosity for what was out there in the world. Maybe it was to spite my father. He went outside every day, not taking me with him, let alone asking me to go with him, or offering to teach me how to do anything I'd need to survive this hell-ridden world. He'd go out and do who-knows-what while I was confined to the inside, obediently waiting—just for him to ignore when he got home. I was like a dog waiting for his master—day after day.

Come to think of it, I'm positive it was the latter reason why I left the house that day.

Chapter 3

I explored like an eight-year-old in the ruins of society. My mind raced while I witnessed the destroyed world with my innocent eyes. My sheltered, caged mind had forgotten how bad the outside was. Or, at least, I learned again how bad the outside could be.

Continuing down the road, a massive gust of wind blew by. I saw it toss and turn the loose dirt on the ground. Buildings creaked around me and cried out in pain. I was unaffected. My father's jacket insulated me from the gust. At that moment, I felt superior.

I walked for what felt like an eternity. I had no destination in mind, but I didn't want to return home. I saw an alleyway to my left; it was cold and dark. I was reminded of the closet back home.

When I left the alley, the area lit up, and I witnessed the most beautiful thing I had ever seen—the city. I was breathless—speechless. It was so gorgeous—how come I'd never seen it before? How come I'd never known about it? Why didn't I leave the house sooner? I never wanted to forget this sight. I fell in love for the first time.

The city held a shade of gray, and a tint of decayed yellow. The colors were so enriching—they seemed to dance wherever they were. They skated across the asphalt and landed in the numb grass. They ran along the sides of buildings and raced up taller ones. One of the buildings was so tall it kept going until the hazy sky which loomed overtop the city engulfed it. This giant was magnificent and beautiful—a marvel to behold. It was visible everywhere in the city, and its size trumped all else in its wake. It commanded attention.

The city amazed me. I couldn't get over how perfect it was; quiet, yet so loud at the same time. I continued to walk through the streets of the city, observing all I saw. Brick structures protruded everywhere, some of which had tents inside them. There were bikes in pieces, rusted, overturned cars, their original colors faded. Street signs looked burned away. They disgusted me—ashes everywhere. There were ashes in places that didn't seem carried away with the wind. It looked like people lived here at some point. Now, it was only me in this city.

I passed a small building with the word "DINER" across the top of its see-through glass doors. The windows of the establishment were cracked and shattered. I found one that I could safely maneuver through and entered.

There were objects destroyed by time. Bright red, sparkling booths were attached to the walls, their posture parallel to the floor. They seemed to have lost their brightness and sparkles with time. Their padding was ripped and torn apart, with the insulation from the seats pulled out. As I approached, a few spiders scuttled out from the places; I backed away.

Lights dangled from the ceiling—old electrical wires pulled from their rightful spaces. Terrified that they would fall on top of me, I shuffled away.

Dirt, dust, and debris covered the wooden counter. I ran my hand across the wood; it was surprisingly smooth. I lifted my hand and observed the mass concentration of dust it collected; it felt a little funny and fuzzy like it was furry. I quickly ran my hand down my jeans to wipe my hands. I looked back at the counter and noticed my hand created a path; an area left behind where the wood seemed to sparkle. I hardly saw my reflection; long, thick brown hair rested upon my head, slightly obscuring my amber eyes. My father's jacket drowned my scrawny body. I sighed, and dust coated the clean space once more.

After leaving the diner, I continued to walk the streets. My head tarried upward to gaze upon the immense high-rises. The hazy sky moved fast; it made me uneasy. My mind wandered while I walked—lost in my thoughts and the questions

I kept asking how everything got into the city, how it was built, and how it became ruined. I'd let my imagination run wild, and I'd create a world in my head where there were people—like my father and me—who laid bricks in a cube-like formation to build houses beside the street. They used enormous animals to assist their work, and electricity flowed through objects to create wondrous structures. The stories my mother told me in fairy tales altered my perception of the city and made it magical, abstract, and safe.

My original pace through the city was casual and calm. Despite the city's alluring presence, I didn't want to run through it. I'd never experienced such pulchritude; I only wanted to stop and stare.

This mindset stayed until I heard a noise amongst my entrancement of the beautiful structures that brooded over me. I froze mid-stride when I recognized footsteps pounding on the imperfect pavement. I swiftly and slyly crouched behind some nearby debris. There was a small breach in the wreckage, where I peeked from my cover. I saw something more beautiful than the city, more beautiful than the buildings, the sky, the "DINER"—all of it. Through the debris, I saw another person.

Up until then, I only knew the lives of me, my father, and my mother. I never had any outside human contact due to my confinement to that house for eight years. I may have subconsciously believed in others' existence, but I'd never seen anything to support that theory. I thought we were the only ones left.

Even though I was excited to see another person, I stayed vigilant—peering through the peep-hole to get a better analysis of them. I only saw the backside of them, but they didn't seem to look like how my father and I looked; they were slightly shorter than I was, but not by much it seemed, about an inch or so. They had longer hair than I did, though. It extended past their lower torso, colored a blondish brown, in contrast to my dark brown hair. A tight-fitting, clean—not dirty and ripped—teal green shirt, jeans, and turquoise shoes cloaked their skin. This person reminded me of my mother in some ways. This other person allured me, but not in the same way the city did. I couldn't describe it at the time, but all I knew was that a little part of me wanted to go out and talk to the other human, but the other part of me was too scared or frightened to do so.

They were looking around left and right as if they were searching for something. I stayed behind the debris for a while and watched through my rusty anonymity. After a few seconds, I quietly and carefully looked up from the rubble and saw another block in the middle of the road I could hide behind, and it was a little closer to the other person. Carefully, I crouched down and slowly trod over to the debris. I was about halfway there, and a gust of wind blew, blowing dust in my face—I coughed by accident. The dead city's atmosphere amplified the cough to extend for miles. The other person cocked their head in my direction. We locked eyes from twenty feet away.

Its face was even more gorgeous; the perfect emerald-green eyes were wide and seemed to shimmer in the city's colors. The face's shape was slightly rounded, yet still defined by its small ears and tiny nose. Its mouth also sparked my interest, a little wider than mine, but the lips were much fuller. The mouth looked dry and trapped shut—as if it hasn't opened in years.

I stared at the petite figure as it stared back—studying me. I slowly stood from my crouching position to be upright, hoping to show I was no threat to them. Its head retracted a bit—out of instinct. We continued standing and staring without movement for only a second or two, but it felt like seconds turned minutes, turned hours. Time slowed as we contemplated our next move. I took a few cautious steps forward, and when I did, I saw the other person smile. A few inches more, and they turned around and bolted off in the other direction. Bewildered by the other human, and upset with not gaining nay answers, I gave chase.

The quiet city now turned into our obstacle course. We jumped over fallen structures and bounced on top of the asphalt with every step. We climbed up sides of buildings and ran downstairs with perfect grace. We jumped over potholes like it was hopscotch and swung off the desperate structures of buildings that no longer lived. The other person was acting like all this was just a big game, and the city was a well-defined arena at our expense.

Up ahead, I heard a high-pitched laugh, and in intervals, the other person looked back at me, smiling and giggling. I couldn't help but smile again.

This person seemed to know their way around the city, as they would run down alleys and come out of the other side to immediately hop over a porch on the right and slide off onto the dead grass. I, conversely, had no idea where I was going. I ended up far behind them a few times. The other person seemed to slow down and wait for me by trying to do a cool stunt, which involved climbing up a wall or jumping over a toppled trash can—which they could have quickly walked around.

An enjoyable wind blew through my greasy hair. It may have been the first time I experienced real fun. Before then, my version of fun was walking around the house every day, tediously cleaning up the house—neatly aligning everything before my father got home. This experience of running through the city helped fuel my drive not only to explore the city more, but it also made me even more interested in this other person. I wanted to catch up to them not only to have "won" our game but also to talk with them, learn about them, and be with them.

At one point, the person made a sharp 90° turn down an alleyway, to which I followed them and their bouncy hair. The alley was musty and a little hazy. I squinted to try and see, and

I slowed down impulsively. When I got out of the alleyway, I no longer saw the mystery person. I desperately searched the area, but they vanished. I ran around, back down where I came from, all to try and find them, but they had gone. I stopped running, bent over, and grasped my knees to catch my breath. While I panted from my exhaustion, I looked up for a moment. Suddenly, the gloom of loss didn't matter anymore; I unknowingly found the sole reason for the advancement of my life, and what drove me to keep coming back outside to the city; the library.

Chapter 4

The building had collapsed in on itself and didn't look like it was standing on its own anymore. The outsides looked scorched and tattered as if a horrible fire once lived on the perimeter of the building. It was entirely encapsulated by debris, which made it look like a distorted dome—it looked nothing like a library at all.

The thought of my mother crossed my mind. I recalled that scene where she and my father discussed the library—where she obtained the fairy tale book. I stood in front of the place where the entirety of my mother's memory came originated. I felt compelled to investigate.

As I gazed upon the destroyed building, a thought crossed my mind: What if the girl I chased was in there? We were playing together, after all. Maybe she hid in the library? A glimmer of hope shined, and I haphazardly approached the building. I saw no sign of the girl as I drew near and paced the library's perimeter. Spikey objects lined the border of the library—construction wire and foundation protruded from the debris. The library was like a fortified palace. Thankfully, I was too thick-headed to take the hint, and I continued to walk around it. On the third lap, I noticed a small breach within the protective coat of the library—a hole, meager enough for one person. I squeezed my way inside.

The small hole was indeed small; I barely fit inside it. I squirmed and dug my way through, pushing debris to the side and behind me to continue forward. I did so carefully, to avoid any sharp edges that could cut me.

Finally, my exhaustion from my long day turned on me; I started to pant uncontrollably. I felt my body getting progressively hotter. It began with a few drops of sweat, but I kept getting hotter—hotter—hotter—hotter until I started madly sweating. My breathing and heart rate shot up exponentially over the next few moments, and I couldn't get enough air to supply my lungs with the oxygen they desired. I hyperventilated while my body kept getting warmer, and my perspiration increased—the salty sweat started to form on my upper lip, trickling down to get caught in my open mouth. The walls began to cave in on me, and I couldn't go back because I felt trapped. So, I kept moving forward, slowly and painfully as my heart—and now my mind—began to race, and I was betting on my heart—not my mind—to win out. I felt every muscle in my body lock up, and my entire body pulsated as I endured every beat of my heart pump blood through my veins, sounding like an angry drumhead. I remember thinking to myself, "Why is it so hard to breathe? Why am I sweating so much? How come I feel this way? My heart's going to explode if I sit in here any longer, but I can't get out...I need to get out. I need to get out!" I screamed in agony as I rammed my hands and my fingers into the sharp, yet smooth debris and pushed them away from me to move forward. My hands scraped against rebar, and I started to see blood on some of the debris I was throwing behind me, but I was in no mood to feel pain at this moment. I kept yelling as if someone out there would hear my cries and answer my plea. My eyes watered from the dust clouds I created. Red covered my hands, and my legs ached from all the work I'd put them through. It felt like I was never going to reach the other side, like this was how it ended; I didn't know how much further I had to go and how long I had been digging this tunnel, or better yet if there was another side to it. My breathing intensified, and I shut my eyes as I continued to dig—dig—dig and kept digging. Dig—dig—dig until I could feel my hands no more.

And then I got out. A bright, warming light blinded my eyes. Dead air filled my lungs again. I rolled out of the hole and rested beside it. The ground felt like a cloud. It was carpeted and dirty, but I didn't care; I just appreciated its comfort. I looked at my hands that were dripping in sweat, dirt, and blood, and wiped them off on the carpet. The blood was still flowing out of my palms, so I decided to get up and find something to halt the bleeding.

I scanned the room. The library was completely different on the inside. Outside, it was rough and jagged, discouraging all from approaching. Its interior was warm and inviting—seats, couches, signs with happy faces, and flowers. There were books directly to my left on a shelf. More books lined the inner walls of the building; some on shelves, some not—some dusty, some not. The outside world's overall gray atmosphere was too present inside the library, but it seemed to compliment a feeling of odd comfort. The library felt more alluring this way. A ray of light shone through a large hole in the ceiling and illuminated where I stood. It didn't look to be manmade; it existed because of the library's crumbled foundation.

I slid my hands in my jacket pockets and surveyed more of the area. To my right was a long stretch of wood that extended to block off one area of the library—used to borrow the library books. There were contraptions behind the desk I never saw before—computers. Their screens were all cracked; their hardware torn from them.

Across from the desks were the children's books—the right led to the teen section and the general adult sections. Each section had a large sign miraculously hung from the ceiling. I gravitated toward the children's section and opened a few books. Everything had a smile attached to it; the clouds, the grass, even this giant orange ball at the top left of the page—the sun. In some stories, the sun had sunglasses; in others, it just existed. The people in the pictures were all wearing t-shirts and shorts and were having fun outside, playing in the alive, deep green grass. Everyone was smiling. Yet, still, the sun fascinated me the most. It was strange to think that something so far away was out there, and helped us regardless of how little we did for it...

There was one story where the sun was not there—it didn't appear on any of the pages. It was cloudy all the time in this story, and they weren't as light-hearted and cheerful as the others. Everyone was wearing a jacket, and the pictures looked cold. Droplets of water fell from the sky onto their coats and slid to the ground, creating puddles of water. People rushed to their homes, seeking shelter from the rain. White arrows protruded from and penetrated clouds, some rising from the pools of rain on the ground. I soon learned this book was about the water cycle.

After spending some time in the children's section, I began to wander around the library, astonished of all that was there. I stood in a house of literature, knowledge, and a link to a prior way of life—something up until this moment I'd never known how much I desired. I felt obligated to read and learn their secrets.

And so, I did. I left shortly after that moment, carving more room in the hole as I exited. It took me about two hours to get home because I didn't know the path back. I arrived at the house before my father did, and just in time, too. Right when I collapsed on the couch, my father walked in the door. Despite how tired I was, I still stood up to greet him as he walked in. I turned to face him, and I noticed for the first time a little spiky circle of red and white stripes, with gold in the center, resting on his jacket. Inside the gold was a large letter, "G." Many other letters surrounded the G in a clockwise formation, like a decipher ring. I'd never seen it on him before.

"What's that?" I asked him, pointing to the spiky circle.

"Nothing…just something I found," he bluntly replied.

"Well, what is it?" I cocked my head to the side as I asked.

"It's a pin. You, uh…attach it to your clothes," my father answered as he turned away and began to walk toward the kitchen.

"Oh. Ok." I was disappointed by my father's nature of brushing me off every chance he got. I glanced down at the floor, feeling shameful for even asking.

My father took a few steps, then looked over his shoulder and back at me. "You're wearing my jacket," he said. It was less of a question, but rather a bold statement.

"Uh...um..." I struggled to draw words in my panic, "I...uh, got cold."

My father paused, pressed his lips together, and bobbed his head. He then continued his walk to the kitchen. I ran upstairs and bolted to my room once he turned his back. I removed the jacket and set it at the foot of my bed. Realizing I hadn't eaten anything that day, and finally letting hunger set in, I climbed into bed starving but instantly fell asleep.

My dreams were filled with the smiling, sunglasses-wearing sun cast over the library, and the person I met that day was with me. We ran around with smiles on our faces, and warmth enveloped our bodies.

For the next year and a half, I regularly visited the library. It started as once a week, then two, then three, until it finally became a daily ritual. I tried to keep my visits a secret from my father—at least, for a while. I believed he would disapprove of me leaving the house and running off. However, I think my father eventually figured out I was going to the city all the time. So, my clandestine adventures continued, so perhaps he didn't care what I did.

Over time, I found a way to reach the library in about 20-30 minutes. It wasn't far from the house—it just took a little time to get there. At the library, I made a few modifications— mainly widening the entrance hole as I got older and bigger, removing the dust off the books and desks, and restocking the shelves to make the place look more civilized and well-kept. I began to fill my father's jacket a little more, but it was still too big for me. I continued to wear it, nonetheless.

Through my reading, I learned about everyday objects of the past: cars, buildings, stores, phones. Weather captured me the most, though, because I never experienced it; it was always dark, gray, cloudy, and cold. To imagine that there used to be the sun, and rain, and storms truly fascinated me. I read every book in the children's section that covered the weather. As my reading level grew, however, so did the technicalities of the weather. It got too intricate to continue reading about after a while.

After countless children's books, I felt as if they were becoming stale, and I could read them all with ease. So, I shifted to teen novellas. They took longer to read, and there weren't as many pictures, but I got the basic idea of what they were trying to say. The Giver was one of those books, and one of the few I still remember. It was about a boy living in a futuristic world where emotions and all kinds of humanistic traits are stripped away and given to a man called The Giver. The boy is chosen to become the next generation's "giver" and learns all about the past world. It reminded me of the world I lived in; how I was learning about this previous life, much like him, and yearning for knowledge.

I didn't know some of the words in these stories, mostly because they were more advanced than the 12-page children's stories. I could decipher them through context clues or by referring to the dictionary, which was conveniently next to the teen books. Nonetheless, the challenge of these books brought me to a better understanding of grammar—expanding my vocabulary and my encyclopedia of words.

I tried reading books in the reference/college section, but they were too expansive. So, I moved to the back of the library, where the adult novels rested. There were rows and rows and rows of books. They were towering rows, much taller than I was. There had to be hundreds of books there. I didn't know where to begin. After searching around, I found in the very back of the library a showcase of various novels titled, "best reads". I decided to start there, and I read all of them. I organized them by the covers; I was always one to judge books by their covers. For the most part, it worked out for me. Don't stop something that works.

It was a nonstop reading festival for me as I sped through all the books in the "best reads" section. After reading one of the books, "The Glass Castle", I began to learn more nonfiction books. I mostly read biographies of notable people (or at least, those who seemed notable), autobiographies, and a few documentary-like books. I was strangely drawn to biographies and learning about the lives of people who used to live in the old world. This was the closest connection to anything from the past world I could ever find. While at the library, I read plenty of stories—some classified as "fiction" others "nonfiction", but all were fiction to me. I tended to gravitate toward these stories to learn about the lives that people used to live and learn about the end of the world— how it came about, what happened, what it was—alas, to no avail. My father called the end of the world, "The Fallout", but I found nothing about it. Despite all my best efforts, attempts, and countless years of searching, nothing came close to detailing those events—nothing documented it. At that time, I felt as if I needed to know what happened so I could further my survival. Although, upon reflection, I mostly wanted to know more about everything, and the fall of civilization was the only thing that couldn't satiate my lust for knowledge.

I quickly honed my skills in other topics, such as math, science, and writing. I picked up the college textbooks again and read through them, now with a greater understanding of their subjects. I challenged myself using the tests found inside the books to quiz how much I retained after reading and wanted to learn more and acquire more knowledge.

These infrequent visits to the library allowed me to work harder toward learning everything I could from the library, and I began leaving the house earlier in the morning and returning later at night. I also tried to look through neighboring buildings for food and bottled water. The library became my little sanctuary. It was the only place that truly felt like home.

Chapter 5

At this point, I'd shut out my father—we hadn't spoken since I asked about the pin on his shirt, and that's how we liked it. I didn't care about what he did, and he the same. Aside from our dismissive glances, I hadn't experienced any other human interactions besides the mystery girl. I always hoped I would run into her again—or even someone else. Seeing that girl gave me hope that there were others around the city, but I was too afraid to see for myself. I stopped believing in monsters as I grew older, but I was still terrified to leave my daily routine.

So, when I saw him at the library, I was alarmed.

I remember dusting off the computer desks at the library when we met. They were cleaner than usual, but I cleaned them off with a rag like I always had. I looked at the amount of dust that stained the cloth and felt a little disgusted. I laid it down on one of the desks, then fingered through books on a moveable bookshelf. I heard a little bit of rustling coming from the entry hole, and my body stiffened. It's not the first time this had happened, though; sometimes the wind clipped some rocks and little chunks of debris fell into the entryway, but it still startled me every time. I continued looking at the entryway in suspicion, saw a head of hair emerge, and heard a grunt. I immediately dropped to the floor, crouched, and took a deep breath. I was excited to see that other person, but was scared for my life all the same.

I breathed inaudibly, trying to hold my breath as much as possible. Their footsteps came closer, and I stayed crouched, paralyzed. I quickly and quietly darted around the cart to its side, where the overhead from the desk shrouded me in an area of darkness. I hid there, hoping the intruder wouldn't notice me.

Soon, the pounding footsteps ceased. A feeling of relief washed over me. I stayed crouched for a few more seconds, until I eventually let out a small sigh and slid down on the ground, sitting with my legs outstretched. I placed my hand over my heart to feel the intensity of its pounding.

"Hey there," I heard him say, as his head popped down from the top of the desk.

My pounding heart skipped a few beats as I screeched. I jumped, bumping my head on the bottom of the desk. The boy laughed at my plight. "Sorry about that, kid; didn't mean to scare you...not that much, at least. Though, it was pretty funny!" he laughed.

"You aren't going to kill me, are you?" I asked him, terrified and rubbing my head.

"Oh wow, you're pretty quick to the point, aren't ya? Well, no, I'm not going to kill you. I'm one of the good guys," he replied with an awkward smile.

"Ok," I said, having to believe him. I crawled out from under the desk, still holding my head. I stood and turned to face him. "How'd you know where I was hiding?"

"Well, you aren't the most graceful kid," he said with a smirk. Still a bit on edge, I studied him. His skin was very dark and dirty; he probably hadn't cleaned himself in years. His short black hair sat atop his head like needles. His small green eyes made sharp movements, and bags of dirt and stress rested beneath his eyelids. His face screamed mixed emotions; even while smiling or laughing, he looked solemn and emotionless. His body sat erect on the desk, his soot-covered legs dangling in the air. The shirt he was wearing was a deep brown color, like the guise of tree trunks in a few of the children's books. It looked like the darkness of color was due to dirt and soot, and it had collected over some time. There were also splotches of black on the shirt.

He cocked his head at me and asked, "Uh...is there something on my face, or what?"

"Dirt," I hastily replied. He had a good laugh at that. I honestly wasn't trying to be funny, but this person found some humor in my words regardless.

"Well," he said, still chuckling, "I guess I do, don't I?" He stopped laughing and looked at me. I felt like now I was the one being evaluated. "I like you, kid. You seem to have a good head on your shoulders. You seem to know—not perfectly, but well enough—how to act in the face of danger," he paused and stared at me. "Nothing we can't work on, though," he said, emphasizing my stance—his eyes gave a condescending look. I then noticed I was still on guard the entire time he was talking. I tried loosening up a bit as he continued, "And, on top of all that, you still seem to be upbeat and cracking jokes, despite the situation we're all in." He extended his hand toward me. "Name's Victor Curl." I looked at his side and back at him. "Ok, don't rush..." he said, very distant, and retracting his hand, "Can you at least tell me your name?"

I stood there, scared, wondering if I could trust him. His appearance wasn't appealing, but he seemed to be smart and could deduce situations quickly. I glanced over him again to see if he had anything dangerous on him. I didn't see anything.

"Well?" he said, growing impatient.

"...Michael. Michael Amit." I extended my hand out and glanced at his. He smirked at it.

"Well, it's nice to meet you, Michael," he said to me. I just nodded my head. He took note of my tone and relaxed his mood. "So," he exhaled as he hopped back up onto the desk, "what brings you here to the library, Michael?"

"This is my home. Well, not really, but it might as well be," I replied.

"What's that supposed to mean?"

"It's just...I spend all my time here—at the library. As soon as I wake up, I walk down here, and I leave a little before sunset to be home safe before dusk."

"Why don't you just stay here then? Why even go home?"

"My father's there; I'm afraid he'll be mad at me or something. Not that he displays emotion ever. He probably wouldn't even care if I didn't come home..." Victor perked up to show interest. I continued, "My father's rather conservative; he keeps to himself a lot and doesn't care about me." I laughed. "I don't think he's ever really cared about me. All he does anymore is go out all day, and he doesn't return until a little after dark."

"That last part sounds a little like you, huh?" Victor said. I was silent and looked away at a boarded-up window. "Your father doesn't seem all that bad to me, though," he said, egging me to tell him more. "What about your mother? What's her story?"

"Good question," I said. "I haven't seen her in years. She just up-and-left one night; didn't even say goodbye."

"I'm sorry to hear that," he said. "Hopefully she's not dead or anything." I shot him a deadly look. "Ok, crossing a line, my bad—just trying to stay positive."

"And my father—he never does anything for me, either. He only ever cares about himself. He's been like that ever since I was young."

"Hmm... say, does your father wear a pin, by chance?" he asked.

"What?" I responded. It wasn't so much a question I wanted an answer to, but rather out of shock that he would know.

"Like a pin? That you wear? It's, like, a circle with red and white stripes, gold in the center with some engravings on it."

"Uh..." I hesitated to answer. I grew increasingly uneasy by how much he wanted to know about me—and how much he already seemed to know. He described my father's pin with such ease and clarity. For a second, I wondered if he had been following me for a while.

"You know what, uh, never mind. Disregard that." He rubbed his hands together for a few seconds and exhaled loudly. "So, what do you do here? At the library."

"Well, I read books here. I've read… " I turned around and looked at the vast collections of events and adventures that are documented around the room, "Most of these books."

"How long have you been coming here to the library?"

"A few years now," I replied, proud of my answer.

"Ah, you are smart! And you've read most of these books in that amount of time?" Vic added, seeming to be impressed. I nodded. "And you've been keeping track of the days?" he asked me.

"I don't particularly, no. My father has a calendar that he makes himself so he can keep track of the days and remind himself of certain events."

"But, you know how one works, and you could keep track if you wanted to, right?"

"I mean… I guess so, yeah. Why do you ask? Why do you keep asking me so many questions?"

"Oh, no reason. I'm just curious." Victor poked and prodded under the surface of everything I said, but then seemed to back off before getting too far in. "Anyway," he once again changed the topic, "I got ya beat. For coming to the library, I mean. Been coming here my whole life, kid," Victor said. I suddenly felt inferior to Victor and involuntarily grew visibly upset, displaying a frown. He took notice of this and began to laugh.

"How old are you?" I asked.

"Me? I'm sixteen," he replied with little to no hesitation. I expected at least some resistance, but he gave up the information easily. "And you?" he asked in return.

"Oh, uh, twelve. I'm twelve. Almost thirteen."

"Oh, wow. You were born the same year as The Fallout; twelve years ago."

There it was, the information I had been seeking. It was my first time hearing about The Fallout outside of my mother or father. I realized that this guy, Victor, might be my link to what I want to know about The Fallout. I decided if I wanted to know anything more, I had to stay near this person. He held the answers.

"You, uh," I began to say, "You said earlier that my father had a pin on his shirt?"

"Oh. Just disregard that; it's not important," he said, trying to brush it off.

"No, it is important. It's a tiny pin that looks like a spiky circle of red and white stripes, with a gold dot in the center. It has letters engraved on it."

Victor looked surprised. His mood changed from annoyed to enthused. "Yeah, that's the one. Exactly..." He stopped and looked like he was slowly pondering something. "Do you remember when he first got the pin?"

"Yeah," I replied, "A few years ago he came home with it on his shirt; he was a little distant about it. I didn't notice it at first, so he could have had it for longer, but..." I trailed off in my thought.

Victor was a mixture of both broken and excited. He got up and walked away, flipped through a few books on the cart, then glanced back at me. "How would you like to join us?"

Flabbergasted and confused, I asked, "What do you mean? Join who? Join what?"

"I..." Victor sighed before he continued, "I probably shouldn't be telling you this, but I have this group of people I live with," he sounded reluctant. "We band together to survive. We all have similar interests and similar pasts, and it all revolves around those pins, like the one your father has."

My ears perked. My interest sparked. My blood ran cold. My bones turned frail as I heard that there were other people out there in the world—people that shared my interests—

people that shared my past—people like me. I involuntarily asked, "Where?"

Victor smiled, chuckling to himself. "In that case, I guess I'll show you." He began to walk away, toward the hole that leads to the outside—I followed. It's incredible how one simple word could set off a chain reaction of events that would create the rest of my life. My one word incited a response within Victor, and he knew precisely what I meant. Human interaction was still relatively new to me then, and it amazed me how we seemed to be so in tune with one another at that moment.

I looked back at the library and reflected upon all the time I spent there. Out of all the books I'd read, all the adventures my mind went on, all the things I'd learned, and all the things I had yearned to learn, none could compare to the series of events about to unfold.

Victor spoke: "Come on, let's go, while there's still daylight."

"Yeah... right behind you, Victor," I replied. I felt sad leaving this place I called home.

"It's not like you can't come back here, Michael," Victor said, sympathetic. I blew a sigh of relief. He chuckled, smirked, then said, "And you can call me Vic; my friends call me Vic."

I chuckled, too, knowing he was trying to make me feel better. While we wormed through the dug-out hole of the library, I said, "And you can call me Mike: my friends call me Mike."

Chapter 6

The city held a different vibe with Vic—far different than when I walked by myself. He took different routes and had a distinct sense of exploration. While I was in awe of everything, he had a more analytical approach—looking for something he could use. He continuously scanned the ground, looked for scraps—canned food, water bottles—anything he could use. Vic was not one for functional fixedness. He would regularly stop to bend down and sift through the gravel and dirt, pull out something resembling a bent wire, and tossed it back. Other times it wasn't a bent wire, but an open can, a cracked bucket, and a bottle of perfume. He picked up the perfume, sprayed it in front of him, and wafted it. He turned around and sprayed my shirt with it—a lot—and I ended up smelling like how I envisioned a field of roses would feel. I liked the scent but also realized it was a bit silly. Vic couldn't stop laughing after he sprayed me with it.

After a while, I became absentminded; I wasn't even conscious of the fact that I was following him; it just became an involuntary action for me.

We soon made it to our destination. I only knew we were there because Vic turned around and said, "Home sweet home, huh?" He presented the "home" with his hands. It looked run-down, like all the other houses and buildings along the streets of the city. It was about three stories tall, some of the sidings had fallen off, and a few windows were splintered. It was colored an even shade of brown and grey, which complemented the rest of the degenerate city.

I followed Vic into the building. I didn't see a door immediately, but there were a few planks of plywood covering an open area, which I guess constituted as a door. It blended in with the rest of the neglected area. Entering the building was paired with dust and dirt flying at my face; nothing I wasn't already used to, though. Cobwebs lived in the corners of the ceiling. Holes splattered the tile floor beneath us. To our left were a set of stairs, which we climbed. We walked forward into a big open room. I looked around and, despite the heavy coating of brown everywhere, something about it seemed homey. There was a candle-lit lamp sitting on an end table in the far-right corner next to a large window, still intact, that showcased the beautiful horizon of the city. To my left was more open space, a few supplies littered around, bags stacked on top of more bags, and a room that had a door cracked open, but all I could see inside was darkness. I entered the room and looked around.

"Heeey, stranger!" I heard a voice say from my right. I turned and saw another person and jumped. I landed on the floor and tried to crawl backward, away from the person.

"Hahaha, ease up, Mike," Vic told me, "That's just Billy."

"Billy Emule, if ya want my full-name!" he chirped. He offered his hand to me. I took it, and he lifted me off the ground with both hands easily. I noted his light blue eyes and his short, fixed brown hair. His shirt was a deep, faded blue, and he wore heavy cargo pants, pockets filled with things. He was heavier set, big-boned, and young, not much older than me. Despite being young, he still was intense—the grip he took on my hand was crushing. When he let go, I grasped my hand and tried to stretch it out. He wore some sort of circular cap atop his head.

"Now I told you," Vic began to say to Billy, "to take that stupid Yamaka off."

"But I like it," Billy said back, rather comedically.

"You aren't Jewish!" Vic retorted.

Billy grunted. He yanked off the Yamaka and slumped away, muttering something under his breath that sounded like, "You're not Jewish... "

I turned to Vic, looking for salvation. He said, "Let's go around and see where everyone else is cooped up."

We walked toward the room with the door cracked, and the closer we got, the louder and louder the sound of people talking became. Vic opened the door first, and walked through "Hey guys," I heard him say to everyone.

"Oh, hey, Vic," I heard someone reply, a male.

"So, uh, hey, I have something I want to show you all."

"This isn't another one of your random finds, is it?" I heard another male voice say. This one was a bit higher-pitched sounding.

"No! Well, I guess maybe... anyway," he turned around and he looked right at me. "Come on, then," and motioned for me to enter. I cautiously crept in and felt the heat of everyone's gaze. I tried to view them, but it was too dark for me to make out figures. Only I was illuminated by the outside light.

"Who's this?" I heard the first voice say.

"This is Mike; he's going to join us." Vic repositioned himself.

"What? You just bring someone in here and decide that he's going to live with us? You know that's not your call," I heard the same person say.

"Sure, but this guy's like us," Vic said, trying to defend me. "His father—"

"I don't care if he's a carbon copy clone of me, we don't just accept people in here without first letting your superior decide."

"You know I hate it when you say it like that," Vic playfully replied.

"Oooh, like I'm scared. I'm going to get him." The body stood up and walked toward my direction. He grew taller the closer he got to me and pushed me out of the way. I looked back at the crowd of people, feeling lower than I already was.

"Don't worry about him," I heard a new voice say. Its pitch was a lot higher than everyone else's. "He's always like that; nothing's ever good enough for him."

Vic turned around and said to me, "He doesn't like me, either." I tried to crack a smile, but my nerves got the best of me. I only contorted my lips to an awkward position, like I had a bad bite of food.

"How old are you, Mike?" I heard the same high-pitched voice ask.

"T-twelve. Almost thirteen." I looked down and rubbed my hands.

"Hey, that's how old I am!" The voice sounded happy and energetic. "Twelve, not thirteen. Everyone else here is older than me by at least a year. It's cool to meet someone the same age as me!"

"See, Mike? Someone else born the same year as society's downfall!" Vic said to me.

I didn't reply and continued to look down.

"Not much of a talkative type, is he?" I heard someone whisper.

"He's probably just nervous to be meeting this many people," Vic whispered back, loudly.

I heard footsteps and felt a presence behind me. I turned around and saw a man towering over me. He sported a faded, dark green beanie atop his flowing white hair. His face was pointed downward, which accentuated his chin. His eyes were brown. He wore a heavy green jacket overtop his white shirt, which stretched to cover his lower body. A black bandana with white marks on it draped around his neck. I nervously smiled back at him, hoping he wouldn't keep looking down on me for too much longer.

"Is this who you were talking about?" he leaned back to ask the person behind him.

"That's right. Vic brought him in," they responded.

"Hmm." The tall man walked over to Vic, grabbed his arm, gentle, but still assertive. "Mind if we talk for a minute, Victor?"

"Oh, uh, yeah, sure," Vic replied, nervously laughing all the while. The tall man leaned back into the room, pointed at me, and said, "And for his sake, turn a light on in here." He shut the door.

Someone in the room leaned over and lit a lantern, which sat on a crate next to them. The room irradiated a red-orange hue, which allowed me to see who was sitting in the room with me. Three people existed; two boys and one girl. They relaxed under blankets and pillows, covered with warmth. The girl wore a pink beanie.

I leaned my ear up against the door. Albeit muffled, I could still make out most of what the others were saying outside:

"You just brought someone here," The tall man's voice said, "without asking anyone? What were you thinking?"

"I was thinking..." Vic started to reply before getting interrupted by the third person.

"No, you weren't thinking. You can't just bring some stranger into here!"

"Now, quiet; we don't just interrupt. Let Victor tell us his side of the story," the tall man replied.

Vic took a few breaths before continuing, "I thought that he could help us out."

"Ok... so, what made you think that?"

"His father bears a red, white, and gold pin."

"He's one of us?"

"Yeah. That's why I brought him here."

"Hmm..." I heard footsteps, so I assumed the tall man began to pace around. "I'm still a little disappointed that you didn't address me first, nor take precaution."

"And I'm sorry about that, but I didn't think I'd have time to come back and get him. I've been studying him for a while now, and he's got a good head on his shoulders. He could help us out, I think. Plus, I couldn't wait any longer. I knew you'd say no, but once I discovered he was one of us, my instinct was to bring him with me. It felt like the right thing to do." Vic sounded insincere like he was trying to seem sorry but ultimately wasn't.

The tall man stopped pacing. "I'm going to trust you on this one Victor but know this: I'll be keeping a close eye on him. We don't usually let strangers take hospitality with us."

"This is the first time we've ever done it... " the third voice said, under his breath.

Vic sounded giddy while he said, "Awesome! Thank you, thank you, thank you! I won't let you down; I think this kid will be just fine. He will be fine, I know it."

I heard them shuffle toward the door, and I scurried away. It swung open and almost hit me across the face. I stood up involuntarily to face the boys as they walked back in. The tall man looked at me—I was intimidated by his size. He stuck out his hand, loosened his face, and said, "Welcome to the orphanage, Mike."

I took his hand and nervously laughed. I remained frozen for a few seconds. His look was unsettling, as if he still wasn't sure what to think of me, yet still wanted to do the right thing. "Here, allow me to introduce you to everyone," he said to me. "You already know Victor here, and this person behind me," he looked outside of the room, and I stuck my head into the doorframe and saw the other boy again. He seemed to be about Vic's age. He was taller than me, probably about as tall as Vic, and he was boney and skinny, too. His hair was short and pressed down. He crossed his arms, covering the splotches of colors on his dark grey shirt. "That is Peter Búlle," he finished saying. I waved to him outside of the room. He didn't budge.

The tall man continued around the room. "That is Jack Baylor right there..." He pointed to the man who was sitting in the far corner of the room, his back resting in the indent of the wall. "But we all call him 'Speed,'" the tall man finished. Speed wore a black leather jacket and a faded red undershirt. He had a few chains wrapped around him, and his hair was spiked. He wore goggles on top of his head, which made his green eyes pop out, but he looked friendly.

"Next to him is Ms. Melody Loveless," the tall man went on to say. She had long, unkempt, frizzy brown hair. She had blue eyes and held a smile that could cut to your core. She wore a leather-looking jacket, like Speed's, and she had goggles wrapped around her neck, along with a pretty, pink scarf. Her shirt displayed a lovely purple hue. It wasn't as splotched with random spots like the other people's shirts, I noticed. She waved at me. I waved back.

"Myles Chamberlain," he continued. Myles was sitting closest to Melody, yet still a fair distance away from her. He was closest to the crate with the lantern, which made his oily face glow radiantly with the flame's crackle. He had a mound of layered blonde hair; it looked like a helmet of hair. He, too, had goggles on top of his head, and he had round, brown eyes and thin eyebrows. He looked shorter than everyone else under the covers. While being introduced, he looked like a turtle receding into himself while he tried to get more comfortable. I shot him an awkward smile. He replied the same way.

"And I," the tall man finished off, "am Chris Sorano." He loomed over me as he sent a warming smile. "Now, with formalities out of the way, let's get on with the next order of business." He paused, then turned around. "Peter," he whispered, "We've never inducted anyone before. How should we go about it?" Peter shrugged. Chris turned back around, looking lost for a few moments, but soon regained composure. "Uh, here, you can follow Victor around for a while to kind of get the hang of things. Victor!" Vic stiffened up. "Make sure you don't lose sight of Mike at any time; he's your shadow. Got it?"

"You got it, boss," Vic replied. I looked over at him, to which he kindly smiled in response.

"Alrighty then," Chris continued, "Meeting adjourned. Everyone, make sure Mike feels at home. He's one of us now." Chris walked away, with Peter not too far behind, tripping over Chris's footsteps.

Vic shut the door as they walked out. I looked around the room again, and the faces I saw showed mixed emotions.

"What does he mean, 'one of us'?" Myles asked.

"He means that Mike is like us. His father has the pin," Vic said.

"Wait, so then that means..." Speed butted in.

"That's right; Mike is G's son." Vic stopped, waiting for the others to take in what he said fully. Everyone in the room looked took back and gasped.

"I don't understand..." I blurted out. "What's so important about his pin? And I'm whose son?"

"You don't know anything, do you?" Speed said.

"Do you have a mother, Mike?" Melody asked me.

"I did. But she, uh, left one day; I don't know where she is right now. She might have just become another victim to The Fallout."

"The Fallout?" she pondered, "What's that?"

I noticed Vic grit his teeth from the corner of the room. He mouthed the words, "Quit it."

I continued: "It's what all this is." I looked around and took in the dark and dank nature of the building—it left me unsettled once more. "It's what I call this world we live in now."

"Huh." Melody looked astonished. "That's not a bad name for it. I kind of like it! The Fallout..." she trailed off for a few seconds. "We always just called it 'Hell.'"

"Hell's nicer than where we are..." Speed interrupted.

"I don't know," I said, "Even Hell can get comfy once you're settled in."

It grew quiet for a few moments. They gawked at me, confused. I crawled beneath the large blanket. Its warmth was inviting.

"So, what's your story?" Speed asked me.

I propped myself with my back against the brick wall behind me, stiff as a board, from being in a situation so unfamiliar and so new. Confused, I dribbled out, "What do you mean?"

"I mean," he said, a bit cold, "what do you do? Your skills. Your interests. Your hopes and your dreams." His tone eventually became less cold and bitter and more sarcastic.

I muttered enough times to mutter the words, "Oh. W-well, uh, I wouldn't say I have...hopes or dreams, per se...but I read a lot."

"Read?" he asked, chuckling. "Where do you read?"

"At the library."

"What's a library?" As Speed asked, both Melody and Myles shared the same expression of stupefied fascination. I glanced over at Vic, who bulged his eyes and pushed his head forward and mouthed, "Drop it." It then occurred to me that these kids had no idea what a library was.

I quickly retorted, "It's uh...nothing."

"Well, whatever," Speed said, "Reading isn't going to get you very far here."

Vic leaned over and loudly whispered in my ear, "Don't mind him. He's just trying to act all tough for 'the new kid'."

"Hey, I'm not acting tough!" Speed said, unintentionally puffing his chest out.

"Oh, Mr. Sensitive's showing his true colors now," Vic sarcastically slid under his breath. However, we all heard it and shared a laugh.

"Ok," Speed added, laughing more with the group rather than at himself, "I'm not sensitive about anything, let's get that clear."

"Yeah, you kinda are," Melody chimed in, with a laugh under her words.

Speed huffed and skunked beneath the covers. The group laughed at this. I smiled at the situation.

Once the laughter died down, Melody spoke up. "No, but seriously, what all do you do? You said you read, so what do you mean by that?"

"Well, I read everything from picture books to books with fewer pictures than words, to ones that talk about things that happened before The Fallout." I scanned the room as I spoke, noticing the cracks and protrusions the room held, "Some books are about monsters and villains and some of saints and heroes."

"How can you read all of that?" Melody asked with wide eyes and an inquisitive expression. "I can barely count to 100!"

"I had to teach myself how to read that well—"

"Can you take me to this 'library'?" she excitedly exclaimed, barely getting the word out without tripping over her own words.

I evaluated the situation for a few moments, trying to get a read on why this random girl would want to go to this library. A few seconds ago, she had no idea what this was. She still had no real idea what it is, yet wanted me—a total stranger—to lead her there? The entire scenario perplexed me, and it caught me off guard.

"I mean, I guess I could..." I slipped out and then eventually trailed off. I didn't want to confirm a definite yes or no answer since I wasn't sure what my status was.

However, that meant nothing to Melody as she quickly responded, "Oh, yes, yes, yes, yes!" She relaxed beneath the covers and sang an original tune of "I'm going to the library..."

slowing down on the word "library," as she still was having trouble pronouncing the name.

Once she stopped singing, she asked the others, "Does anyone else want to go with us?"

It grew quiet for a while until Speed spoke up and said, "I don't have much a need for books. Anything I need to know to survive, I can figure out on my own."

Everyone looked over to Myles, who slinked further beneath the blanket.

While excited about the opportunity to teach my obsession with someone else, confusion was still pained all over my face. I was still trying to identify and dissect everyone's personalities and their role in the group. Melody picked up on my confusion and attempted to erase some of it: "Myles is our 'engineer' of sorts. He likes to tinker with things he finds."

He poked his head out and said, "I guess it couldn't hurt to be able to read a little."

I nodded my head. It was a bit odd to see kids not know things I'd taken for granted. The fact they couldn't read boggled my mind; perhaps it was because of how often I frequented the library and dedicated my early life to education. Still, being able to talk with kids my age was refreshing. I kept going back and forth in my mind about whether staying with these strangers was a good idea or not. I thought that I might be setting myself up for disaster. Though, at the same time, I felt as if they wanted me there, despite all I had going against me. I made a final internal decision to stay.

"Oh, hey, Vic," Speed said, "I wanted to talk about today's run with you..." Vic perked up and scooted a bit closer to where Myles was sitting.

I trailed off not too long after the conversation began. I thought about how much fun I might have with these people, and how I wanted to get to know them inside and out and truly learn everything about them. I also wondered why the pin my father wore was so important, and why did they refer to him as "G"? My decision to stay nestled its way into my mind as thoughts of pristine tranquility overtook me. Pure dopamine sensations rushed into my consciousness, filling every crevasse of doubt I had before. Nothing seemed to matter or exist except for the visions I saw before my eyes. The library also came to mind as I thought about how I would teach Melody and Myles how to read, and how I might have a way of fitting into this puzzle of unknown misfits. I soon brought myself to sleep with my back against the concrete wall.

I had entirely forgotten to return to my father that night.

Chapter 7

I awoke to stiffness in my spine and a crick in my neck. During the night, I had slid away from the wall. Instead, I lolled on the hard, concrete floor. I positioned myself up again and stretched my body. I noticed that Myles, Melody, and Speed were no longer in the room. To my side, Vic was no longer present, either. It was only me—alone in the big concrete block.

My legs popped as I stood and shrugged the blanket off me. It stuck to the fibers of my jeans as it fell. I walked to the door next to me and opened it.

"Oh, there he is. I thought you died on us already," Billy said, not too far away from me. He held a spoon and an open can of what looked like peaches. He shoved a spoonful of the food into his mouth.

Vic stood next to Billy, then walked over to me. He slapped his hand on my shoulder and asked, "So, big man, how was your nap?"

"It was fine," I said, still stretching my back.

"Well, you're gonna have a lot more of those in that room, so get used to all that comfort," Vic joked. He then ran over to an open box and grabbed a can out of it. He used a can opener to peel off the lid and handed the can to me. "I made breakfast for you. Eat up—we have a big day."

I held the can in my hands and hoped for a spoon. I was not given one. So, I settled on tipping the canister in the air and letting its contents fall into my mouth.

"When you get done eating," Vic said, "see Billy over there. He'll show you where I'll be."

I nodded. He walked toward the other side of the room, turned a corner, and was soon out of sight. No one else was in the place except for Billy and me, so I decided to sit next to him. A few cushions were lying on the floor where he was sitting, so I placed myself on one of them.

"So, what's your story?" Billy asked me before I even finished sitting on the cushion.

"Why does everyone keep asking me that?" I replied.

"I just want to know, like, what you're doing here, why'd you come along, that sort of thing. I heard a little of what Vic and Chris were talking about last night, but I try not to eavesdrop too much." Billy scooped around his can and lobbed out a large chunk of peaches and juice and threw it at his mouth.

"Vic found me, uh..." I remembered Vic's face when I brought up the library the night before and decided to come up with a different story. "...walking around and asked me if I wanted to join him with a bunch of other kids."

Billy dug around some more in his can. "Listen," he said, "I know you aren't telling the truth." He paused to chew for a few seconds. "You're a bad liar. But you probably have your reasons. Vic wouldn't just pick up some random kid walking around out there. We've seen plenty of those already. Vic sees something in you, uh, what's your name again?"

"Mike," I said, my voice breaking.

"Well, Mike, Vic must have seen something in you is all I'm saying. I don't know what, personally..." He fumbled around with his can of peaches for a few seconds, trying to get one last scoop out of it, "But he told me that he wants you to meet him out back." He put the last spoonful of peaches in his mouth.

I sat for a few seconds, silent, wondering what exactly he meant when he said that Vic sees something in me. The only thing I'd done was try to hide from him inside the library; what about that shows something special?

"Uh, I don't know where that is," I eventually said, growing impatient.

"I know that!" he retorted, "Gosh, kid. You only just got here, and you already want to run around. Pace yourself, man.

The days here are long." He rested the spoon inside the can and placed it next to him. He wiped his mouth with the inside of the coat he was wearing. He stood up and prompted me to go with him and looked at the can in my hands. "You might want to eat that on your way. You're gonna need the energy."

I worked on my can of peaches, pouring the food into my mouth. I didn't end up eating a whole lot, though—my nerves were starting to get the best of me. Every time I tried to eat, my stomach would attempt to make me expel it back out.

We went down the stairs until we reached the ground floor, where I initially entered the building the day before. Behind the stairs was a door to the outside and an alcove hidden by a mound of concrete rubble.

"What's this?" I asked, walking over to investigate.

Billy grabbed me by my jacket and yanked me back. "Get away from there! It's the result of this place falling apart over the years. It's been there since I've been here. Now come on, we're almost there."

He gripped the collar of my jacket and hauled me away. I looked back at the rubble, observing its sturdy husk.

"Nice jacket," Billy said. "Sturdy, though a bit big. Where'd you find this?"

"Uh, I took it."

Billy pursed his lips. He opened the door at the end of the hallway and led us outside.

The light hit my eyes. I squinted for a few seconds before my eyes dilated. Billy let go of my jacket, which made me stumble before regaining my footing. I looked around and saw metal and plastic torn apart and lying all around. Slides that were broken and tilted to their sides, swings that had the metal bars holding them up in pieces, mulch that had long dried up—dirt and dust everywhere. To the right of the playground equipment was a small basketball court with one of the hoops still standing, as if untouched. A long staff rested upon the pole of the basketball hoop. Vic was on the court, inside of a drawn-on chalk circle, looking much like a traditional wrestling arena.

"Ah, there you are!" Vic said, leaning off a basketball pole. "You're a bit earlier than I thought you'd be."

"Yeah, well, somebody was dying to walk around," Billy joked, his eyes shifting my way.

"Either way." Vic took the staff and put it at his side. He motioned for me to meet him by the basketball pole. "Billy, thanks for showing him here. You can leave if you want."

"I think I'll do just that. Inventory probably needs doing. It probably needs to be done again when everyone gets back. Probably needs to be done again when..." Billy rambled as he walked off.

"Where is everyone else, by the way?" I asked Vic.

"I don't know. They had left by the time I woke up. They probably went out on an early morning run." Vic grabbed a wooden staff next to him. "Here," he said as he handed it to me. "Today, I'm teaching you how to use a staff."

I held the staff in my hands. It was a bit heavy and quite large, considering how young I was at the time. I swung it around and got a feel for it.

"It's difficult to be lethal with it," Vic continued, "It'll just hurt a lot. For both you and me."

Without warning, I saw Vic spin toward me, his weapon connecting with my body. I dropped to the hard ground; the wind was taken right out of me. I sat there for a few moments before I saw Vic stand over me. He extended his hand. I grabbed it.

"Why'd you do that?" I asked, being pulled back up to my feet.

"If you're going to roll with us, you must prepare for the worst—the unexpected." Vic swung his staff underneath my feet, causing me to fall once more. A searing pain shot through my back as I collided with the concrete. "Like that."

I stood up and regained my posture—my guard now up. "Didn't think I'd be getting the hell beat out of me when I woke up this morning," I grumbled.

"Yeah, well, 24 hours ago you didn't even know me, so a lot can happen quickly—something you'll have to learn if you're going to be any use to us." He swung at me again, but I blocked it. He smirked, "Quick learner." Vic then shoved forward and twisted his arms, which knocked the staff out of my hands. "You won't be total dead weight, which is good to see..." Vic looked at the ground, then backed up away from me. He motioned his head toward the staff that he knocked out of my hands. I picked it back up. "Yet, you still have much to learn."

For the rest of the day, we worked on my combat skills. Other than the few times Vic knocked me down initially, we didn't continue to go toe-to-toe. We instead focused on my stature and how I poised myself in battle. He also tried to teach me how to watch my opponents and read their movements, but I only ended up getting struck by Vic every time.

We took a break around midday; I took off my jacket to cool off from our rigorous training.

"You're not doing too bad," Vic said.

"Thanks," I replied. "Once you stopped knocking me to the ground, it got a lot easier."

"I can still do that if you want," Vic said. He smiled.

"What did you mean last night when you said you watched me at the library for a while?" I asked.

"How did you hear that?"

"I eavesdropped through the door."

"You little sneak..." Vic licked his lips. "Ok, fine. I noticed a while ago that when I would head to the library, it was cleaner than usual. It seemed too tidy, and everything was organized. I figured someone had to be visiting this place—and regularly. I usually go out at night, so I could keep the place a secret from everyone here. One day, I stuck around and saw you crawl in—you intrigued me. I thought it was my secret, but you also knew of the library. I felt connected to you in some weird way."

"Why didn't you want anyone knowing? Why did you want me to stop talking about it last night?"

"I don't know. The people here don't think highly of my hobbies, I guess. I love finding things and collecting objects. I saw the library as another one of those pointless findings—something only I can appreciate. That's also why I didn't want you talking about The Fallout. I see them both as 'my thing,' I guess."

"I appreciate the library, too, Vic," I said. "Melody does, apparently—Myles, as well. I think you're too hard on yourself. You know how to fight—I've been learning that all day—and knowing how to read isn't something to be ashamed of. I think it's cool that you have an eye to find things underneath all the dust and rubble of this world."

"Thanks, Mike," Vic responded. He put a hand on my shoulder. "Now, let's get back to training!"

We practiced until evening. We walked back inside to greet everyone, who'd just made their way back. Billy counted a collection of bottles and cans in Melody's arms.

Vic closed the door behind us. Speed and Myles turned around.

"Ah, if it isn't our newest recruit," Speed said. "We were wondering where you two were. Are you showing him around, Vic?"

"Not really—more like teaching him to defend himself," Vic replied.

"More like beating me every 6 seconds," I muttered under my breath.

Speed heard me and chuckled. "Kid's got a mouth, huh? Last night you could barely get an answer out of him..."

Myles nudged him. "It's ok, Mike. Don't mind him. He has a huge ego, is all."

Speed gave Myles a mocking laugh. Myles turned to tap Melody's shoulder, who was busy talking to Billy about her haul. She spun around, noticed me, flashed a smile, and gave a wave. I returned the gesture.

"Vic's been teaching Mike about how to protect himself," Myles told her.

"Oh, really? That's awesome! Just keep at it and you'll do fine; I know it!" Melody seemed overly excited, while I couldn't help but smile back. "Hey guys," she said toward Speed and Myles, "Billy's done counting. Let's go see Chris." The two agreed, and everyone left—leaving Vic and me alone.

"At least they're accepting of me," I told him.

"I'd hope so. We're all fighting for the same cause—to stay alive. Kinda need each other to succeed in that, don't we?" Vic smirked. "You've had a big first day, so I'd say just to go get some food and rest. We'll meet out back again first thing tomorrow morning, alright?" He patted me on the back as he followed the path of everyone else toward Chris. I followed Vic's orders.

Chapter 8

A week passed, with the same routine of waking up early, practicing all day, then going to bed—only to repeat the process all over again the next morning. Halfway through the week, however, Vic decided to ditch the staff idea, as I wasn't getting very far, and wanted to focus more on hand-to-hand combat first. I was a little better at the close-quarters combat than I was with the staff. I could get a read on some of Vic's movements and did relatively well at dodging, not so much at capitalizing on the opportunity to retaliate, however.

One night after we finished practicing, I walked into the central atrium of the building, which everyone called the foyer, looking for something to eat and writing on. I found a used piece of cloth and a marker, which I used to create a calendar. I kept a mental track of how many days it had been since I left my father and picked up where his calendar left off. It felt wrong to be living without some sort of schedule.

As I sat on the floor of the foyer, drawing lines and writing numbers, Melody noticed my scribblings and stopped to ponder.

"Hey, Mike," she said.

"Hello, Melody," I replied, not looking up from my work, "How are you today?"

"The usual." She watched me work. "So, uh, I was passing by and noticed you doing... that." She motioned toward my drawing. I stopped scribbling to look at her. Her hair was down, and her face had a few freckles of dirt scattered across her skin.

"Oh, this?" I said, holding up the cloth to show her.

"Yeah, that! What exactly is that?"

"It's a calendar," I told her.

She looked aghast. It was like I spoke ancient tongue to her and was expecting her to understand the vernacular. "A...calendar," she stammered, "Forgive me, but what's that?"

"It's...uh..." I struggled to find the words to describe it. "Well, it's a grid you use to keep track of the days. Like, see here?" I motioned her to view the calendar with me. She sat next to me. "Today is September 14th, with the yesterday being the 13th, and tomorrow is the 15th. These are separated by weeks, which consist of seven days. Today is Thursday, see?"

She seemed lost but tried to understand what I was showing her. "Ok," she started, "So what's special about this day? With the...whatever that is."

She pointed at September 6th, which I had written underneath it, "The day I left."

"That's the day Vic found me at the library and asked me to come here with him. Couldn't you read that? I know my handwriting isn't exactly that great, but..."

"Mike, I can't read," Melody told me. She looked at me as if I were crazy not to know, or that I was mad for assuming she could.

"Oh." I stopped thinking for a few seconds. It hadn't occurred to me until then that there would be people in the world who didn't know the joy of reading. Education was a privilege I had for so long I'd forgotten not everyone was as lucky as I was. "I didn't know," I said.

"Yeah, I never was taught. I never learned how to do it..." she trailed off. "Sucks, because I could be much more of a help if I could just read simple things." She hit her hands against her jeans and wiped her palms on her legs.

We ended up just looking at each other for a little while. I couldn't take my eyes off her; there was something about her that fascinated me, but I couldn't verbalize it. I found myself thinking about what she was thinking. The thought processes of constant inquiry and openness she possessed contrasted with the objective, formulaic mindset I had. Her mind was freer. I felt as if we could both be looking at the same thing, but her eyes would interpret the scene entirely different than me. There was something I saw in her that I felt like no one else had seen before, even if I couldn't tell exactly what it was—I felt a connection. I wondered if she felt it too.

"Oh, hey, that reminds me," Melody started to say. I snapped back into reality, exiting my interpretive and hyperbolic state of mind. "You still down for taking me to the library? You said you'd be willing to teach me a few things... and I was thinking you could maybe even teach me how to read?"

"Oh... oh yeah! Of course, I'm still fine with that!" I felt a cold sweat run down my spine and a sense of anxiety enter my being. "But, uh, when do you want to do that? I'm supposed to be practicing with Vic until... well, I don't know when."

"I can go ask Chris to give us the day off tomorrow. I'm sure he'll be fine with it," Melody reassured me.

"If it's that easy, then I'm fine with it," I said.

"Awesome! C'mon, let's go do it now!" Melody jumped up and grabbed my arm, tugging me along with her. She was stronger than I thought, as she threw me up from the ground with not even a grunt from her.

"Hold on!" I yelped. She either didn't hear me or ignored my plea, as dragged me across the foyer. I slid the calendar and marker into my back pocket to work on later.

We crossed the rectangular room to reach one of the smaller rooms on the north side of the wall. Melody entered first, tugging me along behind her. The room we entered was pitch black, with the only light being the one emitted from the door we just opened. As the door swung open, I saw Chris and Peter. Chris was sitting behind a desk with some important papers sprawled out across the desk. It was only knee-height, and both characters were sitting down close to the floor to discuss overtop of it. Peter sat away from the desk, in a bean-bag chair positioned directly across from Chris.

"Hello, Melody, Mike," Chris said to us. Peter turned around to notice us. He waved at us but seemed annoyed that we were there. Melody waved back, but I didn't.

"Hi, Chris. Peter. Sorry, are we interrupting something important?" Melody must have realized she was holding on to my arm, as she quickly let go when she started talking. It felt a little weird, having her grip released from me. I had gotten used to the pressure she brought along with it.

"Nothing that can't wait," Chris responded. He looked at Peter. "Could you give us a minute? Find a can of something and bring it back in here. Couldn't hurt to eat something."

Peter nodded and removed himself from the room, brushing past Melody and me.

I looked back toward Chris, who was undoing some locks on his desk, moving it from its knee-high position to about chest-high. He stood up and stretched.

"What do you need, you two?" He asked. He didn't seem annoyed by our appearance, more curious than anything.

"Mike and I were wondering if we could be relieved of our duties for tomorrow," Melody told him.

"Ok. For what reason?"

"Mike's going to take me to the library," she said, her voice giddy. I felt the weight of a thousand anchors on my head as Chris looked over at me. I couldn't look up to face him.

"Hmm..." Chris readjusted his beanie before putting his elbow down on the desk, his head resting upon his hand.

"Oh, come on! I know there's like a million things to do, but we just want one day-"

"Do you know where this library is?" He asked. Melody grew silent and slumped down in her posture. "It's not that I don't want to give you the day off, I just don't want you wandering the city if you don't know where you're going, especially in such a small group."

"I know where it's at," I said. Melody spun around at me and smiled. She mouthed a thank-you to me.

"Oh? You do?" questioned Chris. Once again, not in anger—curious.

"Yeah. At least, I'm pretty sure I do. I haven't been there since I got here, but I know my way around there pretty well." Chris looked at me with eyes that teetered between disbelief and complete faith. He silently stared at me for a few moments. I grew more and more unnerved as time passed.

Eventually, he broke the silence with a smirk and one word: "Sure."

Melody jumped in glee and thanked him a hundred times before running out of the room. I looked at Chris before leaving.

"Please be careful, you two," he said.

I nodded. Peter nudged my back, as he had both hands full of bowls, spoons, and two cans of food.

"Oh, sorry. You need help with that?" I asked him.

"No, I should be good. Thanks, though." Peter shuffled past me and laid the items on Chris's desk. He was ready to close the door behind me. I then heard Chris tell him, "Hang on, not yet. I need to write something down first…"

Melody waited for me in the foyer with a stupid smile on her face. It didn't look to be leaving anytime soon.

"I'm so excited!" She exclaimed. "I can't wait to see what the library looks like and for you to teach me how to read and to—oh man, this is going to be great! Thank you for taking me there," she told me.

"I haven't brought you there yet," I said, smiling back. Chris's door closed.

"Hey," I began to ask, "Why is Chris's room so dark? Is it always that way?"

"It's been like that since I've known him," Melody said.

"Why? Have you ever asked?" I said.

"No," She told me, "I figure that if they don't want to see what they're doing, then I have no right to know what they're doing either."

We left early the next day—around 9 am. I told Vic about Chris relieving us for the day, and he said that was fine. Vic took up Melody's job for the day while we took to the streets, toward the library.

I hadn't left the building since I was brought to the group the week before. Something was liberating about freely walking outside the confines of walls and fences.

"Ok, what direction?" Melody asked once we secured the door. She wore a pair of goggles and a bandana around her neck.

"Uh, this way," I pointed to our right. We began walking away from the building. I asked about her accessories.

"Oh, am I wearing those?" She looked down at her neck. "Guess I am!" She laughed a little before saying, "Sorry. Force of habit, I guess. We usually wear these when we're out, but you probably won't need them."

"What do you need them for?"

"To stay anonymous."

I wrinkled my eyebrows, wondering why that was but decided not to press her on the subject. I felt it simply wasn't necessary for me to know all the details at the time.

"What's the building we're holed up in?" I asked.

"What do you mean?" Melody asked me.

"It isn't a normal house. It served some other purpose; I just don't know what that is. Chris mentioned something like 'orphanage'?"

"Oh," Melody blurted. "Yeah, it's an orphanage. Well, it used to be. Peter told me that orphanages used to house kids who didn't have parents anymore. So, in a way, I guess we fit the description perfectly."

We continued to walk through the city, mostly silent as I led us back the way Vic and I came just a few days earlier. The only sounds were the wind's howling voice, as it skirted across the sides of ruined skyscrapers, and the pattering of our innocent footsteps.

"This city is beautiful, isn't it?" Melody said, interrupting the tunes played by natural musicians. "Just the way everything was destroyed, yet it all seems so deliberate..."

"Uh-huh," I replied. I probably sounded dismissive. The combination of the city's beauty and the outcome of unlikely circumstances brought me to this destination—where I had Melody by my side while we walked peacefully and artfully through a city of rapture—it overwhelmed my ability to create coherent sentences.

Thankfully, Melody was more than happy to narrate her thoughts: "The way the light shines through the clouded sky and bounces off shattered windows to give patterns to walls around them... and how the muted colors around everything bring out the beauty in it all. I love just thinking about-" She was cut off by her coughing, getting tripped up on her words and inhaling the dust and dirt in the air, perpetuating the cycle. I tried to see if she needed help, but she pushed me away.

"Sorry," she muttered between coughs.

"No, it's ok. You don't need to say anything else; I feel the same way."

She looked stunned, either from what I said or from the dust that kept entering her lungs. She slid her bandana over her mouth. "Really? Y-you do?"

"Yeah. I've thought this city was beautiful since I was young. I can't get enough of it."

"Wow... I didn't know there was anyone else who sees the city as I do. Cool... " Melody continued to look at me, staring, until eventually, her eyes darted away, the wonderment left her irises as she jerked her head away.

We soon reached the library. Once we entered, I saw Melody's eyes sparkle again. The sight of all the knowledge paralyzed her. Though she couldn't read any of the signs hanging above the different sections of the library, I could tell there was something in her longing to be released.

I approached her and placed my hand on her shoulder. She jumped at first, but soon relaxed and let my hand calm her.

"Well, what do you think?" I asked.

"It's amazing," she rolled out, as if in a drunken state.

Melody shrugged my hand off her shoulder and darted toward the section to our right.

"What's that say?" she asked, pointing to the hanging diction above her.

"It says, 'Children's Books.'" I replied, slowly making my way toward her.

Melody grew more excited at the sound of "Children's Books" and ran to the back wall. She pulled a multitude of picture books and skimmed them, soaking in all the visual information before her.

While she had her fun, I couldn't help but look around and ponder about how nice it was in the library; forgotten, alone, detached from the rest of the world. It seemed to run based on its own rules, encapsulated within its own time, as it didn't reflect the horrible beauty of the city, but rather a timeless space that seemed unaffected with each passing day. I couldn't help but think about how I was sharing this space with Melody—someone I hardly knew, but one of the few people I feel I could trust. I was excited to educate her, and for her to view the world as I did. She already saw the city as beautiful—like me—I pondered if perhaps she could surpass my education.

"Come over here! Look at this!" Melody commanded. I rushed over, and she pointed to the book she was reading. "See this? That—what's that?" She was referring to a cloud in a children's weather book.

"That's a cloud," I responded. "Do you not know what a cloud is?"

"Sorta. I know what it is... I just never knew what they were called... " She examined the book a little more. "Which one of these words is a cloud?" I pointed to the word. Melody smiled and said, "Ok. Now, teach me more."

And I did. I taught her basic words, mainly nouns, and everyday objects that she would see on signs, papers, etc. I found a pen and paper and began writing words for her to learn and pronounce. I found pictures and associated names with the images. We talked and laughed and bickered as I introduced her to the world of English.

After a few hours of exercising nomenclature, we took a break. We eased back in our rolling chairs for a moment before realizing they were rolling chairs. Melody put her feet to the ground and began rolling around the floor, giggling all the while. I joined in, and soon we were dancing across the library chambers as our chairs glided across the stained carpets.

We rolled across the building until we were exhausted. We soon returned to our work table. Panting and sweating, Melody said, "That was a lot of fun!"

"Yeah," I sputtered through exhales.

It grew silent between us before a gust of wind hit the building, causing some of the rubble above the roof to rustle and creak.

"Oh yeah," Melody began, "Mike, you should show me how that cali-thing works. I don't remember what you called it."

"Oh, you mean the calendar?" I asked.

"That, yes! Show me how it works."

I picked up the pad of paper we were working on, turned to a new page, and drew a calendar.

"Ok, so this is the month, September. Today," I circled one of the numbers, "is the 15th. There are seven days in a week: Sunday, Monday, Tuesday, Wednesday, Thursday, Friday, and Saturday. Each one corresponds with a number. Now, every month has either 30 or 31 days in it, with one exception (February), and once you reach that 30 or 31-day threshold, the next month begins on the next day, starting over again at 1."

I passed the mock-up calendar to Melody. She picked it up and burned the page into her memory.

"Where'd you learn to do this?" she asked, mystified by the whole process.

"No, not exactly. My fa-" I stopped myself. I didn't want to mention my father, especially not to give credit for this. "Uh, someone I used to know did this, and I just picked it up from them."

"Oh, ok." Melody's words cut through me. She continued, "Still... it's cool and all, but what exactly is this used for?"

"It's... well... " I struggled to find an answer. "I mean, it helps keep track of time a bit, but I thought we could use it to remember things, that way we never forget about them."

"That's smart," Melody said, plainly. She reached across the table and grabbed a pen. "Write down, 'Took Melody to the library' on Frii-dae the 15th," she told me, having trouble pronouncing the day. I wrote down her request. She smiled and thanked me. "Hey, why don't we show this to everyone back home? Imagine how useful this could be! We could plan out our days, keep track of what we did and where we went—"

"I don't want to share it," I replied.

"What?" She asked. "Why not?"

I wanted to tell her why. I wanted to tell her how the calendar connected me to my father and how it was originally his idea. I wanted to tell her about my past, about my history, and my fascination with everything. I wanted to tell her how I didn't feel comfortable in the group yet, and how scared I was of everyone there. I wanted to tell her how Chris frightened me to my core, and how I couldn't imagine standing in front of him and professing a new management system when I had only just joined the group. I wanted to tell her everything that comprised my identity. I wanted to tell her I was sorry.

Instead, I told her: "I don't want to talk about it."

As it grew ever closer to dusk, we decided to stop for the day and head back to the orphanage. I went behind the front desk and grabbed a few slips of plastic to preserve our progress. I unlocked one of the rooms behind the counter to reveal a mound of unused black backpacks. I grabbed one and locked the door behind me, putting the key back under the desk.

I returned to Melody, slipped the paper into the plastic slips, and carefully inserted them inside the backpack. I then threw some books into the pack as well. Before closing the bag, I walked over to a few other shelves and threw some more books inside for Melody to read later.

"Where'd you get that?" she asked, while I continually added to the bag.

"Oh, from one of the rooms behind the counter over there. There's a whole lot of them in there."

"Huh." Melody scrunched her nose. I walked back to the table and began to zip the pockets of the backpack, now filled with books and papers and pens for us to bring back. "That thing has a lot more room than what we have back home. What we use is a little bag with a huge pouch on it. This would let us hold so much more..."

"Well, we can keep it. I'm only using it to bring some stuff back for you to work on at the orphanage. But, I don't see why we can't use it for something else."

Melody became giddy at the sound. She got up from her seat and hugged me. "Thank you for today; it was really fun. Thank you for being so helpful, Mike."

I hugged her back and replied, "You're welcome, Melody. Always happy to help."

"You're going to do great things for us—I just know it," she whispered into my ear. Melody broke the hug and walked to the hole we crawled in through.

I lagged, putting the backpack on my shoulders and tidying the library a little before we left.

As I approached the crawl space, she was holding her stomach. "We haven't eaten anything all day, and it's starting to catch up with me. Whoops."

My stomach began to grumble too. "We must have forgotten to stop and eat."

"Well, I forgot to bring anything with us too, so it's a little my fault. It isn't easy to walk around and find something to eat, you know." She motioned for me to go through the crawl space first, which was a little tricky, given that I now had the backpack with me. Nonetheless, we left the library and returned to the world outside once more.

"Let's try and hurry home because I'm starving," Melody said. "Lead the way, Mike."

We walked a little quicker than we did earlier. We wanted to get back to the orphanage as fast as we could without full-on sprinting all the way there. The light faded fast, which put added pressure on us.

It was dark when we reached the orphanage, and we had to squint to see somewhat clearly.

"Home sweet home," Melody said at the door.

"Yeah...home," I muttered between breaths. Melody knocked and waited until Speed opened the door to let us in. He closed the door behind us and locked it.

We were immediately greeted by Chris, who, with open arms, asked us, "So? How was the library?"

"It was amazing!" Melody told him, voice cracking from the excitement and with her hands acting involuntarily. "I looked at a bunch of picture books, Mike taught me some words, he's teaching me to read, and we brought some books home for us to work on!" She pointed to the backpack on my back. Chris smiled to show he was listening. "Mike found this there, and we thought we could use it when we go out searching for supplies."

Chris looked amused by this and shifted his eyes toward me. I felt the weight of an anvil on my head as I struggled to make eye contact with him.

He shook his head and said, "Of course. I'm sure it'll be helpful to us." Chris looked at me. "Thank you, Mike, for finding this."

"Yeah, no problem," I replied, still unable to raise my head.

"It is getting rather late," Chris continued, "You two go get yourself some food and report to your room. Try and get some rest; tomorrow, you'll go back to your usual routine."

"Yes, sir," Melody and I replied and hurried upstairs. We were both starving, and scarfed down two cans of potatoes in seconds, not caring that they were uncooked. Afterward, we walked into our room with no one else there. I dumped nearly all the contents of the backpack near Melody's sleeping area, and she proceeded to crack open the weather book from earlier and browsed through its pages.

I settled into my spot and pulled the large blanket overtop my lap and propped a pillow behind me for support. I reached into the backpack and took out a pen and clipboard. Behind the pillow was my calendar from the day before, which I updated to reflect the current day. I also wrote down, "Took Melody to the library" on Friday the 15th and struck a line through the box to signify the day was over. I then wrote on the next day, that Saturday, "Back to normal."

Chapter 9

The next morning was set to the sound of shouting.

"But this is bullshit!" Vic yelled from outside the room. The closed-door next to me suppressed his volume.

"Watch your language," Chris pressed, "and no, it is not. When I heard what happened yesterday, I was quite frankly a little more than upset. Be thankful I haven't thrown you out on to the streets."

"It wasn't even-"

"Yet, continue to push me and perhaps I will." I heard footsteps growing louder and closer to the door.

"Can I even get the chance to explain myself?" Vic challenged.

"You almost got Myles killed yesterday, Victor," Chris said on the other side of the thin wooden door. "We hold the lives of our own over any random trinket or morsel of food you find. Got it?" It grew quiet. "Now, I need to think and plan for this job we're doing soon, so I'll be in my room if you need me. You just take Mike and continue training him for now." The footsteps grew fainter until the slam of a door in the distances ended them altogether.

There was no noise for a few moments, so I took the initiative. I opened the door and saw Vic standing still, staring at the ground. As I swung the door open, he shifted his stature to look at me. His eyes seemed emotionless.

"Um, good morning," I muttered.

I sensed that Vic knew I heard everything, as he quickly said, "Grab something to eat and meet me outside to practice. Fast. And don't ask any questions."

He turned and walked down the stairs. I followed his instructions, ate briskly, and made my way outside. Vic was already swinging a stick around madly, but with form. He was panting, and a few beads of sweat rolled down his face.

I closed the door behind me, which alerted Vic.

"Mike. Take the other stick there and get ready."

"But, we haven't practiced with sticks before..." I mentioned before being silenced.

"We're trying something different today. Just do it."

I attempted to replicate the actions I saw Vic perform but to no avail. I lost the stick within my hand movements and it hit the ground. I bent down to pick it up, and while turning to face Vic, I felt a blunt object strike my face, knocking me off my feet.

My back hit the floor. I exclaimed: "Dude, what gives?"

Vic didn't reply. Instead, he took a few steps back and motioned for me to get up. I started to stand, then Vic struck the backs of my legs, knocking me back down.

This time I landed with my left wrist taking the brunt of most my weight. I let out a cry of pain with still no response from Vic. He was like a statue that only came to life when it was time to knock me down.

I struggled to hold myself up by my palms, but another whack from Vic pushed me toward the ground once more.

"Can you at least let me get up?" I yelled. I slowly got myself to stand upright again, with Vic watching me while I did so. My stick was across the basketball court, nowhere near me now, so I decided to try and take him on with my fists.

I ended up blocking the first jab he took at me, but he shook my hand from the stick. He then hit me between my shoulder blades, slapped the right side of my abdomen, and finally pushed me daintily down to the floor. I fell on my back, scraping my elbow.

I got up again. This process occurred a few times the same way, with Vic using the same moves and me not learning what to do next. Everything I did got me hurt more and more, and I began to stop feeling pain because my body had become so numb to the falling and the strikes.

After getting knocked down the fifth time from this cycle, I gritted my teeth and jumped up.

"Stop... knocking... me... down." I changed positions, this time a little further away from where I had been before. Vic took a step forward to go for the first hit again, but this time something was different. I felt as if I could see what he was going to do right before he did it—as I could see into the near future. The combination of anger and adrenaline going through me was so intense that I became extremely focused on what Vic was going to do. My mind was so clear—I knew how to stop it from happening.

I instinctively blocked the hit as I had before, but instead of letting him break the block, I pushed up with my hand and grabbed the middle of the stick with my other hand. Vic and I pushed back and forth for a while; then, he pushed me back with the stick, which removed my grip from the weapon. It knocked me back, but I kept my footing and could see Vic charging toward me with a heavy attack. He spun the stick over his head and turned a 360-degree motion to get the most power behind it. I ducked underneath his attack and grabbed the stick with both hands during his retaliation. I used all my might to overturn him, and I toppled him—using the stick to push him to his right. He lost his balance and released his grip on the stick. He was on the ground, and I put the stick next to his neck to show I won.

He stayed on the ground for a few seconds before smirking. He pushed the stick to the side while he got himself back on his feet.

"What was that all about, huh?" I yelled at him. "You just beat me up over and over again? Are you not talking to me all of a sudden? I'm bleeding because of you!"

Vic smirked again and grunted, "At least you're ready."

"Now, what's that supposed to mean?" I asked.

"You tell me. You bested me in hand-to-hand combat. Nobody's done that in a long time." Vic walked past me slowly. I lowered my stance and relaxed myself a bit. "You've been paying attention..." He began. He quickly swiped the stick from my hands before I even realized he did it. "But not too much attention. So far, you seem to be a worthy opponent. It'll be interesting to teach somebody who can kick my ass every now and then."

"Thanks," I replied, confused, "But why were you so distant?"

"I was training you," Vic told me.

"Oh, bullshit."

"Hey!" Vic snapped. "Watch your language; how did you even learn that?"

"Don't act like I'm stupid. I heard you and Chris talking this morning. Just because you're angry at him doesn't mean you have to-"

"I'm not angry at Chris," Vic cut me off, "I'm angry at me. He's right—I almost got Myles killed because I was reckless and curious and thought I saw something, so..." He grew quiet.

"I don't care what you did," I said, "That's not important. Myles is still alive, and that's what matters. You're still alive, and that's what matters. If you learned from your mistake, that's what matters. Taking your anger out on me isn't helping anyone; it just hurts me. A lot."

Vic was silent for a few moments, tapped the staff on the ground, then said, "You're right. Thanks." I smiled at him. Vic then swiftly hit my left knee, forcing me to kneel.

"Ah!" I screamed.

Vic laughed. "But I'm not sorry about that!"

"You're a jerk," I said, trying to stand back up.

"And proud of it," Vic replied.

The two of us went back to our usual training regimen after that incident. Vic saw the potential of my hand-to-hand combat abilities, and began to teach me how to hone in on my defensive-nature, and wait for the perfect opportunity to strike. I struggled at first with the concept but soon began to see actions before they happened—based only on the body movements Vic would do. I could tell which way he was going to attack me, what maneuver I would need to do to block/evade the attack, etc. It took a while, but eventually, I got it down. I still wasn't the best at it, however, but this was at least a start.

We trained until it got dark. Vic called off our practice and went inside. Chris and Myles were talking about something across the foyer.

"Hey, Mike, go into our room and see if the others are in there. I'm going to go talk to them," Vic said. While he walked away, I saw him put his hand on the back of his head and run his fingers through his hair.

I swung open the door to our room, which was slightly cracked open. Speed sat directly across from me, and Melody sat along the wall to his left. Her face was buried deep in a book, mouthing out the words she was reading.

"You look a little beat-up, huh Mike?" Speed said.

"Oh..." I looked down and noticed the cuts through my shirt. Bruises were visible from the sections ripped away from the fabric of the shirt. "Yeah, today was a bit rough."

"I feel ya," Speed said. "We had a pretty good day, all things considered," he looked over to Melody, who quietly murmured to herself. "We couldn't go three feet without her talking to us about books."

"Sorry about that," I told him. "She does seem pretty into it, doesn't she?"

"That's putting it lightly," Speed roared in Melody's general direction. He continued to stare at her, hoping to get a reaction from her. She kept reading. He tapped the back of her book, which startled her. "We're talking about you, you know," he said.

"Oh. That's fine," Melody quietly replied. She then immediately went back to reading.

Speed put up his hands and laughed at her. "What will we do with you?" he said offhandedly. "But yeah, anyway, it got so bad we started calling her Bookworm."

"Bookworm? Why's that?" I asked.

"Because she keeps finding ways to worm her books into our conversations!"

I chuckled at the thought of Melody interrupting Speed and Myles, just to talk about things she read from the day before.

"Oh yeah," Speed interjected, "We found something while we were out today. It's like these black boxes, kind of like bricks—but the cool thing is that when you press this button, you can talk to someone through it!"

"Oh, you mean like a walkie-talkie?" I said, not thinking.

"What? That's what it—wait, how do you...?" Speed was flabbergasted.

"They were used a lot in some espionage and spy books I read in the library."

"Geez, now you're doing it too..." he said in a sarcastic tone. He smirked and said, "Myles is talking to Chris about it, so you can take a look if you want."

I nodded my head. I walked out of the room, leaving the door cracked. I saw the group of boys spread out across the foyer. Vic and Chris were closest to me, with Myles at the other end. As I approached Vic and Chris, I heard Myles's voice screech from the walkie-talkie.

"Can you hear me now?" Myles said. Vic and Chris almost jumped out of their skin when they heard him speak.

Myles began to walk back over from the other side of the room. "See? Cool, right?" he said.

"Cool? That's amazing!" Vic exclaimed. "Dude, this is great."

"I agree," Chris said, "We will use these. I can think of a lot of applications for these tools."

"We couldn't think up a name for them, though..." Myles lamented.

"Walkie-talkies," I said. The group didn't notice my presence from earlier; they shook when I spoke. After the initial shock, their eyes hung on me as if I was speaking another language to them.

"...right, walkie-talkies..." Myles said. "Well, that clears that up, huh?"

"How do you...?" Vic whispered to me.

"I read a lot of books," I told him.

"Well, I have, too," Vic replied.

"Yeah, well, I guess I've just read more," I said. Vic snickered at me.

"Hey, Mike," Chris said. My body stiffened at the sound of his voice. "Can you go tell the others to come out and eat something? It's getting dark; we should all have some food while we still have some light."

I nodded and told Speed and Melody to join us in the foyer. We ate while Billy attempted to entertain the group with jokes. We all laughed, even Peter—who rarely showed a smile—let a chuckle creep out. Vic and Speed started teasing Billy after a while, making it funnier.

Eventually, the group became fixated on Vic, Speed, and Billy's antics of teasing each other. I leaned in toward Melody, who was sitting right next to me. "So, what books have you been reading?" I leaned back.

She moved closer to me and spoke into my ear, "The one where it's about this rain-bou fish. The pictures are super pretty; I end up getting lost, looking at the drawings."

"That's awesome, especially since it's a rainbow fish, not a rain-bou fish," I replied.

"Whatever!" Melody laughed, nudging my arm a little.

"Excuse me, you two," Chris said from behind us. We turned around and saw his tall body looming over us. He continued, "Sorry to disrupt, but I just wanted to let you know of a little change I'm going to be implementing."

"Yeah, sure, what is it?" Melody asked.

"I've noticed how much you've taken akin to reading, Melody. You seem intrigued by it, and I want to fan the flame of that passion. I was wondering if you two wanted to continue to take a day off every so often to go down to the library. I began to think about it some more, and I believe it will benefit you two—and everyone—to become more acquainted with one another, learn, read, all that."

"Of course!" Melody exclaimed. She turned to me. "Mike, you hear that? Oh, I'm so happy right now!"

"Yeah, that's awesome," I told her. Then I asked Chris, "Would you care if we went down there once every seven days?"

"That's a peculiar number," Chris said, "But I'm sure that would be fine. I haven't told Vic this yet, but he'll take Melody's place those days as he did before. I'll try to keep up with the days, and such."

"If you forget, I'll remember," I said. I hadn't told him of my calendar—where I've been keeping track of the days myself. I was afraid to tell him about it; general anxiety overwhelmed me when sharing my calendar with anyone other than Melody came to mind.

Upon hearing my guarantee, Chris shot a finger-gun at me. I was a little taken back by this gesture, but Melody later explained that this was a thing Chris did to thank people.

"I'll leave you two be," Chris said as he began to walk toward the group of kids teasing one another.

"Thanks again, Chris," Melody said.

"No problem, Bookworm," he retorted.

"That's a compliment!" Melody yelled angrily. I saw Chris smile at her response.

"It's ok, Bookworm—calm down," I told her, continuing the heckle.

Melody scrunched her face and nudged my arm again. We continued to talk, and I told her some of the stories I'd read. She was excited and intrigued by all the stories I said and was looking forward to her next library visit.

As natural light faded away, we secluded back to our rooms. I quickly fell asleep after the long and eventful day—my mind occupied with thoughts of Melody, and our next trip to the library.

Chapter 10

Melody and I visited the library every week. After only a month, she read through 30 books—most of which were small picture books about weather and imaginary creatures. Next, she wanted to move on from "little kid books" and into something more mature. Her answer? Comic books.

The perils of Spider-Man, Batman, Wonder Woman, Catwoman, and The Avengers captured Melody. The action, the excitement, the character developments, the lengthy stories—all of it kept her wanting more. She even fashioned herself a cape from loose cloth and wore it around her neck. She ran around, jumped from bookshelves—acting like her favorite comic book characters. Occasionally, I would play the part of her trusty sidekick, ready to jump in if our make-believe excursions went awry.

One day, while on our walk to the library, Melody hopped up on a pile of debris and started making plane noises.

"What are you doing?" I said, laughing.

"I'm a superhero; what does it look like I'm doing?" She had her left arm outstretched to look like Superman.

"It looks like you're a crazy person."

"Well, then what does that make you?"

"The confused bystander," I told her. She chuckled. "Seriously, though, get down from there," I said. "You'll get yourself hurt."

While she climbed down, she said, "Nothing can hurt me. I am invincible!" She emulated sounds from an imaginary audience, who watched her during her graceful descent from the rubble—as if it were to be viewed by the entertaining eyes of an Olympic stadium.

She stood in front of me and asked, "Who would win in a fight? Batman or Iron Man?"

"Why those two?"

"They both have a lot of money."

"Oh, ok. Umm... I don't know. Iron Man, I guess?"

"What?" she said. "How could you say Iron Man wins in a fight against Batman?"

"He's got, like, the laser-things that shoot out from his hands, right?"

"Yeah, but Batman has a gadget for any situation. He could, maybe, pull out a laser deflecting suit or something. Or, he could use a shield that reflects lasers!"

We began to walk toward the library and spoke while we talked. "I didn't know Batman had a gadget for any situation," I said.

"How do you not know that? It's, like, a basic Batman fact."

"Listen, Melody. I don't want to upset you or anything, but... I don't read comic books."

She stopped walking—stunned.

"Whaaaaaat?" she exploded.

"Keep your voice down, Melody!" I put my finger in front of my lips. "They're just not my thing, ok? I tried getting into them when I was younger, but they didn't intrigue me—didn't catch my eye."

"How could you not like comic books? It's got action, it's got fighting, it's got Batman beating up bad guys, it's got Spider-Man web-swinging from buildings! It's got cool supervillains! It's got complex characters! It's got love!" She said the word love with a long, drawn-out 'uh' sound to make the word sound mocking. She also tilted her head onto my shoulder, to further the display.

"I don't care if it has love or supervillains or bad guys getting their comeuppance. I just like the books I like."

"Ok, then what kind of books do you like?"

"It changes all the time. Right now, I'm into biographies and autobiographies."

"You mean, those big books with, like, over 300 pages and no pictures?"

"Sure, I guess—that's a way to describe them."

"Hmm. Lame." She started walking again.

"What do you mean, 'lame'?" I caught up to her.

"I mean, how can you read something with no pictures? How will you know what's going on if you can't see it?"

"I imagine what it looks like! The books describe the scene or the setting, and you imagine how it all takes place in your mind. It's liberating. It's like your own interpretation of what you're reading and how you connect with—" I glanced at Melody, whose face was uncomfortably close to mine.

"Lame," she cut me off, curtly. We shared a laugh and continued toward the library where we made-believe some more.

For a few weeks after that, life became normalized. Vic and I continued training, Melody and I kept visiting the library. She was a quick learner and retained information faster than I could think of things to teach her. I also became more comfortable with other members of the group during this time. Things seemed regular.

On November 21st, however, things went abnormal. During the morning hours, Vic and I worked on my fighting skills using a staff. While we practiced, Vic always left a walkie-talkie outside with us, in case anything happened, and Vic needed to go. We heard Myles's voice over the walkie-talkie.

"Vic? Vic? Come in, Vic. We need to talk. Over," he said, franticly.

"Hold up," Vic told me. We stopped our combat. "Let's take five, yeah?" I nodded and leaned against the basketball pole and placed my staff on the ground.

"Yeah, Myles, what's up? Over." I heard Vic say into the walkie-talkie from across the court. He turned the volume down on the walkie-talkie, so he had to hold it up to his ear to hear Myles's reply. I guess he didn't want me listening in.

Vic grew quiet, and soon an expression of shock spilled across his face.

"You're kidding. That's insane. Over," he said. Quiet for a few moments more, then a reply from Vic, "Ok, uhm, I'm going to tell Chris, ok? Then I—I'll be right down. Just stay calm and stay safe. Over."

Vic looked at me; I must have borne a concerned look on my face. He motioned me over toward him.

"Hey, uh," he whispered, "Something came up. I'm going to meet Myles and the others. I'm going to tell Chris, and we're going to go. You'll be here alone. Is that ok?"

"Wait," I said, "What's happening? Why am I going to be here alone?"

"I don't have time," Vic began, "I need to go now. Stay here for a few minutes, then come inside. Lock the door behind you. You know that." He patted my shoulder and walked inside.

I followed Vic's orders and waited. I worked on my form during this time. I waited for what felt like a few minutes, then went inside.

I locked the door behind me and walked up the stairs. "Hello?" I yelled. "Anyone here?" No reply.

I wandered the foyer and looked in rooms to see if anyone was hiding. Not a soul. I walked around, taking a good look at the orphanage's inside; despite my living there for a while, I hadn't taken the time to look around by myself and explore where I lived. I mostly followed the same routine and never strayed too far from the format.

At the bottom of the stairs, I studied the pile of rubble. I examined the bits of concrete, which created the wall of debris; it looked sturdy. I tried to move the rubble and most past the pile, but it wouldn't budge.

Shrugging off the rubble from my body, I returned to the foyer. I desperately desired to peer into Chris's room, usually locked with him inside it. I received a sneak preview of the place on the night Melody and I asked to go to the library, but I'd forgotten the finer details. I checked the room and noticed it was left unlocked. He must have forgotten about it whenever Vic grabbed him and left.

Chris's room was dark and musty. I opened the door as far as it would go, to allow light to grace the room. There was a desk in the center of the room. Papers were strewn about its top. Pencils, pens, and markers were on top of the documents. I attempted to open some of the drawers on the desk, but I couldn't get them to open. A plastic chair sat behind the desk, and two beanbag chairs were on the floor across from the desk. Some papers were by the beanbag chairs as well.

The papers displayed what looked like schematics for buildings, and had illegible scribbles written in black marker. I did find one article that had a "To Do" list on it, where most of the "to do's" were illegible and/or marked out ultimately. A few of them I could make out though: "Visit the market", "Test walkie-talkies" (this one had a black line through it), "Visit the run-down business building", and "Talk w/Vic about Mike."

Upon seeing that last part, I placed the paper down and covered it up with more paper. What could that mean, "Talk about Mike"? Was it good? Was it bad? Have I not been doing enough around the orphanage? Was I doing too little? Did I do something wrong?

I swallowed hard and noticed another piece of paper—or, rather tiny rips of paper. They had tally marks written on them, and each stopped at seven tallies. I concluded these were Chris's version of a calendar. Autonomically, I grabbed a pen off the table, along with a mostly clean sheet of paper, and began drawing a calendar. I then dropped the materials and placed them all back the way it was before. I didn't want to insinuate I had been there, so I decided to keep the calendar-stuff between Melody and myself for the time being—our little secret. I wasn't ready to openly share my methods with a large group yet. The thoughts of what he would need to talk with Vic made me more and more curious. I wondered if I were to come back the next day to the "To Do" list, would that be marked off?

I left Chris's room and propped the door open like it was earlier. My attention turned to the two doors on my right; they were along a wall—one on the left side, and one on the right. The first door, the one more left, led to a small, empty white room. I paced the room, but it was only big enough for about two people. That said, it was spotless as if the end of the world did not affect it. It even had an odd smell to it—the smell of plaster and drywall.

The next room, which was in the corner of the foyer, opened to a much more expansive room and contained various materials. There were toys, food, utensils, building materials like hammers and some nails, paper, clothes, a few assorted weapons like pocket knives and staves, and some gloves. I was more drawn toward the toys than anything and found a tennis ball amidst the toy cars, dolls, and other balls. I picked up the tennis ball and bounced it off the walls of the room, but it was so big I had to chase the ball after. I decided to leave the room and throw it around the foyer instead.

I leaned against a wall and chucked the tennis ball across the foyer. It bounced back to me, returning the ball to my hands. It was simple, yet fun, to catch the ball and to think of new ways to bounce it off the wall. Eventually, I wondered what would happen if I threw it as hard as I could. So, I did, and the ball flew all over the foyer.

I decided to do the same thing again, but this time I opened the door to the small narrow room relative to Chris's room. Once again, I threw the tennis ball as hard as I could—this time, it bounced furiously inside the small room. However, something caught my interest; as it bounced around the room, it made a very hollow noise as it hit one of the walls. The other walls connected with created a deep sound that made it seem like they were reinforced by something, but one didn't give that sound back. I went and retrieved the ball, then replicated my previous action; the noise continued. After recovering the ball, I went a bit closer to the room, threw the ball against the left wall, and let it bounce around the room again. Every time the tennis ball hit that left wall, it made the hollow sound. Growing frustrated, I threw a punch at the left wall of this room. To my surprise, the entire wall felt loosely held up and shook when I struck it.

I punched again, and my hand went through the wall, creating a large hole. I went into the other room and grabbed a hammer. I started to tear down this odd wall. It wasn't anything logical or rational; it felt autonomic.

The first hammer strike into the wall went straight through it, creating another huge hole. A light shined through while I continued to hit the wall. I thought of Chris walking in at this moment and reprimanding me, but it was quickly shut out by my natural curiosity.

I continued to break the wall until I had enough taken out that I could see the other side—an entirely new room. I still couldn't see much of this new room, which made me want to find out more. I easily broke down the rest of the wall, revealing a spiral staircase in the far corner of the room. I dropped the hammer immediately after seeing the staircase and rushed to the top. The stairs were metal and gave a loud echoic noise as I climbed the stairs. Once I reached the top, I opened the door to reveal an entirely new foyer.

The new foyer was dusty, and I coughed heavily after entering. It looked like the other foyer, but this room had a slanted wall and window to my right. It gave the place an eerie green light as if it was made of stained glass. I approached the window and wiped off a section of it with my shirt. A gentle yellow light shone on my face, blinding me for a second. I stepped away, and the view was beautiful. It was harsh and direct, like a spotlight, highlighting everything was illuminated.

The room was akin to the small narrow room; it was as if the room hadn't been touched or affected in any way by the end of the world. Instead, it looked unattended.

Across the foyer was a single room. The door was open so that I could enter. I found a small bedroom with three beds, one along each wall, with sheets, mattresses, and pillows. There were no windows, but a small lantern sat atop a nightstand in the corner. The room looked dusty but otherwise was untouched. The beds were still all made to look tidy.

This made me even more excited. I thought of what everyone would think of this new, undiscovered area right above us. What would they think? Would they sing their praises onto me? Would they trust me now? Would I receive more responsibilities besides being Melody's teacher? What other uses could this foyer bring, especially with the actual bedroom with actual beds!

I exited the bedroom and found, to my right, a small kitchen. It had a small brick oven and stovetop, as well as an out-of-order sink. Peering inside gave me the idea that we could start a fire inside the oven, and even cook food. There was a small area with dried grass underneath a grate. A pot rested on top of it. I pulled the pot out and closed the oven.

I walked over to the large window and wiped off a bit more of the green from it, creating patches of green color on my shirt. Eventually, I made an area large enough for me to look out of, and saw members of our group outside, carrying Speed. For a while, I forgot they were all out and I was alone. I quickly ran back downstairs into the original foyer and shut the door to this new area behind me. It looked as if nothing was different.

I heard the noises and screams from below as everyone piled in through the front door. They soon made their way up the stairs and into the foyer. First was Billy—the horror on his face conveyed all I needed to know about what was about to appear before me.

Grunts and cries of pain grew louder as the rest of the group worked their way up the stairs. I saw Chris, then Vic, who held the other end of a makeshift stretcher, which had Speed lying on top of it. Stains of red blotted the white fabric, with some of the red liquid seeping through.

"Out of the way, Mike!" Chris barked. I stepped aside and put myself against the wall. As they passed by, I noticed Speed holding a towel up to his left leg, and he was applying any pressure he could to it. He couldn't stop laughing.

Once they reached the center of the room, Chris turned around, looked at Vic, then spoke to Speed. "Hey Speed, Vic and I are going to put you down now, ok? Is that ok?"

"Uh-huh," Speed managed to mutter through exasperated breaths and expedited panting. The two boys slowly lowered the stretcher onto the ground. When it touched the floor, Speed released a loud cry of pain, which soon turned back to laughter.

"Alright," Chris said, "Speed, just stay here for a few seconds. I'm going to get into my room and grab some supplies to fix you up."

"Oh, trust me, I'm not going anywhere!" Speed yelled back. He then burst into nervous laughter, quickly becoming an "Ow!" and he grasped at his leg.

"Here, let me hold it," Vic said and grabbed the towel from Speed. He applied more pressure to the wound. I hadn't seen the gash yet, but I knew it was terrible from the amount of blood I saw.

Speed let out another gasp when Vic applied pressure to the wound. "Don't make me get up and hurt you too, Vic!" He chuckled a bit before going back into a fit of screaming.

I glanced to my right and noticed Melody and Myles. They glanced back.

"Mike!" Melody exclaimed. She let out a loud sigh and rushed over to grab my shoulders.

"Hey. Are you ok?" I asked. I took her hands off my shoulders and held her forearms.

"Yes, I'm fine. Speed was the only one hurt," she told me. She looked back at Speed, still holding my arms.

"What happened?" I asked. Melody turned her head around, but Myles walked up and answered my question before her.

"We were scavenging for supplies, and stupid there," he nodded toward Speed, "decided it would be funny to try and jump off some debris, probably trying to act cool for Melody. Instead, he messed up and got a huge piece of rebar stuck through his leg."

"Jeez," I let out. I released Melody's arms and placed my hands over my mouth.

"Yeah, it was pretty gnarly." Myles looked at Speed. "Hopefully, it isn't too bad, though."

"Was the rebar rusted?" I asked.

"What? Uh, I don't know. Why?" Myles asked, confused.

"Well, you know, he could have tetanus if there's rust..." I replied.

"What's tetanus?" he asked, still confused.

Before I could answer, Chris reappeared from his room. Everyone's attention was on him. Peter also emerged from the stairwell and presented himself in the room.

"Ah, good. Peter, come here for a second," Chris said. Peter rushed over toward Speed. "I need you to take the towel away from Vic and disinfect the wound with alcohol."

"Ok," Peter said. He placed his hands on the towel, releasing Vic's grip on Speed's leg, and slowly pulled it away from the cloth. It revealed a bloodied hole that went straight through Speed's calf. Blood seemed to stop oozing from the cavity, outside of a few spurts pumped every so often. The feeling of air hitting the open wound made Speed wince.

Chris picked up a cleaner towel from his gaggle of supplies and placed it inside Speed's mouth. "Here, bite on this. This could hurt in a minute."

"Plus, it'll keep his mouth shut for a little while," Vic said under his breath.

Chris heard that and chuckled. He then grabbed a cotton ball and gave it to Peter. "Put the alcohol on this, and dab it on the wound. Don't just pour it all over the place."

Peter nodded, took the cotton ball from Chris, poured some alcohol on it, and dabbed it on as directed. Speed yelled, but the towel in his mouth muffled out most of the sound.

The light dimmed with the impatience of the day. Chris stayed hunched over Speed's leg while he performed surgery; he dispatched stitches, disinfecting ointment, bandages, and gauze. Speed passed out from either blood loss or pain after a while, making the operation easier for Chris. Peter did everything Chris told him to do, with Vic administering any additional help required. Vic carefully examined everything Chris was doing. Melody, Myles, and I watched patiently from the side, waiting for the operation to be over.

Just as dusk began to creep through the windows and dwindle at the foyer's illumination, Chris finished. He stood above Speed's limp body and told Vic to follow him and Peter out back and get some water to wash their hands of Speed's blood. They all left, while we three were left to see the results of their work. Speed was still passed out, with the left-pant of his jeans ripped off, and a considerable amount of gauze was taped and secured onto his leg. It looked compact, but Speed wasn't walking anytime soon.

"He's not going to die or anything, right?" Melody asked. We edged closer to him. I leaned in and put my ear to his chest.

"No," I said, "At least, I don't think he will. His breathing is more regulated now, so that's a good sign."

"He's probably just exhausted from everything," Myles said, "C'mon, let's go back to our room and leave him be for now. We've had a rough day."

"Uh, hold on," I told them, "Let's wait for everyone else to get back first. I have something I need to show you all."

We waited for the three boys to return. When they entered the foyer, Myles said, "Mike was just telling us has something he wants to show everyone."

"Oh, does he?" Chris said. He looked over to Speed on the ground. "He's doing fine, I presume?"

"Yeah, he's just sleeping now," Myles answered.

"Great." Chris let out a huge sigh. "Alright, Mike, what is it you want to show us?"

"Yeah, um, just follow me," I said. Chris gathered everyone as I led them across the foyer toward the door leading to the hidden room. "I hope you're not too mad with me," I said toward Chris, "but I tore down a wall..." I opened the door and showcased the now-missing wall and the set of spiral stairs, which led to the upstairs. A face of wonder and intrigue manifested across their faces.

I led the group up the stairs and brought them to the new foyer. Melody immediately ran to the other side.

"Look at how big this place is!" she yelled. Her voice echoed off the walls of the empty room.

"Hey, not too loud now," Vic said. "Though, this is rather nice." He then joined in making loud noises and hearing the slight echoes.

Even Peter was in awe. "I always wondered about the glass pane on the orphanage's side, but we never found anything to bring us up to it."

"How did you find this?" Chris asked me.

"I was bouncing a ball off the walls earlier, and it got stuck in the room below. It made a weird noise, so I, uh, punched through it," I told him.

"Oh," Chris replied. He paused for a few seconds, watching the others meander about the room. He also looked around but was more observant than actively participating in the excavation of this new area. Chris looked at me after a while. "You punched through it?"

"It was, like, drywall, or something. It wasn't very thick, which is why I think it made a different noise from the other walls." Chris looked away and left me hanging on my own words. I continued, "That room also smelled of paint as if it were either new or never touched..."

Chris scrunched his face. "I never thought much of the room because of how small it was and, now that you mention it, the smell. Perhaps I should have..." he trailed off. After thinking for a few brief moments, he said, "Regardless, well done, Mike. I'm sure this new space will be of great use to us."

"There's a bedroom over here!" Melody exclaimed. Everyone stopped whatever they were doing and walked over to meet her.

"Let me see," Vic said. He pushed his way through Melody and into the room; he apologized for pushing her.

"Do you think we should move Speed up here? Lay him on that bed there—against the wall," I pointed out.

"I don't know if that's a good idea," Chris said, "He needs rest. Plus, I want to give the wound some more time to heal before—"

He was cut off by Vic, who interjected, "No, wait, that's a great idea. Give him a bed to rest in, instead of the dirty floor."

"Maybe later," Chris asserted, "I don't want to risk moving him."

"Why not?" Vic asked. "We can move him slowly and carefully; Mike and I could do it easily."

"I said no, and that's final," Chris said, a little louder than his usual volume. Vic was taken aback, as was everyone else. Peter leaned in and whispered something into Chris's ear. I couldn't catch the words.

Peter leaned away, and Chris closed his eyes and nodded. "Fine, do it. But if anything goes wrong, it's on you, Victor."

"Who gets the other two beds?" Melody asked. She had been in the room the whole time during this back-and-forth and had only now re-entered the conversation. "Cause there's still two more. There and there," she pointed toward the two other beds that were on the other side of the room, across from the one where Speed would rest.

"Yeah, what about the other two beds?" Myles chimed in. "Who gets those?"

"I mean, it would make sense for Mike to have one since he did find it," Vic said.

"Ok, but—and no offense, Mike—but he's new," Billy said. "I've been here just as long as you have, Vic, and I don't want to sleep on the floor anymore. If Mike gets a bed, then only one of us veterans gets the last one."

I was ok with the idea of getting one since I found the room to begin with. If I weren't left behind, no one would even know of this floor's existence. That said, the sinking idea of Billy's argument got to me: Why should I be privileged when they ultimately do more than me and have been together longer than me? The only thing I had done was to find this room. I felt isolated and detached from everyone. Realizing my trivial existence within the group overcame me.

In my wallowing, I noticed Chris gave me a curious look. It was as if he was contemplating something, and I felt like he was looking straight through me.

"Let's draw straws," I blurted out. I didn't even think about what I said—another involuntary action.

Billy pointed at me. "Now there's an idea," he said. We proceeded to rip off some wood peeling from the bedroom door and fashion them into flimsy sticks that would allow everyone to draw from them. Chris and Peter did not participate, as they already had their room.

The rest drew sticks, simplifying the results: Melody and Myles would share the room with Speed. I was a little upset by the results, even if it was entirely fair and random.

"That settles that, then," Chris said after announcing the results. "Melody and Myles, you two get the beds. So, if you have anything from downstairs, go ahead and bring them up here." He turned toward Vic, "And you. You and Mike go downstairs, wake up Speed, and put him in his new bed." We started to walk away, but Chris put his hand on Vic's shoulder. His words were ghastly. "Do be mindful; I spent hours stitching that gash. I'd rather not do that again." Vic nodded, shaken, and grabbed me to get going.

We were about halfway across the new foyer when stopped us again, "Hold up!" We stopped and turned. "Mike, did you check these cabinets yet?"

"No," I replied, starting to walk back toward the kitchen area, "It didn't occur to me to check them." I got a scornful stare from Peter upon saying that, and I felt a little hurt. I didn't know why I got such a hateful look from him, but he did not seem to enjoy my answer.

"Well, get in the habit of doing that," Chris told me. "It's all a part of being attentive to your surroundings..." He then opened a few of the cabinets, and let out an audible gasp. "Oh, my..." he said as he frantically opened more and more cabinets.

Food. Cans and cans of food lined in the cabinets. Raw ingredients, canned vegetables, non-perishables, cups, bowls, cooking utensils, and recipes hid within the wooden cupboards.

"Billy, are you seeing this?" Chris asked.

"Yeah, this is amazing! And look, there's even a stove and kettle—we can cook actual meals instead of just eating straight from the can." Billy ran his hands over the kitchen. "I can't wait to try this all out..." he trailed off, and began picking up all sorts of items from the cupboards and examined them.

"Mike, do you know what all this means?" Chris asked me.

"Umm," I replied, looking at Billy as he was overly fascinated by the kitchen area. "We can cook?"

"We can cook!" Chris exclaimed, "We were starving, and you found us this room with enough food to last at least a few weeks with, and we can boil water and—and, we can cook, we can cook! Mike, seriously, thank you." He paused for a moment and could tell I was curious about Billy. "Oh right, Billy's always been good with food. He's always liked to try different food for us, combining foods and all that. This is right up his alley." Billy looked like a little kid seeing the world for the first time as he played with every knob and utensil to get a feel for what everything did or could do.

"But what about the fire?" Peter asked. "Wouldn't that create smoke, and be obvious that people live here? That's a little concerning, don't you think?"

"... Don't take this from me, Peter," Billy told him.

Chris chimed in. "While that's a good point, I don't want to think about that right now. We have food, and I just can't think more negative thoughts right now."

Peter shrugged his shoulders and began to examine the kitchen too. Seconds later, I heard him say, "Mike, did you see this over here?" I walked over to him, and he pointed to a door in the kitchen.

"No, I guess I didn't. I pretty much found this place right before you all came back; I didn't get to explore all of it."

Peter tilted his head to show he understood. He opened the door, which was unlocked. Behind the door was a small room with a few more cooking supplies inside, and a tiny staircase that went straight up.

"Where does that lead?" I asked.

"Most likely the roof," Peter replied, frankly. "Well, at least we can test out my smoke-theory sometime." He yawned. "But I'm not going to check that out right now; I need to get some sleep." He left the room. I surveyed the small, blocky room. It had a wooden floor—unfinished—and had a few empty burlap sacks on the floor, underneath some cans of preserved corn. I closed the door behind me when I left.

Melody and Myles scuttled into their new room, and Vic and I proceeded to move Speed into his new bed. He wasn't cognizant when we were moving him, and we made sure to be mindful of his injury. Right as we placed him into bed, he fell right back to sleep.

Afterward, we all made our way into our new and separate sleeping arrangements. The room which used to hold six now had only three: Billy, Vic, and myself. It was nice to have a bit more room, but the absence of Melody, Myles, and Speed was more apparent.

"It sucks that we're still stuck in this room," Billy said. "I would have liked to be in one of those beds upstairs."

"Yeah," Vic said, "But, it was all fair. And good for them—they both work hard, let them have it. I'm happy for them."

I nodded my head. I was still upset that I was stuck downstairs, but I understood why that was so. I thought more about Chris's expression that night and how he seemed interested in something; however, it didn't seem he was involved in me, per-say. The way he looked seemed as if he wasn't thinking particularly about someone, but rather something—a thought—an idea.

I wondered again about the note in Chris's room: "Talk w/Vic about Mike. What would that mean now? Did my random discovery prove my existence to the group?? I should have felt proud of my accomplishment, yet I felt damned by my lastingness to check the drawers and room like Chris and Peter immediately did. I wanted to feel special, but I couldn't

help but feel anything other than completely, entirely ordi-
nary.

I tried to imagine what was going through Chris's mind,
but in that thinking, I drifted to sleep—eventually forgetting
my train of thought.

Chapter 11

The next morning Billy woke me up. He towered over my slumped body.

"What?" I exclaimed. My arms flailed while Billy laughed at my plight. I sat upright. "Gosh, you scared me."

"Sorry," Billy said, still laughing. "Probably should have stood farther away."

"Whatever," I groggily replied. I stretched my arms. "What do you need?"

"I don't know," Billy replied. "Chris wanted me to wake you; didn't think to ask why."

He walked away and out of the room. I took a few seconds to compose myself and to wake up a little before I followed Billy out of the room. I saw everyone huddled around what food we had in the foyer. A handful of cans rested there, with only a few more in the hands of everyone else.

I waved at Melody, who noticed me walk out of the room. She excitedly waved back. Chris was sitting next to her, and I waved to him as well. He cocked his head in an "Understood" manner and went back to eating. Peter was sitting across from Chris and motioned for him to grab a fork.

"Lucky that I found that room upstairs, huh?" I said to Peter. "We were running low on food."

"Yeah," Peter said, chewing, "We haven't been able to find anything recently."

"Why is that?" I asked.

"Well, not that you'd know because you're still in training, but we typically stay close to the orphanage when we scrounge for materials or food. We're running out of places to check. But now—if Chris agrees with me on this—I think we can start trying to explore a bit further out."

Chris shook his head. He shouted from across the room. "Not yet."

"Why not?"

"For starters, our water supply is running low again."

"Oh, really? It's that time again?"

"Yeah. So, I kind of want to have you guys make that journey today. Some of you."

Peter scrunched his brow and turned his head. He looked interested in the idea.

Chris continued, "I want Billy, Vic, and myself to go get water today."

"Ok," Peter said, "What about me? What do I do? I usually go with you to get water..."

"I want you, Melody, Myles, and Mike to go—"

"Wait, what?" Peter interrupted. "Hold up. You want me to bring Mike?" He turned to me, "No offense to you, or anything," and then back at Chris, and said more quietly, "but are you sure he's ready to go out?"

"He takes Melody to the library every 7th day, and he found us the attic. He's been practicing with Vic since he got here. He'll never learn unless he's thrust into it. Besides, I think he should be ready."

"Yeah, but if we get into any trouble..."

"Let's hope you don't."

"But if we do?"

"You'll manage, ok?" Chris seemed aggravated by Peter's push back, but quickly got over it. "I want you and your crew to go search for a cookbook."

"A what-was-that?" Peter asked. "You're going out to get water, and you want me to take the kids and look for some stupid book?"

"It's not just 'some stupid book,' ok, Peter. Now that we have a kitchen, I'd like Billy to start trying to cook actual meals or make something better than canned peaches."

Billy perked up at the sound of his name. "Wha?" he said, his mouth full of food. Some morsels of peaches spat out and landed on Vic's face. Myles, Melody, and I laughed. Vic chuckled shyly and wiped his face.

"I saw that you were tinkering around upstairs with the cooking materials, Billy," Chris told him. "I think you would be good at it."

"I mean, yeah, sure. I could try it. I can't read, though..."

"That's fine," Chris said, "We'll deal with that problem when we get to it. I want you to be our main cook, but I would sometimes help, too. At least, that's my goal."

"Do you think the library would have a cookbook?" I asked Chris.

"I don't know, Mike. You're there more than me; do you remember seeing any?" Chris answered.

I opened my mouth, but no words came out. Come to think of it, I don't remember the library having anything related to cooking. That was about the only thing that the place didn't have. I closed my mouth.

"Well, either way," Chris continued, "There are a couple of places deeper in the city that I think might have a cookbook or two. Old restaurants, bakeries—places like that."

"Is that why you were asking me about what places I've been to last night?" Peter asked.

"Exactly why, my friend." Chris finished eating and stood up. "I'm going to get the canisters ready and all that, Billy and Vic. You two finish up eating. Join me when you're done. I'd like to get this done sooner rather than later. It's a long trip." Chris walked away.

"Hey, Chris!" Melody yelled. Chris turned around. "What about Speed?"

"What about-oh! Crap, I forgot about him. Thank you, Melody. Um, I guess if you could bring him something to eat, that would be great. Did he wake up yet?"

"Yeah, he's awake," Myles answered. "He was talking our ears off about how his leg hurts and poking fun of how we get to room with him. Just being his usual-ass self."

"Well, that's good. I guess," Chris said.

"You think he'll be fine all by himself here?" Peter asked. "We could leave Mike behind just to tend for him, make sure nothing bad happens."

"No, I want Mike to go with you. As long as we lock the door behind us, and we both take a key, he should be fine." Chris then walked out of the foyer and into the recreational room, and a few moments later came out with an armful of empty jugs to be filled. Billy and Vic scarfed down the rest of their food to help Chris. Melody grabbed a can of peaches, opened them, and swiped a fork for the food. She went up to the attic to feed Speed.

As I finished eating, along with Peter and Myles, Peter told us, "Alright, so I have a few places we can check to find a cookbook or two, but I wouldn't expect to find anything today. We need to walk a while before we even get there, and I don't want to spend too long out today, to be honest. Plus, given this is your first time out, Mike, I'd rather this not be too hard a day for you." I nodded. "If you two want to help me get ready with taking what I think we'll need, that would be great. Melody should be able to find us when she gets done."

We followed him to the corner of the foyer, grabbed four messenger bags, a couple of smaller food items, and a walkie talkie. We entered the recreational room. All the water jugs were empty; only a few bottles filled with water were left. We grabbed them and stuffed them into the bags.

"Mike," Peter asked, "How comfortable are you with a polearm?"

"Uh..." I paused. I didn't exactly know what he was referring to.

"You know... a staff?" Peter continued.

"Oh! Yeah, that's what Vic and I have just started practicing, and I'm not too bad with it."

"Ok, then you can take the staff." Peter pointed to what looked like a broom, but it was torn at the brush part.

"What do I need this for?" I asked.

"In case we get into trouble."

"I don't think we'll get into trouble," Myles said. "You're being paranoid about this whole thing, Peter."

"I just like to be prepared, Myles—that's all." He grabbed a wrench and put it into his bag. "I like to use my fists if I can, but if things get hairy, good ol' Harry's got my back." He pointed to the wrench.

"You named your wrench Harry?" I asked.

"Yeah. Got a problem with that?"

"No. I just find it interesting, is all."

Myles picked up some daggers with sheaths, that looked like they attached to someone's waistline, and stuffed them into one of the bags.

"Is that what you're bringing?" I asked Myles, watching him put the daggers into the bag. "I thought you didn't think we'd get into trouble?"

"I don't think we'll get into trouble. Plus, I'm not fond of fighting. I'll do it if I have to, but I'd rather avoid it altogether," Myles answered. "These are for Melody."

"I always tell him to bring something, but he never listens," Peter jumped in.

"And every time things get sticky, we make our way out just fine without violence," he answered.

"Whatever," Peter said, "I bring things just in case, so does Melody. Never hurts to be safe." He walked away and out of the room.

"Either way, Mike," Myles continued, "These aren't for me. Melody is good with a dagger or a knife. She likes to dart around and sneak if we get into trouble."

"I thought you said you never had a run-in with violence?" I asked.

"Partly true. We've never had to kill anyone. Peter, Melody, Vic—if someone bad shows up, they might injure the bad guys or fight them, but most often, we just run away. Killing isn't exactly high on our list of things to do when scavenging."

I nodded my head. About this time, Melody came down from the attic and met up with us. Myles handed her the bag of daggers, and we left to meet up with Peter.

Peter was down by the entrance to the orphanage rummaging through some apparel. He pulled out some gloves, a black scarf, a black bandana, a hat, and a pair of goggles.

"Here, put these on," he said to me.

"What for?" I asked.

"A few reasons," he said, "One: to hide our identities. Two: there's a lot of dust and dirt out there; keeps us safe."

While hesitant to the idea, I took the garb from him and put it on. It was a little hard to see, and the scarf was a bit too big for me, but I would make do. I looked over to see Melody sharing a bit of the complication with me. However, it didn't seem to affect her as much. She seemed comfortable with it.

We left quickly. We secured the lock on the door before we entered the world. Blurry winds of gray and black matter brushed my clothes.

"Follow my lead," Peter said, to which we lined up behind him while he led us through the streets. Some of it seemed familiar, as it was part of the path Melody and I took to the library. However, a few minutes into this track, and we deviated from my familiarity. I became entirely reliant on Peter's navigation.

A few minutes later, Myles broke the silence: "So, how much of the city do you know?" he asked me.

"Not much, really," I replied. "I only know the area around the library. Otherwise, I recognize landmarks that lead me to the library."

"Well, you'll get to know the city pretty well if you keep with us for a while," he said. "I know a few areas around the orphanage, but nothing out this far. That's why we let Peter lead when we go out. He knows the city the best out of anyone."

"What was that you said about me?" Peter asked from about 10 feet ahead.

"Nothing," Myles replied. Peter turned around and kept walking. He whispered to me, "Everything's an insult with him; never can accept that we are talking positively about him sometimes."

We walked and followed in Peter's footsteps until we reached a run-down and broken-into building.

Melody pointed it out to us. "Hey, what's this?"

"Looks like a market. The windows are busted..." he peered inside. "It's not dusty, which means this was recent." He looked around some more. "It might have been boarded up, and then someone broke into it. Notice all the wood splints and glass everywhere?" We looked at the ground he was referring to. Glass rested atop of broken wood splints on the concrete beneath us. I noticed chunks of wood on the outside of the market, next to the windows. They were still hanging by the nails deeply sunk into them.

"Can we stop and see what we find?" Melody asked. "I bet we'll have room for supplies if we find any here."

"Good idea," Peter said. "Yeah, let's check quick and see if there's anything."

Myles took a crowbar from his bag and started to wipe away some of the broken glass from one of the windows.

"After you," he said, motioning to Melody, who was closest to him. "Watch your head," he added. The entrance through the window was small, so Melody had to bend almost in two to get through. I slipped through next, and then Myles. Peter was too big to get in.

"Leave me out here all alone, huh?" he laughed from outside the window. "I'll survey out here and see if there's anything interesting. Though, I doubt it." Peter walked away, leaving us alone.

The inside of the market was relatively clean. Near the broken-in window was a bit of dust and dirt, newly added. Further toward the back of the building, though, was more well-kept. Some of the shelves were empty, but many had items such as packages of homemade bread, cans of corn, and a few packs of dried jerky. There were also cases and cases of bottled water.

"I think we hit the jackpot," Myles said.

"Yeah!" Melody exclaimed, "I've never had homemade bread before! And we haven't had corn in so long..." she trailed off as she started to fill her bag full of food.

"Homemade bread..." I muttered. It was odd seeing bread this new at the store. By this point, any bread produced before The Fallout would have rotted, molded, or been turned stale as a brick. I pressed on the bread and it was squishy—fresh. "Let's be quick," I said, concerned.

I decided to leave my bag empty, as we still had supplies at the bakery to obtain. I looked around the market more. Near the back was an area that was a butcher; weights and prices of different kinds of meats were displayed behind a glass counter. The glass was transparent, unlike some of the windows on the outsides of buildings were. I could see cloth on the other side of the glass—it looked like towels.

I walked behind the butcher's counter to feel the towels. They weren't wet, but had a slick feel—dampened, almost, with impressions of items left on them. Behind me was a door that was locked when I tried to jiggle the handle. There didn't seem to be a key anywhere around either.

Once Myles and Melody had their bags full of food, they motioned me to leave. They kept boasting about how they were going to have to remember this place, as there were still a hefty number of things left. We exited the building and called for Peter. Within seconds, he showed up from the alleyway to our left.

"You find anything?" I asked.

"Not really. I did find a door leading out into the alley; locked though."

"Yeah, I noticed one inside, too, locked as well."

"Ah well," he said. "What about you two?" he said toward Myles and Melody. "Your bags look filled!"

"There was corn, and-and bread, and-and water, and-and-" Melody tried to speak, but kept stumbling from her excitement.

"Whoa, calm down there, Bookworm," Peter joked, "That's awesome you found all that, but is there room still for our supplies at the bakery?"

"That's why my bag is empty," I told him.

"Hey, look at you! Thinking ahead, and all that." He gave me a little finger-gun—I cocked my head back as if he had hit me with it. He smiled, but it soon faded. "Wait, did you say bread?"

"Yeah!" Melody exclaimed. "It looks so good, too!"

I looked at Peter and made a face of worry. He nodded.

"Let's get going," he said. "Quickly. This put us behind schedule."

And so, we went. While initially excited about her finds, Melody soon grew tired of lugging around all the food. She complained a good portion of the way, with Peter snapping at her now and again about how, "If you're having such a problem with it, why don't you just drop it?"

Then she would mutter, "No..." underneath her breath and stayed quiet for a bit longer until she would eventually complain again. Myles and I would laugh to ourselves when they started going at it with each other, and every cycle seemed funnier. We ultimately took bets on how long it would take for Melody to start complaining again. She gave us some mean glares, but we knew they were empty-hearted.

We walked for what felt like all day but soon reached the bakery. By this point, I became so incognizant to where we were going; everything looked foreign to me. My mind ran at half speed due to the monotony of walking and following behind Peter. My senses overloaded from the dilapidated glorious skyscrapers filling my sights. I was speechless most of the time. It took me a few moments to stop walking when Peter told us that we were at the bakery.

The building itself was gray on the outside, like everything else around it. It blended into the walls—you wouldn't know if you weren't paying attention. A small wooden panel was wedged in the door frame.

"This place was my find," Peter told me, "And we put this little wood panel here, so it would be hard to get in. See, you have to push hard on it..." he pushed on the wood, and it creaked backward, barely enough so someone could fit through it. "Like a doggy-door," he added.

He held the panel open and let us creep inside. Myles and Melody had a harder time getting through, but they were persistent in keeping their bags with them. Peter and I had no problems crawling inside.

The bakery's inside had shown some wear-and-tear. Many of the shelves were falling apart or were ripped from the wall entirely. Our interest, however, was on the workstation in the back. Pots, pans, and aprons and utensils were littered—clinking and clanking when we walked past and pushed against them.

Peter told me to grab anything I could fit into the bag. I grabbed a large pot and pan, some knives, forks, spoons, a thermometer, and an apron that had "Kiss the Chef!" written on it. I figured Billy would find that amusing, right in his line of humor.

We were only in the bakery for a few minutes until we had all we needed, and Peter led us out. "I think if we hurry back," he said, "we can return to the orphanage before it gets too dark."

Upon exiting the building, of which Peter and myself left last, we emerged to a group of boys—about six or seven of them—in a line waiting for us.

"Uh, hello, boys," Peter said to them.

They didn't reply. Under one of their breaths I heard, "Are those the thieves?"

"Thieves?" Peter exclaimed. "Excuse me, but I don't believe we have stolen anything from you. And if we did, I'm sure we would have done so with more prowess than to be caught."

"Oh-ho, so you don't steal?" one of them asked. He stepped forward, toward Peter. He looked to be the oldest of the group, tallest—about as tall as Peter, though short a few inches. His bits of facial hair imitated a beard. He stood firmly, despite having a slight limp. "Well, then," he continued, "what's in the pretty girl's bag?" He pointed to Melody, whose bag was still overflowing with bread and corn, practically spilling out onto the street. "That's our stuff. That little building you guys broke into? That was our place. And we don't take too kindly to people uninvited, taking and leaving our stuff without a little something in return."

"We didn't break into your place," Peter said, inching closer to the kid. "It was already smashed open when we got there; we figured no one must live there. It was a dump anyway."

"You best watch your tongue, boy, before I cut it out," the kid said, and he pulled a knife out from the inside of his jacket. He held it to Peter's chin.

Melody tried rummaging through her bag to get her weapons out, but they were too far on the bottom to reach. Even then, this group outnumbered us. I had easy access to my polearm and a few knives I took from the bakery, but I wasn't about to start a fight if I didn't have to.

"Stop," Peter yelled back at us. "No need to get into a fight. And easy there, champ," he said to the knife. Peter backed away a few steps. "How'd you even find us, anyway?"

"Cute one's bag is leaking," one of the younger boys said from the pack. "We followed the trail."

We all looked at Melody's bag. There was a large wet spot at the bottom of the bag, still dripping. One of the bottles of water got crushed by everything in the bag—which caused it to rupture. We saw the water trail, easily noticeable, as the water was savored by the concrete, which probably hadn't seen any rain for years.

Melody tried to get an apology out, but the words were fragmented and lost to the wind.

"Don't apologize, Melody," Peter told her. "It's not your fault. We'll get through this." He turned back to face the kid still holding the knife. "But I'm being serious. We didn't break into your place. It was already broken into. If we knew that place was yours, we wouldn't have taken your stuff. Now, we can give you back your stuff and forget all this ever happened. Sound good?"

"If you didn't break in, who did?" the knife asked, frantically. He tightly gripped his weapon.

"I don't know, but it wasn't us, trust me."

"Trust you?" The knife laughed. "Trust a thief who stole from us?"

"It wouldn't be stealing if we gave it back," Peter retorted. "And if you would stop trying to impress your buddies with your want-to-be attitude, and knew when to pick your fights, you'd be a lot better off."

The kid with the knife didn't like that. Instead, he rushed forward and plunged the knife deep into Peter's chest. Everyone who was witness gasped, including the other party. The knife kid held a grimace, which turned to a smile. Peter reached for the knife, but the kid drew the knife back out and pushed Peter to the ground. Peter fell into a fetal position, clutching at the gaping hole in his chest.

Red flashed into my eyes. The bag over my shoulder slid off as I seamlessly went in and struck the kid with my fist. He tried to hit back, but I dodged and pelted a few more shots into his side. I ripped the knife from his hand, twisted it between my fingers, and drove it into his shoulder blade. He attempted to grab me, but I shook free, hit him a few more times in the side, then took a shot at his head. It took him to the ground. I sat atop him and continually pelted his skull with my fists. I didn't stop until his head caved in on itself. The world went binary. Yes/no. On/off. Life/death.

Blood seeping out of his puffed mouth, I was grabbed by Melody. She yelled, "STOP" the whole time. I was too caught up in the moment to hear the noise. My ears rang. She heaved and pulled me away from the kid, which brought me to my feet again. My hands were covered in red and felt sticky. My face felt hot, but splotches of blood ran down, cooling my cheeks. The knife's blood gave me a streaked red countenance.

After the initial shock, I heard one of the boys from the other party yell, "Get them!" and they began charging toward us.

Myles yelled at us, "We've got to go!" I stayed, still shaken by all that happened. Melody took hold of my hand and yanked me away. It was so fast. She led me toward Myles, who was already running away. While being guided, I looked back at the mess: Peter, still squirming on the ground, with a red pool growing more abundant around him, a boy with an even larger pool of red, and two bags of silver tableware.

Melody was still clutching my hand. I took hold of my senses again and soon ran on my own—still connected with Melody. We passed through alleys, jumped over trash cans, pushed over boxes—anything to slow down the group of boys running after us. We could hear their footsteps growing quieter.

We turned a corner and saw nothing but a vast stretch of road. We sprinted in that direction, but so did the group of boys—they were right behind us again. Melody started to lag—her bag was too heavy, and it impaired her movement. "Come on, Melody!" Myles yelled. She threw the bag off her body and left it behind. One of the boys chasing us tripped over it and landed on his face.

We continued running and darted down more alleys until Myles eventually noticed a row of shops. He checked one of them quickly and found it was unlocked. We shuffled inside and quietly closed the door. We all sat with our backs to the door to block it. We didn't breathe. Adrenaline pumped through our veins. Our hearts pattered so quickly we feared they would give away our solitude. We held our breaths until we realized no sounds were coming from outside the building. Myles inched his way toward the nearest window and peered outside. He didn't see anything but a piece of tumbling newspaper.

"I think we lost them," he told us. Melody and I took our bodies off the door. I turned around to make sure it was locked. It had three locking mechanisms, and I made sure I used each one.

We collapsed on the floor of the room and didn't move or speak until dark. The normal flow of time resumed once more.

Chapter 12

The blood had dried. My hands were stained red. I took the bottle of water next to me and poured some of its contents over my hands. I tried to wash away the blood, but my hands still held a red pigment to them.

Enough time had passed since our chase that the world was utterly devoid of light. The city felt more dangerous; the sanctity of safety was left behind with Peter and his bag of supplies.

I felt around the darkness to understand my surroundings. I found a few aisles, so I thought this must be a shop of some kind. My hand then passed over some shattered glass, but it thankfully didn't cut my hand. I decided to start padding my hand to get a sense of the room, rather than gliding my hand across it.

I soon felt someone's thigh, and I moved my hand up their body until I eventually felt hair—long hair. I knew it was Melody, and I threw my arms around her. I felt her do the same to me. I felt tears run down my cheek. We stayed together until I heard her whimper, "I'm sorry." Her words sounded wet. I couldn't reply.

After a few minutes, I felt her head turn. "Myles?" she asked aloud.

"Yes?" he replied. He was on the other side of the room.

"Come over here; sit with us," she said. Then, we heard some shuffling across the floor, a faint "Oof!" from him hitting a couple of the aisles, and a chuckle from Melody amidst her sniffles. He soon sat down, across from us, with his back against another one of the corridors.

I took my arms away from Melody and laid with my back to the wall. I put my hands to my side. She grabbed them. Her force was so strong. It felt like she never wanted to let go. I didn't want her to, either. She fell asleep using my shoulder as a pillow. I leaned against her and passed out from exhaustion.

The next day came, and we ate some of the corn from Myles's bag; he never dropped his during the run-in with that other group of people. It was cold and didn't taste good. We also broke a piece of bread and shared it, along with some bottled water. I held the food in my hands but refused to eat the part near where I held it.

We ate in silence. The only noise joining us was the creaking made by the building when a gust of wind whizzed by. The shop itself wasn't destroyed, but it was ransacked long ago. Only remnants of things were left behind: half-empty bottles of water, stale chips, and dry bread.

Melody held my hand all morning, refusing to let go. Her breathing was fast, and I could practically feel her heartbeat in her fingers. I wanted to comfort her, ask if she was ok and wanting to know the contents of her mind—but I was too afraid to ask. All I knew was she was scared.

Myles broke the silence: "What now?"

Her question loomed for a few minutes. Stale air made my lungs feel collapsed; every breath was a wheeze. "I don't know," I eventually said. "I don't even know where we are."

"Me neither." He paused. "That was Peter's job..." he trailed off.

Images flashed back to me of Peter's bloodied body, and the face he made as the knife pulled out a part of his life when it ejected from his body. Then, how my fists were shoveling blood out of the boy, and it felt like I was smearing it on my skin as I threw more punches. My face felt dirty, and I only imagined a war-tribe symbol like those depicted in books from the library.

"I didn't mean it," Melody eventually said. She immediately broke into tears, but she wiped them away. "It was my fault. I led them to us. It was my fault."

"Don't say that," Myles told her. "You didn't do anything wrong."

"Yes, I did!" She cried more. "If I hadn't filled that bag so full, or put the water on the bottom, then it wouldn't have leaked, and Peter wouldn't be gone, and we wouldn't be stuck here."

"No," Myles asserted, "Don't think like that. If you want to think like that, then it was ultimately Peter's choice to stop and get stuff from that place—otherwise, the group would have never wanted to follow us." Melody stopped crying for a moment. She still had a firm grip on my hand. "It's nobody's fault."

Melody wiped away her tears. "Thank you," she muttered between broken breaths.

"Mike," Myles said to me, "How are you holding up?" I didn't reply. He noticed Melody's hands gripped around mine like we were two flimsy beams supporting each other. "You look like hell, Mike. Don't beat yourself up, either, ok? Just don't—don't think about anything except how to get home, ok?"

"What do you think the people at home are thinking right now?" Melody asked. Her eyes stared into the cracked concrete. She sounded monotone—a departure from her usual happy-go-lucky, chipper attitude.

"I don't know, but that's not important. We need to try and get home." Myles held his bag in his hands. "We have the supplies to last us a long time in this bag. But we can't stay in this hole forever."

"Do you think they're out there looking for us?" Melody asked, eyes still stagnate.

Myles didn't answer. He looked away.

"Yes," I said. "I'm sure they are."

We sat for a few more minutes until Melody let go of my hand and stood up. She helped me to my feet, then Myles arose, too. "Let's go," she sniffled. Her voice sounded dry and dead.

Myles and I nodded our heads, unlocked the door, then left. The tinted light from outside hurt my eyes at first. The cold, dirty air made me cough. We slipped our bandanas on and walked in a trio, side-by-side.

"Oh wait," Myles said and started to dig around in his bag.

"What?" I asked.

"Walkie-talkie," he answered. "Why didn't I think of that earlier..." After spending a few moments ravaging, he came up empty-handed. "Ah, I think it was in Peter's bag..."

"We can go get it," Melody said. "We should head back there anyway, don't you think?" Her words made me shutter.

Myles bit his lip. "It makes the most sense. I don't have any idea where we are. Gives us an objective..." he trailed off and started walking. We followed.

Plans for how to continue were nonexistent. Capricious and erratic movements were how we operated. Once we had the opportunity to take a corner, we took it. Hours we wandered until we recognized something familiar: the shop we stayed in.

Myles threw his hands up. "I don't know what we're doing. We're just wasting time."

"No," Melody said. "We haven't wasted time. We just learned what doesn't work." We passed the store.

We didn't cross the shop again and instead kept finding new areas: dilapidated parks, wacky mirrors, and benches to rest on made up an area of the city. We lost ourselves in enjoying its beauty. I sensed a smile cross my face—it felt like cracking away caked-on mud.

Night came quickly. We traveled until it was impossible to see anything. We broke into a house and stayed the night. It had an odd smell to it, but we weren't about to be picky. We felt around the inside, bumping into furniture, eventually set-tling on a couch for Melody, and another for Myles. I took a chair. I nodded off once, I think.

The next morning, we got a better look at the house we were in—someone had lived there until recently. We could tell by the corpse in the kitchen, with dried blood seeping from the breast and pelvis of a newly dead woman. A window was broken near the back, prompting the killer's escape. A red line traveled from between the woman's legs to the window. We found a few cans of food, as to not take away from Myles's stash anymore, and some canteens filled with water. I took the knife from the woman's body and wiped it on her blouse. Her eyes glazed over—a thin film formed over her iris, and her lips were cracked. Dried blood crusted the corners of her mouth. Melody had no physical reaction to the woman. She just stared. I stashed the knife in my back pocket.

We exited through the back of the house. Upon our en-trance into the city again, we heard footsteps in the distance and hid behind a nearby fence. The footsteps came closer, and I heard them speak.

"Hey," said one, "Check this out."

"A house, a broken window..." said a second.

"Should we go inside? See if we find anything?" asked a third.

"Go for it. But make it quick," commanded the fourth. More glass shattered, and we heard their footsteps meet the carpeted flooring. We bolted away into the streets and didn't look back.

We continued to walk, and walk, and walk, and walk for what seemed like forever. The once incredible towers turned oppressive. Dust fell from windows like decayed snow, laying on the streets as we pushed through its mess. A cold wind cut through our clothes, stirring up the dust once more and coughing fits ensued—our bandanas could only help us so much. The landscape seemed to shift along with the wind, making us forget which way we were going, and where we had already been. We wandered depressed, desperate, but there was a sense of freedom to it. The ability to roam anywhere we wanted was nice, but it was still more fearful than liberating.

By midday, we came across the death site. Peter's limp body remained—contorted and cold. The other body was gone—all that remained was a pool of red, staining the concrete, with a streak leading away from the market building. It stopped not too far away, with only a few drops of red giving any indication of a direction. It turned a corner.

I examined Peter and saw his eyes were still open. They stared into nothing. A light film calloused itself across the eyelid, perhaps dust, or maybe the body's reaction to its death. The rest of his cadaver looked a lighter shade of pale skin. He looked like the dead woman we saw earlier. Underneath his corpse was his bag—surprisingly untouched—which Myles and I carefully took off while Melody stood several feet away. She couldn't help but stare at Peter. She didn't cry—only stared, like a golem. After we moved the body, we couldn't return it to the position he died in, so we rested him face-down on the asphalt.

His bag only contained a water bottle, Harry the wrench, an orphanage key, and a walkie-talkie. Myles cried into every channel. The only response was its own set of static screams—putrid and plastic.

Myles threw the walkie-talkie to the ground in frustration. He quickly picked it back up, though, and stuffed it inside his bag. He then pulled out a water bottle and poured it over his hands to wash them clean of Peter's blood, which flowed away. I did the same, but the red remained.

I looked further at the cadaver and noticed the point of impact; a wide gash, now tender, had blood still slowly dripping out. Dust tried to get inside, but his body covered the wound with a now red-stained jacket. After being moved, the wound was more open, and dirt already stuck to some of the exposed flesh. I looked around the area for my bag of utensils, but it was gone.

"What should we do?" Myles asked.

"What?" I answered. I zoned out, looking at Peter.

"Like, do we move it somewhere else?"

"Where would we move it to?"

"Inside the building, maybe?" He pointed to the market.

"Myles, I'm afraid if we stay here too much longer, that group will return and kill us. I'm scared. I think we need to leave now."

Myles nodded. We turned away from Peter and walked away. Melody couldn't move, and tears welled around her eyes the longer she stared. They never left her eyes, though. Myles took her by the arm and walked her away, with the two leading the way ahead of me. She kept looking behind us until Peter became a distant figure. We followed the bloodstains.

After turning the corner where the blood trail continued, we saw no trace of a body or blood anymore. I noticed on the ground a small pin. A circular white, red, and gold pin with an engraving in the middle: C. It reminded me of the pin my father wore—it had been so long since I'd seen it last, but its sight terrified me. I snatched the pin and placed it in my inner jacket pocket. Myles and Melody didn't notice.

We left the site, turned another corner, went down another alley, and we were lost again.

"This sucks," Melody said.

"Yeah, I know," I replied. "We still don't know where we are."

"No, not that. About Peter." She wiped her nose with her sleeve. "I can't believe he's just gone. Just like that." She snapped her fingers. "He's been there for so long, for me."

"I've known him longer," Myles interjected. "This hurts me, too. I just can't grieve right now. Not until we are safe."

"Peter was like a big, older brother to me," Melody said. "Sure, we bickered, and he might not have liked me because I annoyed him, but I still looked up to him." She paused. We stopped. She whimpered. "I'm not used to this."

Myles started to cry. "Me neither."

I began to tear up. I looked away.

Melody said, "I don't want to end up like him. Dead, lying on the ground somewhere alone, because someone wanted some freaking water."

"Hey," Myles said, voice breaking between sobs, "Don't speak like that. You're trivializing it."

"What does it matter if we don't get back home! He was dear to me, and I don't even want to go back home if it means I don't get to see him again." Melody took a deep breath, unclenched her fists, and kept walking.

We didn't speak again—only in simple grunts, nods, and the occasional simple question of which direction to try next. Every alley looked the same; each street varied slightly from the others. Cars littered the street, either in the middle of cracked roads or off on the sidewalks with busted windows. We should have stopped to check them. We should have seen if there was anything to try and give us some direction. But we didn't. The only constant was a single tall building, which we could see everywhere we walked. We never drew close to the tall building—which rose atop the hazy sky—but it stayed as a constant reminder of our illusion of progress.

After some time, we ran into another group of boys who tried to attack us. I hardly remember what happened—we were tired and broken, relying on adrenaline to power us. I only remember that Melody hurt herself in the flee. We had to help carry her to get away in time. We dropped some of our supplies as we ran; the group seemed content with our scraps.

Night crept in, and our eyesight grew slightly dimmer, then we heard footsteps. We froze. We couldn't handle another group of boys; we had no food, no energy, and no healthy person to fight. A silhouette slipped out from the shadows, drawing a weapon on us. We didn't try to run. Melody could hardly walk by this point—we would only make fools of our selves attempting to escape again. I accepted my fate.

As the figure drew closer, I recognized the face. It was from Vic. He noticed it was us and dropped his weapon. He still had a large stick attached to the backpack he was wearing, but he dropped it also. He ran into us, enveloping all three of us in his embrace. His arms felt sturdy.

The three of us lost ourselves in our collective crying. Vic's eyes were watery, but he never shed a tear. He only said, "I'm so happy to see you." Our hug soon concluded, and he looked around. "Where's Peter?" He asked. We hesitated to answer.

"I don't know where he is," I said. Maybe no one would need to find out. Myles shot me a look of inquiry. I couldn't tell if he admired my lie or was disgusted by it; his face sent mixed signals. I only chose to lie because I was embarrassed to tell Vic the truth—that we watched him die—that we let him die. "We got lost—split up."

Vic put his arm around Melody and helped her walk back home. He told us to follow him, and we trudged through the light-fading dusk to get back home. My legs began to ache.

Chapter 13

We returned to the orphanage later that night, following Vic's guidance. He didn't seem to have issues navigating the city at night. Amidst the confusion of our travel, Vic seemed to enjoy taking us through the city during the night. He tried to hide it, considering the situation and panic, but I could see in his stature that he thrived in the dark as he paraded us back home.

Our arrival at the orphanage was met with hugs and sighs. Melody and Myles received the most affection while I was embraced more because I happened to be there. The orphanage was an oven compared to the cold outside. I just wanted to curl myself in a blanket. I kept my hands in my pockets.

Billy said, "I'm so glad everyone is all right."

"Not everyone," Vic said. "They said Peter is still missing."

"Really? Huh. Guess I didn't notice he wasn't here. Usually hides in Chris's room at this hour anyway."

"What should we do? Do we go back out and find him?" Vic looked to Chris for answers.

"For sure, but not now. You were putting yourself at risk, Victor, by being out past dusk. I don't want you or anyone else to be out tonight." Chris seemed sullen.

"We can't just leave Peter out there," Vic retorted. "He'll die if he's left out by himself another day!"

"Myles, when did you three and Peter split ways?" Chris asked.

"Yesterday. We, uh, we haven't seen him all day." Myles looked at his hands as he spoke.

"Then I'm sure he's fine," Chris continued. "If anyone knows Peter, it's me. He wouldn't let something silly be the end of him. He's too proud for that." I coughed.

"So... what do we do?" Vic asked, with an almost sarcastic tone.

"We go to bed. Unless we put ourselves at risk, there's no way we can get to him."

"What about the walkie-talkies?" Billy asked. "Couldn't we try and get on and see if he answers?"

I glanced over at Myles and Melody. Melody seemed checked out, not paying attention to the conversation at all. Myles looked spooked.

"Uh, when we split up," I said, knowing that the walkie-talkie was sitting comfortably in Myles's bag, "Peter gave us his walkie-talkie, in case something went wrong."

Chris inquired: "Well, why didn't you try contacting us?"

"We tried," Myles spoke, "We couldn't get it to work." Chris looked at Myles seriously. The eyes tried to pierce through the veil we were cleverly displaying, but Myles wasn't lying about this part. "I'm not lying!" he shouted. "Why would we have wandered for two days if we could have called you and asked for help?"

Chris backed off. "Fair enough. So, then, Peter's been out there for two nights, with no way to communicate with us, and might be lost?" We shook our heads. "Great." He threw his hands up and turned around, looking flustered.

"How could he be lost?" Billy asked. "I may not like the guy too much—sorry, Chris—but if I know anything, it's that he has a good head on his shoulders. Man's never got lost in the city before."

"This is also true," Chris said. "He could still be looking for these three."

"Not sure he'd care that much..." Vic muttered under his breath.

"Nonetheless," Chris thundered, glaring at Vic, "we'll search for him tomorrow. Billy, you can go with me. If anything, I think it's obvious the plan derailed, and they didn't reach the bakery."

"Alright," Billy grunted. "Last time I went out, though, is when Jack got hurt…"

"We'll be fine," Chris said. He turned to face us, peering for any clues. We were solid. "Everyone else can get the next day or so off. You three have been through hell, it seems. Rest up—we can take care of things for a few days. Take it easy." He turned and entered his room, closing the door quietly behind him.

Melody spoke: "How is Speed?"

The break from the vow of silence she had taken during the past few hours alarmed the room. Her voice was quiet, broken, but firm. It was as if a sense of responsibility began to flow through her, radiating positive energy across the foyer.

"Uh," Vic spoke, in chunks, "Well, he said he wants to go by Jack now."

"Really?" Myles said. He chuckled. "Did he realize the world doesn't revolve around him anymore?"

"Technically, it still does," Vic said, "We've been taking good care of him. He's still in no condition to move, but he seems better."

"Well, that's good," Melody said. "And good for Spe— Jack." She paused. "I hated the name Speed anyway." She started to chuckle, which eventually erupted the room into laughter. It felt good to laugh—to forget about the scarring experience we'd been through—Myles, Melody, and I. The night didn't seem so scary from inside the brick walls and with friends—laughing—enjoying the company of thoughtlessness.

We dispersed into our separate rooms after explaining our experience with Billy and Vic. They seemed thoroughly invested in the story of our survival. Myles helped Melody upstairs, though her condition was better since she entered the orphanage. Vic and Billy led me into our room, where I instantly crawled underneath the blanket and made myself snug and safe.

"So, you guys never said," Billy asked, "how did you and Peter get separated from each other?"

His question angered me. Not only from the mental gymnastics I had been performing to keep our lie intact, but from the absolute exhaustion I had let out all over my section of the room. I didn't want to move. I didn't want to talk. I didn't want to think. I only wanted to become one with the blanket and feel its warmth overtake my body. I knew about the truth, and I knew I wasn't ready to tell them yet. It would only raise more questions to tell them about our encounter with the group of boys, or about the stabbing of Peter, or about the other groups we ran from, or about the pin I found lying in the alleyway. I feared their response to my murder. I feared Chris would make me never leave the orphanage again, never let me go to the library again, never let Melody go with me again.

I clutched the pin, still lying in my jacket pocket, and answered. "We walked away."

The next day was calm. We woke up, ate breakfast together, then Chris and Billy left for their search. Vic and Myles went out back to the basketball court to do some combat training. Myles asked Vic to help him out, and said he was, "Feeling a bit rusty." Vic agreed (he was going to practice outside anyway), and the two departed. Jack was upstairs, still lying in his room, with Melody helping feed him. I waited until she was done and approached her in the upstairs foyer.

"How's he doing?" I asked. My left hand clasped my right arm. I wanted to be closed off.

"Fine," she said. "He told me himself that he wants to be called Jack from now on, though. I don't know why, though; he didn't want to say."

"Is he bored? Does he want something to do?"

"No, I don't think so. He didn't seem to want to talk or joke with me or Myles last night; he only wanted to listen."

"Listen to what?"

"Our story. Our event."

"Ah. Yeah, Billy and Vic tried to get me to talk about it more after we went to bed..."

"Can you do something for me?"

"Sure, what's that?"

"Can you take me to the library today? I'm out of books to read, and I want to get some new ones."

"You want to go back out? After what we just went through?

"Yeah."

"Ok."

We packed up some bags and left some food for Jack to nibble on while we were gone. Out back, we saw Vic destroy Myles in their training; Myles tried as hard as he could, but Vic bested him every time. We watched for a few minutes before telling them about our plan. They agreed to let us leave, so long as we returned before Chris and Billy returned; Chris wouldn't want us to be out again. We were willing to take the risk.

Melody and I were soon on our way. We moved quickly—the fear of Chris returning within hours of his departure filled our thoughts. We'd be dead, for sure.

"How are you holding up?" I asked during our travel.

Melody was ahead of me, powerwalking with a strut of determination. She didn't seem to hurt anymore and walked faster than me; I had to jog now and again to maintain my pace. She didn't hear me. I repeated the question. "How are you holding up?"

"Oh, sorry," she said. "Fine."

"Fine? Or not fine?" I caught up with her again. "You can't just be fine—I thought you hurt yourself yesterday?"

"I'm better now."

"Yeah, I can tell—I can't keep up with you. Can you please slow down?"

She steadied her pace a bit better. We were already half-way there.

"Thank you," I said. She stopped a moment to let me catch up completely. She turned her head, trying not to make complete eye contact with me at any moment. We started walking again.

"What are you going to get—at the library?" I asked.

"I don't know. Just something new." She babbled.

"Well, you've been reading a lot of picture books, so are you getting more of those? You haven't touched The Magic School Bus—those are classics. Or, so say the covers."

"Something bigger," she said. "No pictures. Just words."

"Like young fiction? Junie B. Jones is a good start, as is Tales of a Fourth Grade Nothing."

"No." She continued walking.

"Hey, what's going on with you? You're being curt."

"I'm trying not to get us hurt."

"What do you mean by that?"

She stopped walking and turned around. "If we stop moving or talk too much, people will come out and get us."

"I don't think that will happen, Melody."

"It did yesterday."

"There was a lot more going on yesterday. We didn't know where we were. Everything was scary. But this isn't scary; it's just to the library."

"Well, still." She continued to walk again.

I stayed. "Hey," I said. "Hey!" I yelled. "I'm trying to talk to you." I paused, seeing if she would wait for me. She pressed on. She kept walking as if she didn't hear me at all. "Are you scared?" I shouted. She finally stopped. Air cut through the air, and I felt goosebumps along my arms. My hair bristled against the lining of my father's jacket.

Without turning around, she yelled back, "Why are you lying to them? About Peter. They're going to find out the truth anyway."

"I feel guilty." I took steps to approach Melody, who was still not looking at me.

"Guilty..." she said. "Guilty? Why are you guilty?" She turned around and flung herself into me, beating me with her soft palms. "If anyone is guilty, it's me! We stopped because of me! He left because of me! We got caught because of me! He died because of me! You don't get to take this from me, Mike! This guilt is mine." She stepped away, beginning to tear up. She breathed heavily, looking directly into me. "Just let me have this."

"Melody," I said, approaching slowly, "Are you scared? Because I'm terrified."

She sniffed and wiped her nose with her jacket sleeve.

"I see him when I close my eyes, lying in the street, life abandoning his body. I see those boys in the corners of my eyes. I still feel the kid's blood on my hands, spilling from his head. I still feel the cold, stiff body I examined to pilfer the walkie-talkie. Every muscle and every bone in my body aches when I think about it. I hate this. But I want you to know that I care, too."

I held her arm, not realizing I ever grabbed it in the first place. Melody seemed to notice it, too and shook me off her. She said, "You didn't know him as I did. He was like a brother." She took a heavy breath and spoke, "You needn't always fix my problems, Mike."

I had no more words. She sucked them all out of me. My mouth dried, and air wouldn't leave my lungs. I tried to make sounds, but my vocal cords wouldn't string the syllables to speak. I only looked down at the ground disheveled before she walked away from me. I followed her.

We didn't speak until we reached the library, where we made tiny gestures and quick remarks to get inside and let each other know where we were. Melody returned her books precisely and neatly, as did I. She hovered over to the adult fiction aisle, past the young fiction and young adult sections of the library. She began thumbing through action and sci-fi novels. She stuffed a few into her bag—over 300 pages. No pictures.

I grabbed a few books: August Wilson Century Cycle, The Complete Shakespeare Collection, and The Collected Plays of Tennessee Williams. I became engrossed in theatre and plays—the idea of performing for people and memorizing lines fascinated me. At the time, it seemed like a logical conclusion to showcasing love and appreciation for art. I came across a few books which referenced famous playwrights and their influence in fiction. I wanted to read up on them; I wanted to let stories infiltrate my mind.

Once we were content with our selections, we led ourselves out. Usually, we would stay and read in our sanctioned silence until daylight became dim, but today we left early. We wanted to be back before Chris returned with what I knew would be some fraction of Peter's truth.

We returned to the orphanage without uttering a word to each other. Vic and Myles were done with their practice by this point. Myles had a few bruises on his knees, and a large red spot on the back of his legs; he had switched into shorts. He was still sweaty and panting. They must have just gotten done, or Vic called it off. Myles was still restless.

Melody and I were putting away some of our extra supplies when we heard the front door open and close. Pounding footsteps plumped and clopped up the stairs until figures appeared in the foyer. Chris and Billy returned.

Everyone (except Jack) was standing in the foyer when Chris's booming words echoed off orphanage's brick, boring walls: "Peter's dead."

At first, the words kept Vic and the others in shock. Myles, Melody, and I had to feign ignorance, as we knew the whole truth, but Vic was a virgin to the news. Chris detailed how he and Billy found Peter outside of a market, with a knife wound in his stomach—dried blood, indicating he's been dead for a few days. They described the wretched stench, which led them to the body. I asked, in my fake sadness, what they did with the body. They said they pulled him down an alley, following other bloodstains, and placed Peter under some rubble for the time being. They'd go back the next day to bury him properly.

Chris quickly made his way into his room. Billy followed him and stayed with him overnight. Myles and Melody went upstairs to inform Jack of the news, and Vic and I placed ourselves underneath the floor-wide blanket in our room. We took Billy's pillows and used them ourselves.

"How are you feeling?" I asked him.

"I don't know," he replied. "I'm not upset—Peter was an asshole, to me, especially—but I still feel remorse. It's all so surreal to me."

"Why remorse? You didn't do anything."

"Remorse may be the wrong word. Survivor's guilt, more like." He sighed. He didn't seem like he wanted to talk about it.

It grew quiet for a few moments.

"How did it go with you and Myles? I tried to change the conversation. "I saw his bruises. You look pretty good."

He laughed. "I always look good." We both laughed at his joke. "It went ok, I guess. Myles never was much of a fighter. He's like you, where you can see something before it happens—intrinsically. He just doesn't know what to do with that information."

"Is that why he has all the bruises?"

"Sorta. I didn't go easy on him."

"You didn't go easy on me."

"For a while."

"What does that mean?"

"When we started, I went hard on you. I didn't let up. That's how I teach." Vic leaned back. "If you can't deal with someone who knows what they're doing, you're dead. I make my students die several times so that living feels like an accomplishment."

I didn't reply immediately. I was lost in the philosophy of Vic's words. It felt good to knock Vic down after he batted me around for several days. But I also know I sure would have liked to have been eased into knowing how to deflect everything he did. Once I trial-and-errored my way through one thing, he'd throw something entirely new at me, just to get at me once more. It was like every time I thought I outsmarted him, he presented me with a new problem. That said, the time I finally bested him made me stronger; I learned from my creativity rather than Vic walking me through everything. It felt rewarding. It reminded me of how I first felt learning to read. It reminded me of Peter's death. Living felt like an accomplishment that day.

I said back, "Yeah, I know Myles doesn't like to throw up his hands and give up."

"What do you know about Myles?" Vic said in an accusatory tone. His eyes turned sharp. He acted like a completely different person.

"Well, I mean," I stammered, "from what little time I've had..."

Vic chuckled. "I'm just messing with you, dude. Don't take everything so literally."

"Oh," I replied. He kept quietly laughing to himself despite me. "Sorry. It's just that the sudden death of Peter is all I can think of right now. I'm not in the right headspace, I guess."

"Ooh, 'headspace'. Big word. I like it." He smirked. "Yeah, but know what? —Fuck him." He slithered into his pillows and down below the blanket. "I'm still here, and he's not, so I guess I win."

"That's a crude way of looking at it."

"Crude? Yes. True? Also, yes." He took a big breath and exhaled, "I wouldn't want to be in Chris's shoes right now."

"Why's that?"

"Oh, that's right. You're still new." He sat up. "Chris and Peter knew each other for a long time."

"Really?"

"Yeah. Like, since they were kids. Well, you know. Younger than you. A long time. Anyway, he doesn't like to show it, but Chris needs someone to keep his head straight. Peter was his right-hand man."

"Right-hand man? I'm sorry—I'm not familiar with the term."

"Hmm," Vic perched his lips. "I'm surprised you haven't; all that time you and Melody spend down in the library." I gave him a dirty look. He continued. "Every so often, every few years, we do a vote to decide the new leader of our group. Chris came up with the idea. If we ever disagree with his leadership or anyone else's leadership, we could, in theory, vote them out in favor of someone else. We've only ever had one leader, though: Chris. None of us have ever voted against him."

"Why's that?" I asked.

"Dunno. It's not like he's the greatest leader, but he's the best we have. I don't know if I'd want anyone else leading us right now, and perhaps the others feel the same way. That or they are too afraid to be the only ones to not vote for him."

"So, where did Peter fall into this? The right-hand man?"

"Once we decide a leader, they choose their second-in-command. Chris always chooses Peter."

"So, there's a vote for leader—which never changes—and the leader gets to pick their second—which never changes."

"Bingo. But I'm glad the system is there. In theory, it means any one of us could rise-above and become the leader someday..." Vic looked away. "All of that is to say that Chris is without a right-hand man at the moment. I guess Billy is filling that void for the time being, but it could be anyone. Me, you, Jack, Myles, hell, even Melody. Though she may be a little too talkative and over-zealous for that job."

"You know," I said, "She wasn't very talkative today. Usually, she wants to talk to me and loves making conversation. Today, though, it was quiet. She got mad at me. I feel stupid."

"Hey," Vic started to say.

"No, I just asked things I probably shouldn't have. It was too soon. I didn't know Peter all that well, but she said they were pretty close. She was worried about him, and I took it too far."

"Well, if those two were close, that's news to me. She just likes to attach herself to everyone. It's how she is." Vic put his hands behind his head and leaned back.

"I don't think that's true."

"Dude, come on. You're telling me she started talking to some dirty, self-righteous punk—who just started squatting with us one day—because she likes you? Get real. She's too sweet for her own good."

"Then I don't think you know her that well."

"I know her better than you ever will, dude." He looked at me from across the room and from halfway under the blanket. His eyes were piercing again. I had to look away. He continued, "Don't try me. I've taken a fondness to you because you remind me of myself. I don't get that too often in this world. If I were you, I wouldn't be going around trying to get all friendly with the only girl you've probably ever seen; might begin to turn some heads."

"I don't know what you mean."

"I think you do," he growled. Once again, his eyes pierced, but I didn't look away this time. While I was close with Melody, my mind frequently flickered back to the girl I saw jump through the alleys during my first trip into the city. Everything about her still mystified me. I hadn't brought up this mystery girl to Melody, though. It never occurred to me until then. Perhaps she knew something.

"Anyway," I said, trying to change topics, "what's Chris gonna do with Peter gone?"

"Immediately? He's going to say goodbye to his best friend."

"Should we all go?"

"I won't be going. I don't see any point in respecting the dead. There's more of them—the dead—than us—the living. It's harder to live than it is to die. We're the minority. Every time someone dies, we join their side. I'd rather not honor that—only the weak die. The strong survive. That's why we're still here, and he's not—that's how I see it."

"What about Chris's 'right-hand man', or whatever. Who will replace Peter?"

"I'm not sure. Could be Billy? I know Chris thinks pretty highly of him."

"What about you?"

He shot up. "Me? Why do you think that?"

"I don't know. You're smart, and you know your way around the city—like Peter. You're the best out of all of us at survival, and combat, and finding things."

"That's true. I am a good scavenger. I always had that over Peter." Vic mulled it over for a few seconds before saying, "Nah, I'm too hot-headed. Chris and I would just argue all the time, let's be real."

"I don't think so," I said. "I think you'd be a good leader."

"If you think so," he said, sinking back under the blanket. He turned away from me.

"No, seriously. He trusts you—I think everyone here does. You would be next in line if something were to happen to him, I'm sure. If that's what 'right-hand' man means, or whatever."

"Sorta. How's about this: If I'm the new mini-Chris, I'll give you my share of breakfast for a month."

"If you're Chris's co-star, I want you to teach me how to be a survivor."

Vic raised his eyebrows. "Seriously? You want that over food? You can already defend yourself; what more do you need in this world?"

"I don't always want to fight, though. I know I can fight—I've already done it. Surviving those two days was hard, and I felt useless. My fighting ability can only go so far. We wandered forever. I want to know how to find things—how to make things—how to—"

"How to lead?" He cut me off. I bit my lip and looked away. "Sure. If I'm right-hand man, I'll teach you." He paused. "I never thought anyone would say they liked that about me. Chris and Jack and Peter—everyone always criticizes my scavenging. They say it's stupid—it wastes time—it doesn't help anything. It means a lot that you would say that about me."

"Well, it's true. You'd make a good leader." It grew quiet once more. The light had escaped from the room completely, and I only knew of Vic's presence by his speech and breathing.

After a while, we said our goodnights and went to sleep. I knew the next few days would be exciting, and I slept good.

Chapter 14

The scene was set before I awoke. Chris left early in the morning to bury his friend. Billy awoke sometime after Chris's departure; he assumed Chris wanted to be alone. Instead, Billy tried to make breakfast.

Chris and Billy got the supplies they needed from the bakery the previous day, and Billy was anxious to get started. He went upstairs to see if he could figure it out but only learned how to light the fire. Melody tried to help him; he couldn't read the cookbooks. At first, Melody taught Billy how to read from the book—recognizing words and associating them with objects—but it didn't go well. He was not a fast learner and a lousy student; Melody said me much later—he wanted to run before he could crawl, she put it. He would only want to make the food and didn't want to learn to read, per se. Melody eventually got fed up with him. Her solution was to get some paper and draw images of exactly what he needed for each recipe/dish. She wrote little notes next to the pictures, though her penmanship was sloppy; she could read, but I didn't teach her to write properly. She included simple numbers in her notes, such as "x3 (image)", or what-have-you. Billy picked up on the numbers quicker than he did the words.

I awoke to her exasperated grunts—so loud it echoed through the building and woke me from my half-asleep state. I waddled my crust-covered eyes up the stairs, my primordial brain following the scent of cooked food—something I hadn't known since leaving my father. Upstairs, a nearly-completed breakfast was laid out on mostly clean plates. We ate burned bread and seared peaches. They didn't pair well together, though the toast had a somewhat pleasing taste to it. Overall, it was a decent first attempt—but not great.

After breakfast, I watched Melody teach Billy how to read the various cookbooks and help him understand what each utensil did. They would bicker, and I would laugh. Their interplay between a desperate teacher and a slack-off student who wanted the C average was like a choreographed stage play. The symbolism of her tone toward each word she read from the book—flawless, with a wet, wispy rasp in her voice—represented the diverging direction of our state; she would glance at me, then angrily return to the book. The student became the teacher, though her teaching was flawed—an enthusiastically steadfast, guileless devotee.

Chris returned around midday. Melody noticed him while she looked out at the city from the sizeable tilted windowsill on the top floor. He entered, leaving the shovel covered in dirt and sand by the door. He called together a meeting in the main foyer. Billy offered him some of the burnt bread from earlier, now cold. Chris took a bite, winced, and watched while the crumbs fell to the floor.

"How is it?" Billy asked.

"Well," Chris said, attempting to minimize the sound of his crunches, "It's something different." Billy got a chuckle from that.

Chris finished his food, and everyone gathered around him. We grabbed things to sit on. Vic and Myles carried Jack downstairs from his bed and placed him against the wall. He was supported by multifarious pillows to keep him comfortable. I took a sip of water while everyone else sat down.

"I'm holding this meeting," Chris began, "to address some topics I feel are best discussed together. As we all know, we do routine votes to establish a hierarchy of leadership here. Normally, I would wait a bit longer before doing a revote, but given the recent passing of my second-in-command, I feel it is appropriate to perform said revote now."

"You sure?" Billy asked. "We can wait a bit if you want. No one is forcing you to speed things up, Chris."

"While I appreciate your concern, Billy, I'll be fine." He took a pause and swallowed. "My concern now is with the betterment of the group. And as the current leader, I say we do a vote."

I looked around to try and get a grasp on what was happening. I picked up context clues on the situation but didn't know anything for sure. Soon, I saw Jack raise his hand.

"Well, you know my vote goes to you, dude. You fixed my leg. I trust you with my life." For the first time, I saw Jack as a man: open, honest, vulnerable. It was like I was looking at an entirely new person.

Melody's hand was next. Then Myles, Billy, Vic. I raised my hand out of obligation but also with a sense of purpose.

"Thanks," Chris said. "I humbly accept the reelection. Now, for the next order of business, and the real reason I wanted this meeting now: As you know, the acting leader gets to choose their second-in-command without the need of a vote, and with no objections. For as long as this system has been in place with the group, it was always an obvious answer. However, with my second-in-command gone, a new partner must be chosen." He paused and looked around the room. His eyes darted from person to person, scanning for reactions—looking for inquiry. He stopped at Vic. "Victor Curl, I would like you to be my new second-in-command."

Everyone turned to Vic. He looked shocked. He didn't look happy, nor sad, nor enthusiastic, nor upset. He just looked like his mind was somewhere else.

"I... " Vic stumbled. He shut his eyes, "...ok."

"Good," Chris said. He clapped his hands and rubbed them together. "Then it's decided. Does anyone have anything to ask? Anything to add?"

My mind flooded with questions. What was going on? What just happened? When was this system adopted? How long has everyone else been at the orphanage? What exactly does Chris do? What will Vic do in his new position? What is a right-hand man, or is it second-in-command? Where was Peter buried? How does everyone else feel about Vic becoming a leader? Is Billy upset? What caused the change in Jack's demeanor? What is Melody thinking right now?

But I didn't say anything. Nobody else did, either. We swiftly adjourned our meeting. Myles and Vic helped Jack back upstairs, with Jack attempting to walk on his own. He didn't get far before needing help. Chris followed him with some medical supplies to check up on his leg and bandage it again. He was afraid of infection with a gash that large.

The rest of the day went by fast. The questions still pounded in my head, but I was too afraid to ask anyone about them. The concept of making others dwell on things only I cared about was one I didn't want to pursue. My head felt compressed. I read through Hamlet.

Later that night, Billy cooked his first real meal: cooked, canned meat and corn. Considering all we had to eat the past few weeks were cold peaches, it tasted amazing. While cooking, though, Peter's concern of how smoke would affect things—if others could see that people live in this building through the smoke from cooking—was overseen by Vic. Vic took the staircase in the small room next to the kitchen to sit on the roof. There was a smokestack on the top of the building, precisely over the oven, which caught its smoke and fumes. After Billy finished cooking, Vic came down and said he didn't notice any smoke, or at the very least, it was minimal. He said it didn't make much difference to anything unless you were standing right next to the exhaust due to how dusty the world is.

We ate our food, made small talk, conversed over stories I had read, and told them to the group. I recalled Julius Caesar and Of Mice and Men to them, and how the story of Ashfall was eerily like the world we lived in. Outside the realm of fiction, Billy told us about his first encounter with Chris and Peter, and how they almost killed him.

"I used to run with my father," Billy said, "That was before he joined Congress—when it was just us two. I was still very young. My mom died in childbirth, so it was just my dad around to take care of me. We would scavenge for food together, ran from bandits together. My father wasn't a quick man, though—he ran super slow. So, often my father would have to fight to make sure I was unharmed. I can recall the bruises and lacerations he always had when he took his jacket off to give to me when I got cold.

"When I was around seven or eight years old, I got separated from my father. We were running away from something—I don't remember why, but I remember my father telling me that morning we had to leave immediately. We left most of our stuff got left behind because of how quickly we went. We ran down a few alleys, turned a few corners, but my father ran too fast for me. He always waited for me—always. He never ran because I believed he was slow. Even then, I thought that he was faster than he let on, but he would slow himself down so that I was safe. It was unlike him to put himself before me. He ran ahead and turned a corner. By the time I caught up and turned the corner, he had vanished.

"A few seconds later, I was pinned to the ground. I was able to scuttle my way away from the perpetrators, but I turned and saw two boys looking at me. One held a knife at me. It occurred to me, at that moment, that my father meant to leave me. He intended to get me frazzled, leave most of our things behind, and forget the way back home. He was likely waiting for a chance to finally run away at full speed, and whatever we were running from would catch up and kill me.

"The boy with the knife demanded I hand over my bag. It was the only food I had left—the rest was lost, likely stolen by other looters by then. All I had were the clothes on my back and the food in my bag. At that moment, I would have died if I gave over my stuff, or I would die from those kids. Even if I managed to get away, how long would my measly few cans of food last? I was dead no matter what I did—it didn't matter. All I could do was crouch in a corner and covered my body as best as I could with my bag and scream for my father.

"That was when the other boy, the one without a knife, asked if my father wore a pin. He asked if my father's pin bore a letter on it, surrounded by smaller letters all around it. I nodded my head yes. It grew silent. I looked out from behind my thin cover and saw the boy with the knife withdraw his weapon. A hand extended. I took it. I was given an ultimatum; go with them or be left to my own devices. I decided to go with them because that was the moment I met Chris and Peter for the first time. I was the first member of this little group, aside from those two."

"Wow," Melody awed, "I never knew you all went back so far."

"It was only a few years ago—maybe four or five," Billy replied. "They brought me back here—to the orphanage. It was much dustier back then," he chuckled. "Much quieter, too. But now we have all of you guys here and yada yada yada, we're here now, eating a real meal together!"

"Yes, and thank you for the food," Myles said. "It's delicious!"

Once we concluded our meal, Billy volunteered to wash the dishes with Chris and Vic. He said he would go the next day to replenish our water, as we were running low. Vic returned to the roof, and everyone else turned in early for the night. I followed Vic; I wasn't quite ready to go to bed yet.

I climbed up the ladder and saw Vic perched on one of the air-conditioning ducts, staring into the barren city. The roof was beautiful. It was plain—cream floors with nothing on them. A few scattered, abandoned air-conditioning units rested atop the orphanage, acting more as chairs than cooling units. A few assorted pipes lay sprawled out amongst the vacant plateau. I had to step over a few of them to get closer to Vic.

"What are you doing up here?" I asked him.

"Not much. I was just enjoying the view. I noticed it while I was up here earlier. Needed to get a better look, though."

I looked around. Tall structures, some strong, some fallen apart, surrounded us. There was a giant tower directly in front of us. It was the same tower that was apparent throughout the city, and the one we used as a marker when Melody, Myles, and I got lost a while back. Its menace traveled straight into the skyline until clouds of smoke and dust devoured it. It hid in the horrors caused by the aftermath of The Fallout, but it's aura still shined through. The building housed something awful, but I couldn't help but feel satisfied as my eyes got lost in the sea of clouds which enveloped the concrete and steel giant. In a way, I had fallen into its divisive and clever trap.

There was a tint to the sky, unlike any I had ever seen, bouncing off the high walls and windows of the other monoliths. The usual dim, brown light seemed almost green and blue; it was a solemnly beautiful sight. I watched a piece of rubble fall from one of the tops of the towers and rocket toward the earth.

"What did you think of dinner?" I asked.

"Eh," he grunted. "Better than anything we've had the past few years. I'm more excited about what he can make once he's more seasoned."

"Did you see what Melody did to try and help him?"

"Yeah." He chuckled. "Not the most patient teacher, is she?"

"No," I said, laughing back. "She's barely a patient student."

He laughed. "Not everyone can be as good as you or me, eh?" I flashed a smile.

"What'd you want to talk about?" he asked me. He patted his hand on the open area next to him.

"Huh? Oh, nothing. I just wanted to see what you were doing up here."

"Nononono, don't lie. You're getting better at lying—since the first time I met you at least, but it takes a lot to get past me. Something's been eating at you; I can see it." I didn't reply. "Look, you want to be a leader? Do you want to learn how to lead? Then the first step is you can't keep secrets from people—especially me. You need to start being honest, Mike. No one can depend on you if you're not honest." I stayed silent. "Is it related to Peter?" I scrunched my lips. "Alright, fine. Here: sit next to me." I took his offer.

"You promise not to tell anyone?" I asked.

"These lips are sealed. Our talks are confidential, Mike—always have been and always will be."

"Ok. Because I lied about how Peter died." I told him about how we stopped to loot supplies, our run-in with the other group, and how Peter died to a knife wound—stabbed in front of us."

"Geez," Vic said. "I'm sorry you had to go through that. I can see why Melody has been so stand-offish lately."

"That's not all," I said. "That part isn't what makes me sick. I've moved on from—I'm over that. Vic, I... I killed a person."

His eyes widened.

"After he stabbed Peter, I took the knife and stabbed the guy right in the shoulder. Then, I—I jumped on the guy and—and just started pounding. It was like something came over me. I just hit and hit and hit and hit and hit and hit until there was just a hole. Vic, I beat him so hard I broke his skull. His head was a bowl."

He nodded.

"I can still feel that kid's blood on my hands. His life still strung between my fingers. I can distinctly remember Peter telling me before we left that day that we don't kill. I feel like I let him down. I feel like I let everyone down. I'm a failure to myself and my friends. I'm not sure I can ever get over this."

He spoke. "You will get over it. I'm not sure if that's what you want to hear, but you will. I remember feeling the same way after my first kill."

"First?" I said. "There were more? But, I thought Peter said—"

"The important thing is that you live another day, Mike," Vic said quickly. "That is the most important thing out here. Only the strong survive; only the weak die."

I didn't say anything for a few minutes. I soaked in the view, which now dimmed with the ending day, signifying sleep. Vic's words still mystified me. I hadn't completed telling my story.

"We came back," I continued, "the next day, after wandering for a while. Peter was still there, but the other boy—he was gone. There was a dried blood-trail that led into an alley, where Chris and Billy found Peter because we moved him there. Anyway, when we initially followed the trail, the only thing I found was this pin." I dug the pin from my jacket pocket and showed Vic. He examined its design. "It looks like the one my father wore when I was younger. I remember you saying something about it when we first met, so I thought maybe you would know what it means."

"What it means?" he said. He scoffed. "What it means is—wait, have you shown that to anyone?"

"No."

"Ok, good—what it means is corruption."

"Huh?"

"Look, don't worry about it. Seriously. It's something you shouldn't be involved in." He turned away and folded his arms. Under his breath, he muttered, "It's silly, anyway."

"No." I stood up. "What did you just say a minute ago? 'You need to start being honest'? You need to be honest with me, too. I want to know. You seem interested in these pins—and whatever they mean—and I want to know too."

"I just don't want to get you hurt," Vic said. He egged me on, his words sounding mocking.

"If I want to lead someday, I need to know dirty truths. I want to do something with my life outside of the walls of the orphanage. I don't know what that thing is, but I have ambition. I have hope. I'll do whatever I need to find my purpose in this world."

He sighed. "Ok, if you want to know, then fine. It's a long story, though." I nodded. "What do you want to know first."

My mind struggled to find a place to begin. Vic, at this moment, was my conduit to the past. I felt like he knew anything and everything, and the only divide between his knowledge and my learning were the words I used to coax information. Initially, I wanted to ask what the pins mean—what they represent. Why did my father have a pin? Is it good? Is it bad? Then, I wanted to know about how Vic got involved with the group, and why he's still here. Then, I wanted to know why Vic wanted me in the group and how it related to the pin. But my mind flashed back to what I wanted and needed to know the most: The Fallout.

"Tell me about The Fallout," I said.

"Starting at the beginning, huh? Alright." Vic clapped his hands and cleared his throat. "Around 13 years ago—the same year you were born—a terrible war broke out across the world. I assume you're familiar with World Wars 1 and 2, Mike? Well, this was what would have been World War 3, which was titled The Fallout. Back when the world wasn't destroyed, there were other nations—think larger, grander cities—all across the globe. The one we live in was called America. During this time, America had grown power-hungry and corrupt. They wanted to try and take over other nations, inflict their influence on them, and rule the world as dictators. They threatened wars, sanctions, broken trade deals, etc.—all so they could have this imaginary advantage over everyone else as if their values were worth more than everyone else's. Other nations didn't like this. The nations Russia, China, Korea, and assorted countries in Europe joined forces to take down this power-corrupt America. They launched a full-scale barrage on the country—missiles, large-scale bombs, more missiles, and worst of all: nukes. Nukes can level an entire city, and radiate the land for decades, making it uninhabitable, and killing everything in its radius. The threat of nuclear war was always present in that world, but now that a nuke was dropped—especially on one of the most powerful countries in the world—it became a fire sale. Every country chucked nuclear weapons everywhere—bombing every major city they could find, to try and frag out a victory through attrition. This war lasted about a year, until there weren't enough cities or enough people, to continue it. In the end, the world was left on fire and in ruins. Every nation's leader was incapacitated or disintegrated through nuclear warfare. The fires burned and burned and burned until that flame fizzled out on its own, leaving the world with dust and ash.

"Which brings us to now. Where we live wasn't hit by a nuke, or else we wouldn't be here right now. Ours only received a large-scale bombing, destroying much of the city's infrastructure, and disbanding our government. However, other cities went unaffected. The more prosperous and populated cities before the bombings were destroyed, and the less affluent ones remained mostly untouched. Cities like that are known as Prospects. Cities like ours are known as Forlorns.

"The closest Prospect to us, that I know of, is a long-distance away—across the Barren Wasteland. The Barren Wasteland is a treacherous desert of sand and earth, hosting many dangerous creatures and people. The Barren Wasteland exists because those were the parts of the country hit by nuclear weaponry. The atomic energy killed everything in sight, obliterating all in its radius. Now, the radiation is mostly gone, so it's safe to be around. However, going to the Barren Wasteland is still dangerous; many thieves and brigands lie in wait to pounce on people who approach it. The Barren Wasteland is also where we get our water. What separates our Forlorn from the Barren Wasteland is a small river of water, enough to swim across. No one has ever crossed the Barren Wasteland—not alone, at least. Most people die either by running out of supplies or by the rogues which wait out by the river, hoping for someone dumb enough to cross it.

"Are you following along alright, Mike?" Vic asked me. I was looking at the ground, periodically making eye contact with Vic. I imagined horrors in my mind.

"Yeah, I think so," I said. "But how does the pin fit into all of this?"

"I was getting to that. That pin belongs to an organization called Congress. Every member of Congress wears that pin—bears that insignia—so everyone knows who they are."

"What is Congress?"

"Congress is a group of powerful men, for each their own merits, who control the city. They exist to break up contraband, gang activity, and stop other groups from becoming too powerful. Think of them as police from some of the stories you read, Mike. In the case of Congress, however, they aren't looking out for the good of the community; they care only about themselves. Congress's main goal is to make themselves the strongest group in our Forlorn and take control over everything; set up an empire where they are the beneficiaries. That way, they can rule like kings—like dictators." Vic scowled as he spoke.

"I don't believe I've ever seen someone from Congress," I added.

"You have. The reason your father had this pin?" He twisted the pin between his fingers, feeling the groves and pointed edges with his fingertips. "He's a Congress member. Anyone who has this pin is a member of Congress."

"So, you're saying my father is a bad guy?"

"I'm not saying that exactly. I'm just saying it' s—by all counts—very likely."

"How come I haven't seen them patrol the city?" I asked.

"Well, to be fair, you haven't been out in the city all that much. Outside of your library excursions, you've only been out once. It's a big city. Their influence hasn't reached us yet, thankfully. It's mainly up where Peter took you guys—that area is in the thick of Congress influence. Our city is divided into two distinct districts: The Inner City and The Outer City. Where we live is The Outer City. Congress reigns over The Inner City, with much of their ideals and corruption localized to that area. We hardly ever venture into there. That's why Peter was so hesitant to visit that bakery; it's located near the outskirts of The Inner City. You likely wandered The Inner City for those few days after Peter's death.

"The orphanage is located so far away from The Inner City that it takes a day or two of walking to reach it. In a way, though, being so far into The Outer City shelters us from their influence. The path to the library is relatively safe; as mentioned, Congress hasn't reached this side of town yet. Besides, Congress typically patrols at night. During the day, they stick around their base—wherever that is—and if they need supplies or anything, they send out a guy or two to fetch it. They wear these pins as identifiers, so no one messes with them—no one wants to mess with Congress. They have power over everyone, way more supplies, and loads of weapons. Anyone who goes up against them or aggravates them might as well have a death wish. Therefore, we typically stay inside when it's dark."

"How do you know all this?" I asked.

"About what? The Fallout or Congress?"

"All of it. The war, the cities—how do you know so much?"

"Mike, I was alive before The Fallout," he said, plainly yet mockingly. I had forgotten he was about four years older than me. I was born right when The Fallout happened, so it would make sense for him to know about life before the end of the world. I imagined what it must have felt like—to have your whole life turned upside down and readjust to a worse reality. I only ever knew that worse reality.

Vic continued, "I still remember how the world used to be and what it used to look like. I remember the deep blue skies, with white, pillow-like clouds. I remember the touch of grass across my hands as I ran through fields of crop and acreage. I remember the smell of urban life—greasy cars that used to work, and busy people that used to live. The city felt alive back then, but it died along with its inhabitants."

"How do you know so much about Congress, then?"

"Funny you should ask." He leaned back a little and put his hands behind his head. "My father founded Congress."

"Really?" I gasped.

"Yeah, I know. Years after this city truly fell into chaos, he and a few friends he met started Congress. He's Congress Member' A'."

"A?"

"Oh, I forgot to mention: Congress Members don't use names—they lost them when they joined. Instead, they're identified by letters. It makes them more autonomous and cult-like that way. My father is Congress Member' A'." They're given letters based upon when they joined, and my father was first. Next was Chris's."

"Chris's father is in Congress too?"

"Yep, Congress Member' B'. Everyone in our group is the child of a Congress Member. That's why we're together; we're all orphans to the same degree."

"What about mothers? Why do you call yourselves orphans; you still have parents."

"Congress Members are all men, only initiated if they have at least one child and are widowed. It doesn't matter how they are widowed, though, just so long as a child is born and the mother is dead. This way, their heir can be continued, potentially; severing ties with their child, and without a wife, they are tied to no one. If they pass this check, they then go through a rigorous physical exercise. If they survive, they become a newly inducted member."

"So, then everyone in the orphanage is motherless... "

"Correct. Fatherless, too. They are Congress, and as such, they gave up their livelihoods to serve. They eat, sleep, and prey for their 'work'. While they are technically alive, they are completely detached from us—their children—and want nothing to do with us." Victor scowled. "I hate them all."

"How does my father play into Congress?"

"Your father? I'm not too sure." Vic looked away, trying to think. "Well, ok." He spun around. "Let's put it this way. My father is Member A, and Chris's is B. The rest goes: Peter was C, Billy is D, Melody is E, Jack is F... so I guess that means your father is Congress Member G."

"G, huh?" I looked down at my hands and interlocked my fingers.

"I only assume. Unless someone was inducted before your father, but if you remember your father coming home one day wearing the pin, but not his entire life, that means he was inducted later."

"So, my father's pin had a G on it ... he's Congress Member G now... "

"He's not your father anymore, Mike. He's a part of Congress, and they don't care about us—their spawn."

"What about Myles? Which member is his father?"

"His father is Member H. We knew there had to be a Member G child before you got here, but we didn't know who it was. That's why I needed you here so badly; I felt that you were the missing piece to the puzzle I needed." Vic looked at the pin once more. "This one has a C on it, which means it belongs to Congress Member C. Tch. How fitting... "

"Do the letters on the pins correspond to which Congress Member wears it?"

"Correct. This was Peter's father's." He looked away. "He must have seen his dead son in the street and left him there to rot. If you found this pin near Peter, his father was likely there at some point."

My mind flashed back to that moment. We dropped Peter in the alleyway, following a streak of dried blood, and that's when I found the pin. Peter's father moved the other kid's body—or moved the body out of the alleyway—but did nothing to his son. My fingers clutched the side of the air conditioning unit. Its jagged metal pierced my skin.

We sat on the roof a while longer. We didn't speak. I was still processing all the information I was fed. The confines of the world I'd lived in before that moment was crushed. The world seemed vaster than it did before. Other cities? Other nations? The whole world? The revelation that the entire world was like our Forlorn made me feel empty—hopeless. I wanted my life to mean something, but what? If everything was destroyed, what would there be left to build?

Vic broke the silence, "Can I tell you something?"

"Haven't you already told me 'something'?" I said with a smirk.

"It's stupid, really. But..." he sighed. "I want to take down Congress."

"What?" I replied, flabbergasted. Take down Congress? Vic just spoke about their awesome power, and how agitating them was a death wish. Did Vic have a death wish? What was his motive? Did anyone else agree with this?

He continued. "I just—I hate them. I hate all of them. They left their children—some killed their wives, our mothers—to play pretend-police and pasteurize the city? They don't even care about us! They only care about themselves, and to quench their thirst for power! To leave behind a child who must fend for themselves in this world—how could a good person do that? They're corrupt—they're corrupting the city. Not out where we are—not yet—but you wandered The Inner

City. You saw its desolation, I'm sure. Anyone who dares object to their rule gets killed, and if no one does anything, we'll all be slaves to them. I'd rather die than serve them. I'd rather fight." He took a big breath and hung his head. "I just don't know how to do it. It's not easy trying to get everyone convinced to go out and kill their fathers, you know? I'm afraid they still care for them, even though they left us. We're all together—the sons of Congress—"

"We can take the crown," I said, autonomically.

"Yes!" Vic shouted. "Yes, that's exactly it! Oh, I love it. That's it—we start a rebellion."

"I'm sorry—what?" I said, still not fully aware of what I just said.

"We rebel against them. We get other groups on board, we build an army, and we take down Congress once and for all!"

"Vic, are you sure you want to do this?"

"I'm more sure about this than anything." He stood up from the air conditioning unit and paced the rooftop. "I have this new leadership; I want to use it for something. I don't want to just hang around inside the orphanage, trying to make ends meet. I want to save the city—restore it to its former glory. We can start a new world—a new government. One that fights for its people—protects its people and cares for them. We can overthrow Congress. Ugh, if we could just have one ounce of their power... "

Vic's eyes shined brightly in the night. I could barely make out his face, only hardly saw his enthusiasm; I heard his conviction in his tone.

"Do you think we can convince everyone else?" I said as if we were starting a cult.

"I think so, with a mission statement like that: Start a new world!"

I straightened my back and thought about the prospect: a new world—how inviting! A place where we could decide what was right and what was wrong, establish a life worth living, and rebuild the city to what it once was. We could turn our Forlorn into a Prospect—be leaders of a new free world. My heartfelt light and my hands felt shaky.

Vic tapped my arm and placed the Congress pin in my hand. "But it's a fight for another day. Let's sleep on it, yeah?" He walked away.

"Vic," I said. He stopped and turned. "What did this city used to be called?"

"It was Chicago. Now it's nothing." Vic turned away and descended the ladder back into the foyer. I stayed alone on the rooftop for a few minutes longer, gazing out toward the dead roads, my eyes bouncing from building to building, bounding from each marvelous angle of the city above the thick haze of dust and smoke.

Reflecting from one of the windows, I saw a pair of lights—illuminating the structures around it. I heard the purr of an engine echo through the empty streets—It infiltrated the natural whirrs of wind cutting across the city's sanctioned beauty. Where did the lights come from? Was there electricity in The Inner City? What wonders did our fallen little Forlorn hold? I kept looking up. I reflected upon the tall, central building which ascended mightily above the smog. It seemed to be the only constant in this world of change.

Chapter 15

Months passed since the conversation on the rooftop. Emotions and tensions had mostly plateaued. Chris continued leading and organizing our next raids—what we called scavenging missions. I became a regular on said raids, while Myles and I took turns training with Vic now and again. My main goal was to calm myself while my adrenaline pumped through me. I started to use the staff more defensively, steadily blending that into offensive tactics. Myles, on the other hand, was still struggling with hand-to-hand combat. He wasn't terrible by any means—rather, not acute enough to quickly process fights. He was determined to keep trying, though. Myles was the kind of guy who would get knocked down, get right back up, only to make the same mistakes again.

Billy heightened his cooking finesse. He continued receiving help from Melody and me on reading recipes from his various cookbooks. He deduced what materials to be on the lookout for and kept stock of what he had. Overall, we ate better from Billy's newfound hobby and ate more; we had more food to eat instead of peaches and other assorted canned goods.

Jack started to get better. He was beginning to walk again, albeit slowly, and needed someone to walk with him. He would trounce around the orphanage to get his muscles acclimated to walking again but walked with a large bandage compressing his wounded leg. He'd only just moved to a limp when he told the group that he no longer needed someone by his side. Seconds later, he tripped and landed face-down on the foyer floor. Jack's situation humored us, but he was coy with it.

Jack's assistant, when not out on raids, was Melody. She developed a specific schedule: In the morning, she helped Jack get up and move around. Then, she'd go on a raid, and that afternoon she'd help Jack some more, then at night, she'd read from one of her action or sci-fi books. She and I drifted apart, only speaking in simple statements while out on raids together in groups of three or four. She devoted herself to helping others: helping the group, helping Jack, helping Billy. The only person she seemed to neglect from her mercy was me.

To be fair, it wasn't like I was doing anything proactive for the group. Where Melody focused on the betterment of those around her, I was preoccupied with bettering myself. From my training to having Vic teach me how to be more attentive and creative with what I find on raids, to reading and dissecting stage-plays for my enjoyment. I thought about myself first without realizing it.

Vic and I hadn't told anyone about our conversation on the rooftop. I kept a checkmark next to the date in my calendar to remind myself how long it has been since I knew the truth. Three months had passed and we hadn't told a soul. The secret was killing me.

Recently, Vic came across a massive find. He was off on his own, doing his exploring away from the group when he found an enormous stash of canned food items and bottled water. The area looked deserted for a long time, with dust lying atop the canned food and bottle caps. The building they were in looked ransacked long ago, but they weren't as observant as Vic in picking the place over. It took several trips to bring everything back to the orphanage. Due to Vic's find, we took off a few days from going on raids and searching the city for anything serious. Vic took this time to comb the city and explore on his lonesome—to the dismay of Chris—and I took more trips to the library.

Melody stopped accompanying me on my library trips to take care of Jack, and to help Billy with his cookbooks; he was still being stubborn about learning to read. I always asked her if she would like to accompany me—extending my hand to mend our friendship—but she declined the offer every time. I continued bringing her the next book in the series she read through. Her reading speed increased tremendously. A few months ago, she was barely working on comic books, but now she was destroying 300+ page novels like they were nothing. It took me years to get to that level of reading proficiency. I admired her intelligence.

While it was less exciting to go to the library by myself, I didn't mind too much; I went to the library for years before meeting the group. The library was still a muse for me. Everything good seemed to happen at the library; it was a safe space for me, away from the day-to-day upkeeps we had at home.

Another aspect of going alone was it gave me time to think—time to reflect. I would attempt to make sense of all Vic told me about The Fallout. I remembered reading about countless wars in history books—they were portals to a past world where I could see remnants of all around me. I could see the propaganda from the war plastered around the city, urging people to join the battle that ended the world. The posters read, "The Fallout: Them or us—there is no compromise," and "Saving the world for our children." How naïve.

Nonetheless, my mind always circled back to my father. With all the information Vic gifted me, new questions arose about my father. What was his involvement in Congress? Was he always in Congress and I never noticed? I remember my mother being alive for a few years, so it must have been after that. How long has my father wanted to be in Congress? Did he kill my mother so he could get in? The more questions I thought up, the more I hated him. I developed a biased hatred—completely blinded by emotion. I wanted to get stronger and takedown Congress—not necessarily to make them repent for anything, but to uncover more truths.

The longer I thought about Congress, the more I tried to distance my father from them. If what Vic said was true, and they acted like barbarians attempting to build their power and eradicate any threats, how could I lump my father in with them? He never acted like that when I knew him; he was dismissive, sure, but vindictive? It just didn't add up—and I obsessed over finding out.

At the library, I would first pick out the books Melody asked me to pick up for her, as well as anything that struck my fancy. Then, I would scour the building for any information about The Fallout, Congress, other nations—I did this when I was much younger, but I thought I might find something new.

I never found any books written about The Fallout: no newspaper articles, no magazines, no documentaries—nothing. I did find a lot about Congress; however, it was about the Democratic system of government before The Fallout—not the version of Congress in our Forlorn. Their version of Congress was an amalgamation of two groups that met to discuss policy and legislation to govern their country. They decided laws, declared wars, and oversaw everything legislative in the old world. Our version of Congress stole the name, and acted similarly, but didn't adopt the conventions. In the old world, Congress was elected directly by its citizens.

History felt empty without written information on The Fallout. Therefore, I started to write my experiences in a journal, hidden away at the library. I wrote down all I knew about The Fallout, about Congress, and all the questions I still needed answered. It was a notebook, but also a checklist.

After writing some basic experiences into my notebook, I placed it behind the front desk under some assorted materials, hidden from the inattentive eye. I stuffed my books into the various compartments of my backpack and crawled out the entry/exit hole. On the way back, I scanned the area and practiced the skills Vic taught me about noticing areas of interest around me. Usually, I found nothing around the library. It was an untouched part of town as if no one even knew it was there. Although, I noticed skid marks on the ground. Black stains on the cracked concrete. They were thick where I stood but then disappeared a few meters ahead of me. They went out and down the perch that the library sat upon and onto a nearby road. I thought it odd to see tire tracks, especially since cars didn't seem to run anymore. I decided to follow them.

The road they led me to was one I hadn't been on in years; they were part of the path I used to take from my father's house. The road was mostly barren and devoid of any noticeable objects—not that I could find, anyway. Eventually, I saw the marks again—more defined. They had small rifts in the markings. I followed them until they stopped at a large vehicle. It was a clean-looking tan truck, though it looked more tank-like than a truck. The marks on the ground were tire marks created by the truck. I wondered how that was possible—there weren't any cars that worked in the city, as far as I knew. Plus, any gas in the cars would have been rendered unusable. How were there tire marks leading to a car that couldn't work?

I scanned the area to locate its owner but found no one. The only noise was the wind cutting across the low road. I turned my attention to the truck, which was devoid of any dust. I could see my reflection in the car. My hair was dark brown and greasy—longer, with my bangs needing a trim. My amber eyes faded into the tan-tint of the truck. My body was lean, my arms appearing elongated by the curved metal. My father's jacket was still draped over my scrawny body, still slightly too large for me. A dark blue t-shirt covered my bruised stomach, with skinny jeans sticking to my untrimmed legs. I was stuck in awkward puberty, where growing pains were masked by unruly body development.

I heard a noise behind me. A loose can rolled by me. I spun around and noticed a figure, skinny and tall like me. They wore a teal shirt and a brown jacket. Their hair was longer, blonde, and perfect emerald eyes stared into mine. The hair was in a ponytail, and their chest bumped out slightly—a girl. She bit her cherry lips and ran away. I gave chase.

We felt like kids again—running through the old streets I hadn't explored in years. We ran and hopped over obstacles in the roads, tumbled over tops of cars, and under sharp street signs. The air flowed through my hair and hit my face with a stale coldness, reminding me of how I saw the city as a child, unexplored and mysterious.

I gave chase for a while, but soon she tried to lose me; for a while, she played—making decisions to see if I could hold my own against her. It felt like a game of endurance, and she saw me as a worthy opponent. She turned down an alley, jumped off a wall, and grabbed onto a loose fire escape. She pulled herself up, then proceeded to climb up the sides of the fire escape, using the safety bars as a make-shift ladder. I watched them with amazement. I tried to jump like her but fell back to the ground. I looked up and saw her reach the top of the building. I found an empty dumpster and climbed it, which gave me enough height to bounce off the wall and grab the fire escape. I jumped into it and shamefully took the stairs up. She waited until I almost reached the top, then started running again.

She changed the rules of gravity when she moved. She bounded across the air-conditioning ducts of the buildings seamlessly, even climbing some of them to specifically get be-hind me, returning us to where we were seconds earlier. I couldn't do the flips and tricks she was doing, but I managed to navigate the environment well enough to keep her in my sights. Once the roof ran out of space, she jumped off. I rushed over—afraid she fell to her doom. I failed to notice the large drainage pipe that took her down the side of the build-ing, safely returned to the concrete ground. I slid down the pipe, and she ran once more.

We bounced off more obstacles and climbed over more roadblocks until I learned her tricks. She tried to climb houses, using windows as footstools, and I soared next to her. She jumped and rolled on the ground, and I followed.

She tripped over her shoelace down an alleyway, trying to jump from wall-to-wall. She rolled and shrieked, "Hold on!" Her voice was high and feminine. Her petite figure extended into her voice; innocent and fragile. I froze when she fell, and I slowly approached to help her up. "I'm good," she said. She batted my hand away and stood up on her own. "You aren't going to hurt me, are you?"

"What? No," I said. I was out of breath from running but also flabbergasted at her question.

She didn't seem out of breath. "Good. I thought so, at first, which is why I ran. Thought I'd play around until I gave you the slip, but you followed me pretty well." She lobbed spit at the ground and wiped the residue left on her lips. She undid her hair from her ponytail. She ran her hands through her hair; it was straight, clean, and beautiful. "No one's ever caught me before. You should feel proud."

"I wouldn't say proud—mostly tired."

She laughed. "I'm surprised you know parkour."

"Par-what now?"

"What we were doing back there. Jumping from buildings, climbing up structures—parkour."

"Oh. Well, I'm a quick learner, so... "

"I'd say. It took me years to get as good as I am. You found a way to keep up in minutes."

"Regardless, I didn't chase you to hurt you. I was just curious."

"Just curious? What's that supposed to mean?"

"You don't see a lot of people around this part of the city. Especially not girls."

"Tell me about it. I don't think I've ever met anyone like me—a girl, that is." She put her hands behind her head and stretched her arms. I thought about telling her about Melody. I thought about inviting her to the orphanage—she could meet her and have a friend. I thought about inviting her into our group. Her beauty was unmatched—the world was filthy, but she was pristine.

"Isn't that jacket a little big on you?" she asked.

I spread my arms and felt the sleeves dangle over my hands. "Yeah, it is. I'm growing into it."

"Huh. You know, you remind me of someone from a long time ago... wore an oversized jacket, too... "

My mind processed her words. Did she know me? Did I know her? But where from? I felt like if I met someone like her, I would have remembered it. I examined her perfectly deep green, emerald eyes. They glistened and sparkled back at me. Then I remembered.

"You're that girl I chased when I found the library!"

She looked away from me and blushed. "Might be. Oh yeah, I think I remember you running after me. I brought you to that open area by the library and gave you the slip." She smiled. "Wow, that was so long ago. Doesn't feel that way, though. Life goes by fast, especially when you're running everywhere." She walked up to me and extended her hand. "My name's Sarah Jasmine. It's nice to meet you again."

"Michael Amit, but you can just call me Mike."

I shook Sarah's soft hand then released it. She smirked and said, "I've thought about that day for a while now, hoping I could one day find the guy who put up a chase. Nice to see you've improved over the years." She looked up and down my body.

"Same to you—you've improved, uh, too." I looked up and down her body.

"What are you doing out here?" Sarah asked.

"Visiting the library. I've been going there for years."

"Really? Huh. Never been in there; I like using it as my escape route, though, if things get hairy."

"What do you mean, 'if things get hairy'?"

"I'm a thief. Gotta eat to live; gotta steal to eat." She chuckled. "Anyway, I typically pickpocket unsuspecting travelers. Then, I run away, climb a building or two, and they leave me alone."

"Why didn't you steal from me?"

"You said it yourself. You have a jacket that doesn't fit, and what I presume is a backpack full of books. Not exactly the things I need."

"Where do you live?"

"Around here. I live on my own, hopping from rooftop to rooftop. I have a setup, but nowhere I call 'home'. I generally stick to this area, though; the library is a landmark to tell me where I am."

My eyes then gravitated toward the jacket she was wearing. It looked like an aviator jacket, with a patch sewed on the right arm sleeve. The patch was the same design as the Congress pins; the letter J was prominent.

"What's that?" I asked, pointing to the patch. "Why is the Congress pin stitched into your jacket?"

"This jacket was my mother's a long time ago. My father stitched Congress's logo into my family's clothes; he was obsessed with joining them. He was nervous to try and join because of the physical test and didn't think he could pass. The other problem was my mother, but she died of illness when I turned five-years-old. That's when I left home; I couldn't stand my father. I was sick of him—I just wanted to be free to do what I wanted, when I wanted. When my mother died, he became controlling—wanting me to do exactly what he wanted."

"Wait, you know about Congress?"

"Yeah, as I said, my dad was obsessed with them. Why are you acting it's such a big deal?"

"Nothing." I was so new to the idea of Congress that it felt like a secret. The plans Vic and I made were a secret, but Congress itself was not. "Hey," I said, "I know a group of people like you. Not girls—though there is one—but who also ran away from home because of their fathers. We live in an orphanage a little bit past the library. If you want, I could bring you there. You can still make your own decisions, but a roof over your head and a steady place to sleep."

She mulled it over for a few moments. "Normally, I'd say no. But, I don't know, there's something about you I'm drawn too." She looked down and murmured, "Is it... " She looked back up. "Let me get my things. I'd love to go with you."

I waited while she climbed up a building a few blocks away and jumped back down with a small messenger bag. She didn't share its contents, but she seemed excited to go. I thought about her deceiving me—and all this being a clever ploy—but I didn't believe that would happen. If what she said was true, then I thought she admired me somehow. It might have been because I was the only one to keep up with her, but it could have been something else. Something drew me to her—her beauty flooded my senses when I looked at her. When she spoke to me, I felt blessed that she acknowledged my existence. I grabbed her hand to lead her to the orphanage. We ran through the streets, hand in hand, like children once again.

We reached to the orphanage. I didn't have a key, so I knocked on the door to have someone open it for me. Vic was on the other side.

"Hey Mi—uh... " he paused when he saw Sarah.

"Oh, Vic. This is my friend, Sarah. We met a long time ago, and I thought she could live here with us?"

"Hmm... how about you two come inside for a minute?" He led us inside and told us to follow him into the foyer. He left to get Chris.

Chris approached and said, "Mike, who is this?"

"This is my friend, Sarah. I thought she could live here with us."

"Mike, you can't just bring strangers in—"

"She's not a stranger," I said. "I knew her a long time ago, but we ran back into each other."

"I don't know," Chris said, "I'm not sure I can trust her. No offense," he said to Sarah.

"None taken," she said. She cupped her hands behind her back.

"No, you don't understand," I pleaded. "There's a reason I brought her here. Look." I showed them her jacket, with the Congress design stitched in. "It's Congress's logo."

Sarah said, "My father is a member of Congress."

"Wait, he is?" I whispered to her.

"Yeah. I eavesdropped on some travelers one day, and they spoke of a new Congress Member—member J—who'd been inducted recently. They said he had a daughter, but she ran away at a young age—which is me. Then I, you know, stole from them and ran away." She grinned.

"Regardless," I said, now at Vic and Chris, "she's like us— she's one of us. Now can she join?"

"She could be lying," Chris said. "That patch could be an indicator that she works with Congress as a scavenger of sorts. She could have stitched that herself!"

"With all due respect, I think you're being superstitious," Sarah said. "If I wanted to steal from you guys, I wouldn't ask for permission." Chris stared at her. "Listen, if you don't want me here, I can leave. I lived on my own for a long time; I just thought you'd all be different." She started to walk down the stairs. I ran after her, and I heard Vic say something Chris as I descended the stairs.

"Don't go," I pleaded. "Please. I want you here."

"Yeah, well, big guy up there doesn't."

"He doesn't like change, that's all. His best friend died a few months ago, so he's being overly protective of us. If you stay down here, I will go back up and talk him into it—I think he trusts me."

About this time, Vic came down the stairs. "You're in," he said to Sarah. "Chris said you can stay here—if you provide for the group, and not only for yourself."

"Of course," Sarah replied. "It was getting lonely out there by myself. I appreciate the hospitality and will do whatever you need me to do. I'm a good thief if that helps any?"

"It could help. I like to find things hidden around, but if you can be sneaky about it—get in and out of places efficiently—you could be a good scouter."

"I mean, I know the area around the library pretty well, but I've ventured out farther into the city and can fend for myself. If you want me to scout, I'm your girl."

"Awesome! Glad to hear it!" Vic smiled then glanced over to me. It read an expression of 'We need to talk'. I let Sarah go upstairs so I could speak to Vic; Chris alerted the group of Sarah's presence. I let her introduce herself while I stood by the entrance.

"You're lucky," Vic told me. "Chris was about to throw her ass out until I stepped in and saved her."

"Thank you, Vic," I said.

"Don't thank me yet," he continued. "She's on some thin ice. I know she said her father is Congress Member J, but this presents another issue: The newest member we knew about was Myles's father—Member H. Now, if she's J, then we have someone missing..."

"Congress Member I's child," I said.

"Exactly. I thought I had all the pieces in play when I found you, but now there's a missing piece again. I don't feel comfortable announcing our plans to take down Congress if we don't have everyone on board—and by everyone, I mean every single Congress Member's child. I don't need one of them messing up the plan."

"Fair enough, but what does that have to do with Sarah?"

"I don't know yet," he said, exasperated. He pulled a loose hair from his face. "What I do know is that Chris expects her to go to the moon and back to prove her worth. She better be the best-damned thief I've ever seen."

"She is," I added, trying to sound confident. "How'd you convince Chris to let her stay?"

"I said we needed another number."

"And?"

"And what?"

"That wasn't all."

"Ok, fine." Vic rolled his eyes. "I also mentioned how I brought you in, and how we took a chance on you, and said, 'Look at all he's done for us.'"

"That's better," I said. I knew he must have used that argument to win Chris over. It's the most obvious one, aside from her affiliation with Congress. She fit the schema of our group perfectly.

We went upstairs and found that Sarah already made friends. She was talking to Myles when I reached the top of the steps, and she didn't seem to notice me. She was talking to him about different combat maneuvers and how she avoids fights altogether if she can. Melody ate alone in the corner.

I approached Melody and said, "How are you?" She grunted. "Aren't you going to talk to Sarah?"

"We spoke," she stated. "She said you talked a lot about me."

"Yeah, I guess I did. Well, I mean, it's hard not to. You're both girls, so I wanted her to know there was someone like her at the house."

"I'm not like her, Mike," she said. "And I would appreciate it if you don't go around telling people about me without me knowing."

"But... I didn't say anything bad about you, I just—"

"End of story."

"Ok. End of story." I watched as she shoveled a spoonful of instant potatoes into her mouth. "Oh, I got those books for you!" I said, showing her the books from my bag.

"Don't worry about it right now," she said. "I still have a few nights before I finish the one I'm on now."

"Oh, alright," I said.

"So, what's her deal?" she said to me, motioning her spoon at Sarah.

"I don't know. You could have asked her that when you two met earlier." She did a fake-laugh and made a mocking face. I continued, "She's a thief."

"Oh, so she's good at taking things that aren't hers... "

"I mean, that's a way to say it. But don't we do the same, kinda?"

"Hmph. Let's just hope she doesn't take anything of mine, or else she'll be wishing she didn't." She angrily shoved her spoon into her instant potatoes.

"I don't think she plans on taking anything from us... "

"Mike, you are so stupid." Melody stood, tossed away her food, and stomped her way upstairs.

I waited a few seconds, then ran upstairs to grab some food for myself. I brought my plate downstairs to share with Sarah. I pulled her away from the group and gave her half of my plate. She thanked me. Sarah seemed happy not to be alone, and she smiled while we ate and talked as a group. She and I shared our adventures, how we initially met, and how we ran across our little area of the city.

At night, she sat beside me underneath the blanket in our bedroom. She touched my hand under the covers; her palms were ice cold. She rested her head on my shoulder and quickly fell asleep. It didn't take long for me to join her.

Chapter 16

The next day was Sarah's test. We still had plenty of supplies from Vic's find a few days ago, so this assignment was a small one. There was a small group we dealt with recently, called Beringue. We took from one of their hideouts, and they were on the hunt for us ever since. They recognized us by our attire. They were only a group of 6 people, but then again, so were we before Sarah joined. Beringue used warehouses to store their materials, supplies, weapons, etc. Chris had recently found their main stronghold and wanted to get into their warehouses to raid their supplies. He wanted to weaken them.

Sarah's assignment was to sneak into their stronghold, swipe the keys, and return unnoticed. If seen or captured, however, we would bail to save ourselves. It was a suicide mission, and Chris knew that. He saw Sarah as an expendable. If she succeeded, he gained the upper hand in this feud. If she fails, he can sever ties with her and have no connection to the attempted robbery. It was a win-win for Chris.

"Are they all men?" Sarah asked when she heard the stipulation.

"Yes," Chris said. "Roughly 16 years old or so."

Sarah mulled it over some more. She pulled out a nail filer from her bag and ground away at her fingernails, making them rounded and slick. "So, if I get caught, they'll probably..." she trailed off.

"Most likely," Chris replied. I had no clue what they were talking about.

Sarah bit her lip before saying, "I think I can do it. It's just keys, right?" He nodded. "Oh yeah, let's do it now. Let's go."

A group of four went out on this mission: Chris, Vic, Sarah, and me. We didn't take our standard garments of masks, goggles, and hats—without the garments, Beringue wouldn't know who we were. Odd, how at that moment we needed to lose our disguise to become anonymous. Chris went with us to make sure it went smoothly and to show Sarah where their stronghold was. Vic came along, not only as Chris's right-hand man but also so to see Beringue's location. I came along to support Sarah.

Along our way, Chris and Vic naturally walked vanguard while Sarah and I walked rearguard. Chris and Vic talked ahead of the group, but they were so far away we couldn't hear their conversation.

"I have to ask," I said, "Why did you ask about them being all male? What does that have to do with anything?"

"It's important because if I get caught, bad things could happen."

"What kind of bad things? Like, they kill you?"

"Well, that's always a possibility, but I don't think they will. It'd be worse than that."

"Like...?"

"There are some things girls have to be more cautious of in this world than boys."

"I'm sorry, I'm not familiar with..." I trailed off. Sarah made symbols with her hands, insinuating sex. "Oh, ok, gotcha."

"Girls in this world have to think about that all the time," Sarah said. "It's an issue that women face in this world."

"Is it because you could get stuck with a child?" I asked.

"No. I wouldn't expect you to understand, I'm sorry..."

"No, tell me. I won't know unless you tell me. Don't keep me ignorant."

She took a deep breath. "While getting pregnant is a fear, yes, it's more than that. They use you ... it's horrible. It's deprecating. It's humiliating. It's a loss of control. It's a loss of yourself. A loss of innocence. You lose who you used to be and have to live with the experience and consequence forever." She paused. Her fingers trembled. I took her arm. "You feel like property to someone else. You're no longer Sarah, or Jane. You're some guy's sex toy."

"Has this happened to you?" I asked, softly.

"No, thankfully not. But my mother, Jane... it's how I was born—a product of one woman's loss of independence. I feel like I shouldn't exist."

"Don't think of yourself like that," I said. "You can't help you being born. And it shouldn't matter how or when or where your birth took place. I see you for who you are—not under what conditions you were brought into this world."

She sniffled. "Thanks, Mike." Her words were dry. They didn't feel real.

"I don't mean to pry, but is that how she died? Jane, your mother?" I improvidently continued.

"Yeah, she got sick—really sick, a sexual disease from my father. He abused other women, too—I always wondered if I have brothers and sisters somewhere out there—and he got a disease from someone else and gave it to my mom, but she's the one that died. That's what allowed my father to get into Congress."

"Wait, I thought a Congress Member had to be widowed?" I asked. "If that's the case, your mother and father weren't married."

"In theory, that's how it works," she replied. Her tone grew angrier. "But no one can officiate marriages in this world. It's done on here-say. So, a man can confiscate a woman, breed, and claim her as his wife. Then, once the child is born, he can slaughter her, fulfilling the requirements to become a Congress Member. A born child and a dead wife."

"It's that simple, huh … that's terrible."

"That's where a lot of men fail, though. They think that's all you need to be a Congress Member. In actuality, there's a test to become a Congress Member—a series of physically excruciating exams and tests to prove they have what it takes. It's torture, I'm pretty sure, or as lose as it can be without being called that. Most candidates die in the initiation process. That's why there aren't that many Congress Members overall."

My blood boiled. Her story reinvigorated the fire I felt against my father and Congress as a whole. It was the same fire as with Vic on the rooftop. I knew Vic would have felt the same way if he heard Sarah's story. I put my arm around hers as we continued walking.

She continued: "I've never been caught, but I'm afraid if I ever do, that will be my fate. I'll just become another doll used to make a man's desires come true. I'm afraid of being anything but myself. That's why I learned to run fast, and climb, and practiced parkour. I came across some guy when I was young, and he showed me how to maneuver the city; he taught me how to scale the city. He's dead now, though."

"I'm sorry to hear that."

"I killed him."

"Oh." I loosened my grip around her arm.

"He tried to convince me that I needed to give myself to him as a return for the 'favor' he did for me. So, I drove a knife through his heart." She paused and bit her lip. "But that's what I'm saying, Mike. I was six years old when I had to kill a man because he wanted my body. You don't know what that's like for people only to see you for your looks."

I looked at the ground.

"I had to learn to get away quick, or else my fear could come true. I'm not as scared of it now, because I trust in my skills, but that looming terror is always in the back of my mind.

I've had to put on this super-tough exterior for so long to convince myself and everyone else that I'm no one to mess with. But I don't want that life anymore. I want to have fun—confident that I have people who'll care for me and will take on the burden of looking out for me. That's why I want to be in this group with you, Mike. You're the only one who's ever caught up to me, and you've been nothing but helpful to me. I want that support in my life. I want to feel safe."

We walked for another half hour before stopping at a small apartment complex. One of the windows on the third floor was open, and we heard the booming bass of male voice chatter.

"Up there," Chris said, pointing to the open window. "That's where they are." He looked at Sarah. "Now, I need you to get in there and look for the tall guy with blue hair. He's their leader; he should have the keys somewhere on him, either in one of his pockets or on his belt."

"Ok," she said. She threw her jacket to the ground and tucked her maroon tank top into her jeans. She undid her ponytail and fashioned her hair into a tight bun.

"Are you going to be ok?" I asked her. "You'll make it back, right?"

"Don't hold your breath," Chris told me.

"Do hold your breath," she replied. "I'll be back before you run out of air." Then, she hopped onto the rims of one of the windows and started to scale the building.

"That's awesome," Vic whispered.

"She is impressive; I'll give her that," Chris said.

She jumped around, trying to find any kind of footing to keep her ascension going. She reached the window, but instead of going in, she slid open the window to the right of the open window. She climbed through that one.

Only a minute or two passed until we saw one of her legs hop out the window and brought her body entirely over the side. She closed the window and descended the building. She landed quietly, on all fours. From her back pocket, she pulled out a keyring with multiple keys on it. She spun it on her finger.

"These keys, right?" she said, sarcastically.

"How did you do that so fast?" Chris asked, confused.

She tossed the keys into Chris's hands. "Because I'm not an amateur." She waltzed to her jacket, still lying on the ground, while she untucked her shirt, and redid her ponytail. She was so quick it felt like nothing changed.

On the way back, Chris thumbed through the keys and tried relaying the locations of Sylum's storage units to Vic.

"We can go right now and start trying keys," Vic said to him. "We still have the whole day ahead of us."

"What if we didn't, though?" Chris said quietly.

"I don't know what you mean," Vic replied.

"I mean, what if we don't just steal everything they have. We can wait."

"How could you say that? We have the upper hand—we should strike now!"

"No, we shouldn't. We can live for a while off what you found—and I bet we can find more before we run out. We're in no need of supplies." Vic shifted positions. Chris continued, "While bleeding out their supplies will no-doubt make us win, we shouldn't beat them."

"... because—" Vic snapped his fingers.

"Yep," Chris said, confidently folding his arms.

"We shouldn't beat them; we should use them," Vic smirked as the words slipped out of his mouth.

"That's what I'm thinking. I plan not just to steal and consume their supplies but also to use them as a bartering tool."

"So, are we going to blackmail them?"

"Not exactly. Blackmail would insinuate we're manipulating them with malice intent. We'd be more like 'partners,' of sorts."

"You mean, we'd work together? I don't want to work with them."

"They don't want to work with us, either. But, while we have these keys, they have no choice. They can't fight us, because now we outnumber them. They can't steal from us, because we have this badass to get anything back and then some." He pointed at Sarah, who blushed. "If they try anything, we hold the literal keys to their survival. We can starve them out if needed. They are in our control, and we get to decide their fate. Let's not waste it."

Vic nodded. "That's probably the smartest thing I've ever heard from you, Chris."

"There's a first time for everything." The two laughed and went silent. We walked a few more minutes until we reached the orphanage. Before entering, Vic stopped.

"What's up?" Chris asked.

"Just one more thing," Vic said, "Why would we want to work with Beringue? Why partner with them?"

Chris snickered. "You'll see in time. For now, though, they'll be our broker. We can use their supplies as trade materials for other groups we come across. It'll build us up as trustworthy and loyal, but mostly powerful."

"Won't that attract the attention of Congress?"

"Only if we're not careful."

That night, Billy made cornbread from a box found in Vic's haul. It was stale but filling. Batter painted the pans, and crumbs clung to its sides. It took Billy all night to scrape them clean, but he seemed happy that everyone enjoyed his meal.

Sarah was still restless come nighttime, so I told her stories from books I had read over the years until she fell asleep. Vic and Chris talked in the foyer, and I drifted asleep to their plotting.

Chapter 17

A week passed and Sarah became another member of the group. After proving her abilities, Chris took a greater interest in her. She went on missions best suited to her skill set. She would check rooms on higher apartments and other buildings, giving us more supplies. Many buildings collapsed near the ground-level, so having access to the upper floors was extremely useful.

Chris's plan of blackmailing Beringue was successful; Chris negotiated an agreement to have us combine our materials, and we would scavenge while they bartered and grew our supply chambers. This agreement was mostly hush-hush; we didn't want talk of our collusion spreading outside of the two groups, or else Congress would no doubt break it up. While Beringue's members were initially hesitant, they soon realized it could be in the best interests of both parties to join forces and work together; we both lost responsibility and could focus on one thing more efficiently.

Due to combining efforts with Beringue, they introduced us to two other affiliates: Sylum and Gramble—allies of Beringue. They told us they'd work with us in the form of materials, storage, and several types of scavenging. Overall, we could all work together in an honor-among-thieves and find strength in numbers. Chris orchestrated negotiations with Beringue's leader, Dominic. He and Chris would meet up now and again when they had a new idea on how to be more efficient, or when they had an issue with one another and would talk it over. While their meetings were cordial, Chris always had a sharp knife sheathed in his belt if needed.

During this time, Jack recovered to nearly good health. His wounds healed and scabbed over; his most immediate hurdle was learning to walk again. Melody assisted him for a while, but Jack soon stopped wanting her help. He tried to move on his own, and if he fell, he would have to pick himself up on his own.

He started walking on his own after a few days, but it took a noticeable toll on his strength. Sarah noticed this and acted. I watched while I snacked on some canned green beans.

"Excuse me," she said to him one day, "Do you need some help?"

"No," Jack replied, "I got this." He grabbed the ledge of the window while he walked up and down the foyer to keep himself upright.

"You look tired. You sure you don't need help? I can hold you up or help you go lie down."

"Look, doll, I appreciate the concern. There are some things I need to do on my own, though, with no help."

"True, but hurting yourself in that process isn't helpful to anyone."

Jack stopped. "I'm sorry, I know you're new and all, but I haven't caught your name."

"Sarah. Sarah Jasmine."

"Well, I'm Jack. Sarah, I'm gonna let you in on something: I do things on my own around here. I don't need anyone to babysit me."

"That's not what Mike told me. He said you hurt your leg so bad that you were on bed rest for the past few months— needed constant attention and help. Hardly sounds like a lone wolf to me."

Jack gritted his teeth. "Nonetheless, I don't need your help with this." He started to walk again, this time without the window ledge. "Besides, they don't call me 'Speed' for nothing!" He quickly limped across the room towards my bedroom door, then turned around to make his way back to the ledge. He looked like he was in immense pain.

"Speed, huh?" Sarah asked.

"Yeah. That's what they used to call me around here. It's because back before this," he motioned to his leg, "I could outrun anybody. I could get in and out of situations so fast no one would even know I'd left."

"That's so cool! I think of myself as pretty fast, too."

"Really? Huh. That is kinda cool, I guess." He leaned against the windowsill.

"I'm a thief. I scale buildings and sneak around to get what I want without anyone noticing. Plus, I can outrun any guy I see."

"Oh-ho, is that a threat, Ms. Pretty?"

"It's certainly not a compliment. You and your gimp leg couldn't possibly keep up with me."

Jack glanced at his leg, then put a hand over his bandage. Sarah chuckled.

"We'll see about that," Jack said, still clutching his wound, "How's this sound: When I get better, we race. You and I go at it and see who's truly the fastest."

"You're on, dude." Sarah offered her hand, and Jack took it. Jack's stature slipped from the windowsill and fell toward Sarah. She caught him in her arms.

He looked up and flashed a smile. "Ok, so maybe I do need some help after all..." They quietly laughed together, and Sarah walked him upstairs to his bed. I grinned when I noticed Jack hobbled worse than usual when Sarah held him. Sarah had to hold on tighter to continue moving Jack, but he seemed to enjoy her company.

The next day, Jack approached me after Sarah helped him down the stairs into the main foyer. Afterword, she left with the rest of the group—she taught them basic parkour maneuvers and general awareness strategies she used. Chris was intrigued by her abilities in the field and wanted her to show everyone some of her insight so everyone could benefit. We needed someone at the house, though, so that's where I came in (I already knew her tricks), and Jack would gain no benefit in his current state.

Jack made his way toward me while I added to my calendar. I saw him approach, and I hastily hid the paper from him.

"Hey, Mike," he said, not noticing nor caring about what I was doing, "What do you know about Sarah?"

"Hmm? What for?"

"Just curious. I haven't spoken to her much, and I'm a little embarrassed to ask basic things at this point."

"Wow, the self-adoring Jack is embarrassed? What's with this change of character?" I teased.

"Shut up. She's new here, so I should get to like her. Now tell me her story."

"Well, she lived out in the city since she was young, away from her father—a Congress member. Her mother died when she was young, which sparked her rebellion toward her father. I found her while I was out, and we kind of hit it off."

"Sure, you did... " Jack muttered under his breath.

"What?"

"Nothing. Ok, that's a good starting point. Thanks." He started to hobble away before turning back. "Oh yeah, one other thing. I'm not a fan of going up and down those stairs all the time, especially in my current condition and all. Would you want my bed upstairs?"

"Really?" I gasped. "Why wouldn't you want to have a bed?"

"A few reasons. One, the reason I just mentioned. Two, I hate the comfort. I prefer the old living arrangements, but the bed was necessary for how little I would be moving. Now that I'm active again, I want to do away with comfort. It made me too relaxed and distanced from the real world. I want to be on-my-toes again, and the comfort makes that hard for me."

"A little down-to-Earth today, huh, Jack? Something is different about you... " I mocked him.

"Stop. Third, you're closer to Melody and Myles than I am; turns out we don't have much in common. And I can only make fun of them so much before it becomes boring. I need to give Billy and Vic some heckling, or I'm going to go mad." We laughed. "Besides, you found that room upstairs. It only seems fitting that you get to reap the benefit of what you gave the group."

"And fourth," I interjected, "You have a crush on Sarah."

"What?" Jack replied, his face burning red, "Who told you that?"

"You just did. Right there."

Jack grimaced. He stared out the window. "She just seems cool, and we seem to have a lot in common."

"Jack, don't try and tell me you aren't switching beds because you want to be closer to her. You always get flustered when someone figures you out; it's an easy tell." I nibbled on a piece of cornbread.

He blushed. "Heh. Guess I should work on that, huh?" He scratched his head. "Just don't tell anyone, ok? Especially not her. I know you two are close and all... "

"As friends, Jack," I replied. "She's not my type, despite her beauty. You two are cute together. Have at it, Speed." I flashed a smile, and he nodded. I continued, "Ok, I'll take your bed, but if you ever need it again—"

"I won't. Trust me." Jack walked off toward his new room. I followed, grabbed some of my things, and moved upstairs to the bedroom.

I flopped on top of the mattress. All my worries and stresses seemed to float away once I rested my body on its spring-loaded repose. I laid my bag down next to me while the aches and pains of my body washed away. My thoughts wandered, thinking about a cosmic reality, recalling books of solar systems and floating planets. I felt like those planets—weightless and held in suspension by a more significant force beyond my control.

I heard a THUMP, which brought me back to reality. My bag had slid down from the bed to the floor, and the books I had in the bag loudly connected with the hardwood flooring. I turned my body to its side to reach for it, having to move the covers and bed skirt to see down the bottom of the bed. There was just enough room to allow my bag to slide down. I saw my bag and hoisted it onto the bed. During this process, I noticed a small, white casing on the wall with a three-pronged port—an outlet. It looked like the ones in my father's house when I was younger. It occurred to me I hadn't noticed any other outlets around the orphanage.

To further my curiosity, I jumped off the bed and looked underneath the bed skirt. A cloud of dust flew at my face and my eyes watered. I wiped away the dust and saw a CD player and an accompanying CD in its jewel case. A CD was already in the device, and a cable on its back looked to fit into the three-pronged port on the wall.

When I was young, I would explore my father's house and attach appliances to the outlets along the walls. It was both a ritual I created and a glimpse of hope that I could get the magic of electricity to flow out of the walls of the house. Out of instinct, I reenacted my childhood curiosity, and a light flashed atop the CD player. It was blue, with a bunch of numbers displayed. I hit the button that said, "PLAY", but I didn't hear anything come out of it. I hit every button and turned every dial, but still, no sound came out. The speakers on the player seemed dusty, and I assumed they were broken.

In the library, there were pictures of kids listening to CD players using headphones. I searched underneath Melody and Myles's beds, and eventually found a pair. I jacked into the machine, smashed the play button, and blasted my eardrums with loud noises. After adjusting the volume, it was a more comfortable listen—no longer an attack on my eardrums.

I was captured by the music's rhythm. The conjoined efforts of multiple instruments and styles brought together into one working piece mystified me. Different elements came together to capture the spirit of one emotion. Every song on the album performed a specific function, while also contributing to the whole assembly. Every song was an actor—with their own stories—contributing to a larger narrative. The consistent beat held throughout every song kept the rest of the ensemble in line. Their leader was unannounced and was only there to make sure everyone else performed their functions on time, setting perimeters to ensure everyone followed their path. What I enjoyed most, besides the drumbeats, were the lyrics. I listened to the album twice in a row and read the lyric sheet found in the CD case. It reminded me of my current situation. Every word seemed to connect me with The Fallout and my current situation. It felt like the performers wrote this album for people like me—in a world ravaged by people too proud to admit their mistakes. It gave me confidence that Vic's idea of a revolution was plausible—although I still hadn't confronted Congress. I felt capable of anything while I listened to music. The album was Appeal to Reason.

I thought about sharing the CD player with everyone; I wanted to showcase my findings to the group and receive their praise for yet another grand discovery. My mind flashed back to my father's house, and the dreams I had about electricity. My father's face appeared in my thoughts, flickering like a flame. I could smell the burning wood in the fireplace. I shook my head and regained myself. I thought about sharing the CD player with someone, maybe Melody...

I slipped on the headphones and delved into my second listen-through. Soon after the album ended, the group returned from their session with Sarah, and I quickly hid the CD player. I was told all about their trials and tribulations. Myles had scratches along his back from falling too much; he had bruises and wounds all over. He was a good sport about it, though—joking and making light of the situation, despite the constant teasing he received.

Before bed, Sarah gave me a big hug. "Thank you again for bringing me to this group. I really appreciate you, Mike. I just wanted to let you know that."

"No problem, Sarah; anything for a friend," I replied. I looked over Sarah's shoulder and saw Melody watching us. She scoffed and shuffled into her room. I subtly pushed Sarah away from me and motioned Jack over. Sarah helped him limp his way into their bedroom.

It took me a bit longer to fall asleep that night; it was odd to lie in a bed again, but the sight of Melody and Myles made me feel not so lonely. When they both were asleep, I slid the headphones over my ears and listened to my music one last time before eventually letting dreams rule my thoughts.

Chapter 18

Two weeks passed. Chris and Vic worked to maintain friendships with Sylum, Beringue, and Gramble. Diving the work between the four groups allowed us plenty of free time. Jack was with Sarah more often; his leg had completely healed, and the two would often run away together. Sarah spent her time teaching Jack her parkour skills. The two seemed happy together; they would crack jokes only they would understand and had an unspoken language where they used their eyes to communicate. Jack seemed completely different around her—someone I'd never seen him be—modest. It was like he admired Sarah more than he admired himself—and he admired himself a lot. Sarah still spoke with me often, the same amount as everyone else. Our youthful connection always defined our closeness, but now we seemed better off as good friends.

Billy took walks in the morning. He'd put on a few pounds from all the food he was making, testing, and eating. Unlike the rest of us, his primary duty was to stay inside, protecting the orphanage, keep track of our supplies, and cook our meals. Billy wasn't the most active in this role; he mostly sat around waiting. His walks gave him time to think up new recipes and resolve problems he'd encountered while he cooked.

Myles continued to train with Vic. Vic didn't mind Myles's continual attempts; Vic used his extra time to hone his skills with the staff and used Myles as his test dummy. No matter the time he put into this training, Myles didn't get better. Every day he stopped incrementally earlier due to the accumulation of bruises from Vic. He was determined to win someday, though.

Melody would mostly read. When Jack moved on to Sarah, thus not needing Melody's attention or supervision, and

Billy learned to understand his cookbooks, she had no one to occupy her time. She had a large backlog of books to read, as I brought her the rest of her series the last time I went to the library. She came to me one day, though, when she finished.

"Mike," she said, "can you get me my next round of books from the library? I'm done."

"That was the last book in your series," I said.

"I know. I meant could you get me a new series?"

"How was this one?"

"Eh. Not as good as the last one."

"You picked out the last one. This was the one I recommended to you."

"Yeah."

"So, you trust me to get you another series you won't like?"

"I never said I didn't like it... It just wasn't as good as the other one I read."

I didn't appreciate the way she treated me like an errand-boy. Not that her disapproval of the book series hurt me too much; it was how she dismissed the time and thought I put into it. Then, she wants me to go and get her something new? If she wants to get something, she should get it herself, I thought. However, I needed to visit the library soon; it had CDs, and I was dying to get new music in my ears.

"Why don't you just go with me?" I said, flustered.

"Because I don't want to," she said. "Besides, I have things to do around here?"

"Really? You've been reading for at least a week straight—you don't have things to do. Your last time-sink was making sure Jack healed, and now that's over. We haven't needed to go out on a raid for a while; you have the time."

"Fine. Let's ask Chris, though—make sure he knows where we'll be." She walked past me, slamming into my shoulder.

We went to Chris's room. He and Vic discussed logistics for future supply runs for their "business." Vic seemed comfortable in what used to be Peter's bean bag chair.

"Hey, Chris," Melody said, "Is it fine if we go to the library today?"

"Of course," he said. "I trust you to go as you please. It's been a while since you two did anything together, so I'm sure it will be good to get out of the house, bask in your education, etc."

"I just wanted to let you know where we'll be," she added offhandedly.

"Thank you for letting me know. Close the door on your way out, please?" Melody and I exited the room; the two broke into logistical babble right when we turned our backs.

We threw backpacks on our bodies, filled some bottles with water, and headed out. I gathered the goggles and such to hide our identities, but Melody knocked them back to the floor. She threw a hood over her head and tucked her hair behind her ears. We spoke little on our journey, with only occasional stops to pick up a few lone pens and pencils that appeared to have fallen out of someone's bag. We also noticed new wooden structures erected along our path—they looked like watchtowers. No one was around these structures, though they looked imposing.

We stopped at one of the mostly completed towers.

"What are these?" I asked. "These are new..."

"I don't know," Melody replied.

"Should we be concerned?"

"No. There's nothing we can do about them. Let's leave them alone for now."

We walked away from the tower, only to notice more along our path. "How much would you bet that if Myles were here, he'd try to climb this?" I said.

Melody sneered. "I wouldn't doubt it." She exhaled heavily. "I worry about him, you know? He's pushing himself so hard with Vic; I'm afraid he'll hurt himself beyond repair."

"Yeah, he does have a lot of bruises..." I kept admiring the tower. It was a blueish-purple color, the wood painted. There was an outline of some drawing on the bottom of the tower's base, but it was so faint I couldn't make it out.

"While we're at the library," Melody said, "I want to find something for Myles. I don't think he can take much more of Vic's relentless beatings; he's just not that kind of guy."

"What do you have in mind?" I inquired.

"Well, since I ended up coming along, I figured I'd look for something he'd be good at."

"Which is...?"

"Oh. Sorry. Myles has always been good at creating things, building, etc. He has a knack for working with his hands—they're super steady, even when things get nerve-racking. I want to try and find some 'How-To' books, so he can start crafting basic stuff—without needing to read too much, of course. I think it could be like how I worked with Billy; he just learned the words for things in the books he needed. Myles could do the same thing, I think."

"So, another side project for you, then?" I replied. She rolled her eyes and continued toward the library. "You do this a lot, I've noticed. You needed to work with Jack, and then you moved on to Billy, and now you're wanting to move on to Myles. Why do you do this?" She kept walking.

We soon reached the library. We crawled in and went separate ways. She sauntered toward the children's books section to survey crafting books while I rushed to the CDs. They were near the Sci-Fi books, so it didn't look like I was exclusively looking at CDs. I grabbed everything I saw from all genres: funk, pop, rock, metal, rap—their difference meant nothing to me. I saw them as different book types, in a sense. Melody approached me, so I quickly shifted to the Sci-Fi books, pretending to look around. I grabbed a few of them and stuffed them into my bag. I wanted to look like I was getting something besides my secret CDs.

Melody picked out her new book series—The Hunger Games—and we promptly left. The day was still young, but we did not need to stay any longer at the library. She went first and seemed eager to get back to the orphanage; her stride was brisk and confident.

"Hey, wait!" I shouted, still maneuvering my body out of the crawl space. I covered the hole and rushed to her. She continued at her brisk pace. "I wanted to ask you: How do you feel about Sarah? I know she's another girl and all, but we haven't talked a lot since she moved to the orphanage... Plus, the last time you spoke to me, you didn't have positive things to say about her."

"She's fine, I guess," Melody replied. "You can't ignore her ability to climb, nor her agility. She ran circles around us on that parkour day. That said—I don't know—there's something about her that puts me on edge... "

"On edge?"

"There's something about her that sets me off... "

"I don't think she's going to rob us or anything," I said.

"That's not what I meant, Mike... "

"Well, what do you mean?" We stopped walking. A gust of wind blew dust in the air. "Yeah, she's a bit outspoken and quirky, but that doesn't make her a bad person. She's trying, alright? It's not easy to walk into a group, not know anyone, then try to make friends, or else it's life back on the streets. I know that feeling. I've been there—and I sympathize with her. She's cunning, she's witty, capable, beautiful, and while I like those things about her, she—" I was cut off.

"Right there. You ask me what I have against her? That right there," Melody interjected. Her voice broke.

"What?"

"You...how you—you—idolize her! You had me in your life, but now it's like you don't even know me! Do you know how that feels? I'm right here—I feel betrayed, Mike. You care about this stupid Sarah more than me."

"What? Melody, that's not true—"

"I feel left out of this little "club" you two are a part of. What happened to our friendship, huh, Mike? You barely give me a sideways glance when we pass each other in the foyer. But you're all-too-eager to give her a big, fat, sweaty hug before bed every night. We were close, or at least I thought we were. Now, all you want to do is talk about Sarah, think about Sarah, do things with Sarah, be all cutesy and close with Sarah; you never want to do anything with me."

"Melody, I've asked you to come with me to the library every time I go," I pleaded. "You're always the one who says no!"

"And why do you think that is, huh? You think it's just because I'm being mean to you?"

"No, Melody, don't say—"

"Do you think it's because I hate you, or something? Do you think I want to be this way? Mike, I still see Peter's face when I close my eyes—lifeless—a husk. I never got to say goodbye...I can hardly live with myself. The more I think about it, the worse it gets, and the worse it gets, the lonelier I feel. Have you ever tried to talk to me about it?" She paused, staring intently at me. I could see her trying her hardest to hold her tears. I looked away. "No—no, you haven't, Mike."

"Melody, I'm sorry—I didn't know you felt that way, but—" I was interrupted again.

"You want to know why I cling to people? I know that what people say about me—I'm not stupid. I'm not mindless. You wanted to know why I keep having these 'side projects', as you called it? It's because I want to cling to you, Mike, but you won't let me."

"That's what this is about?" I asked chuckling. "You're jealous of her?"

"I'm not—"

I laughed. "That's all this is! You want to be buddy-buddy with me, but when someone else comes along, you get all defensive and passive-aggressive and distant. You preach togetherness and compassion, but you can't even reciprocate that with the person you claim to care the most about! And why me, huh? Out of everyone at the orphanage, why am I the one you gravitate toward? And because you can't follow me at my heels, you jump around to other people until they realize they don't need you, and you move on again? Where am I on that list, huh? When are you going to be done with me?"

"No, Mike—"

"You're still crying over Peter? You two hardly had a thing in common! Why do you still feel so connected to someone who's gone? You can't keep holding on to past feelings; that's what will be your death. You need to live in the moment and keep adapting to the world's change, or else you fail. That's how life works now; it isn't like in our stories and our novels. They thought of life differently; they didn't have to worry about their next meal or the different ways they could die that day."

"Peter and I were close—don't you dare say we weren't!" she declared.

We both screamed at each other through tears. Our words echoed off the empty buildings in the streets of fragile lives. We paused our lashing to take breaths; my lungs were on fire, and breathing was difficult with no mask to filter out the city's gray noise.

"Besides," Melody continued, "how can you be over it? You were with us—you comforted me—you held me. I hadn't forgotten that. I want to be held again. How can you put that behind us? I wake up in cold sweats just thinking about that feeling." Her shouting shifted to screaming. "And how do you live with yourself, Mike? You killed a man! You took a knife out of your dying friend and stabbed a child. Then, you beat him until he was a puddle. His blood stained your pre-pubescent hands. How can you disregard that? How does that not haunt you every second of every day?"

"Because I don't worry about the past!" I shouted. "If I wanted to revel in my past, I wouldn't have come to the orphanage—I wouldn't have met you!"

"Don't' say that," she retorted, "The only reason you came to the orphanage was because of your father! If that's not a fixation on your past, I don't know what is—So, I ask again, how have you blocked out the death of another human being? The Fallout took two lives that day—how did you get your hands clean of their blood?"

"You want to give me a lecture?" I wiped my nose and sniffled. "Hmph. Here's one for you: Get over it. I'm obviously over it—yes, it was hard for a while, but I moved on. That's why. You still can't because that's how you are. You still blame me for our distance—but it's all you! I was nothing but nice, and patient, and kind, but you kept pushing me away! And eventually, I got sick of it. I stopped trying because I knew you weren't. You'll always be a friend, but these days it's getting harder to convince myself of that."

"You don't understand, Mike," Melody pleaded. She looked away.

"I've been trying to tell you something this whole time—but you keep interrupting me—Sarah and I are not an item. I don't like her in that way. Maybe at first, but not now. She and Jack are perfect for each other—it's obvious. Even then, there's something off-putting about her to me... something I don't quite understand." I clenched my fist. "I want to like you, but you make it so damned hard. I try to open up to you, but you slam me shut. I try to be with you, and you brush past me. I've moved on, and you haven't—and do you want to know why? Do you want to know why you can't move on?

Huh? Do you want to know the crux of your life? Do you want to know why you need to cling to people so tightly? You attach yourself to others because you can't stand having to think for yourself for a fucking second. Melody Loveless has no initiative, no drive—not without someone else directing her, standing as an example of what a normal person should be."

Her legs quivered.

"The only reason you cling to others is because you don't know what it's like to be yourself—you need to feel important somehow because being yourself isn't good enough. You're a parasite—you need a host to survive."

She ran and shoved me with all her might. I stumbled to the ground, my back connecting with the cold, dusty concrete. The clash from the impact exploded agony throughout my body. My eyes squeezed out fresh tears. Dust engulfed my acuity.

I sat up and wiped my bleary eyes. I heard Melody run away, and I looked to see where she ran, but she already turned a corner. I stood then rushed around trying to find her, calling her name. I checked alleys, looked under piles of rubble, but no luck. I screamed at a far-off building in frustration.

I spent a few hours aimlessly walking the area around the library. My tears of anger evaporated from the redness of my face. I felt like a volcano ready to burst. I wanted to throw up. I felt awful. I'd taken it too far with her; regret filled my lungs with every shortened breath I took. A saddened sigh succumbed to the silent air of the streets. If I could just find her— if I could just see her—if I could just know she was safe, it's all I wanted. Her words sank into me. The statements which punctured my heart began to tear notches. Why have I blocked out my murder? I took the life of another, but all I could say was, "I'm over it?" You can never get overtaking someone's life. The look in their eyes—fear, desperation, mercy—how could you forget? Why did I pass the blame onto her? Why was she always in my sights? No matter what I did, the outline of her face when we held each other in that market pressed an imprint in my mind. There was a world behind her eyes I knew nothing about.

I felt empty. Lost. I'd forgotten which way was home, and my brain wanted to burst from my head—it throbbed so much. I collapsed onto the ground and screamed at the dirt. I screamed what few tears I had left out of me. They fell like raindrops to the dark ground; the dust drank it in seconds. My hands felt sticky.

Eventually, I reached the orphanage—no sign of Melody. Myles greeted me at the door and asked where she went. I said something dismissive and brushed past his shoulder—mindless, like a zombie. I had no emotion, no pain, no feeling—only vacancy.

The rooftop became my sanctuary for the next few hours. I sat atop the air-conditioning unit, looking out at the slowly darkening world. I saw a light come on in the distance, pointed up toward one of the buildings. My eyes became fixated on the light. How did it get there? Who turned it on? What was powering it? Were there other sources of electricity in the city, more than just the outlet under the bed?

I heard the door to the rooftop open and close. I stiffened and looked over. Melody hung her head. I wanted to run. I wanted to embrace her. I wanted to leave. I wanted to never leave. But I couldn't; I was catatonic.

She sprinted and threw her arms around me. She tried to cry but couldn't generate any more tears. "I'm so sorry," she whispered, "For everything."

I faintly replied, "I know. I'm sorry, too."

She tried to loosen her grip from me, but I pulled her tight. "No, please. Don't leave," I trembled.

"Ok," she said.

Our embrace was strong. I couldn't shut my eyes harder; I wanted to take in every ounce of her. Our breaths were synchronized—our hearts beat in time so they could touch through our connected chests. I buried my face in her frizzled, dirty hair. The salty residue from my dry eyes prevented more tears from appearing. Everything I had become, and everything I was, poured itself into my hold on her. The possibility of losing her was far worse than any thought that flickered through my volatile mind. The magnanimous indemnity she exuded was beyond words. The words don't exist to represent giving all of yourself to someone—to feel anonymity for a moment, because the condition of another reigned supreme. For this suspension of time, we were one.

We let go once our arms gave way. We rested our heads on the other's shoulders. We could do nothing but breathe in each other's presence—that was enough.

My eyes were still closed. "I've thought about it," I muttered, "I haven't blocked out Peter or my murder. I've embraced it." She grasped my loose hand, and our fingers laid like rag dolls, intertwined with one another. "It's become a part of me. It's my new normal. Death is not normal, but it's my new normal. I don't think I'll ever get over it, Melody, and I'm sorry I judged you. I'm sorry I viewed my weaknesses as strength."

"I don't care," she said. "I just want my best friend back." She nestled her head deeper into the abyss of my neck. "I want to tell you about my day. I want to tell you the stories I've read. I want to share my ideas with you. I want to share my every day with you. I'm sorry I've pushed you away; you're right—I was jealous, and I should have just talked to you about it. I just want you back in my life. I just want you."

"I want that, too," I said.

"Let's make a promise," she said. Her breaths were shorter—the inflammation in our lungs limited her inhalation. She took her head off my shoulder and sat more honest, her hand still inside mine. "I want to ask you any question I wish. Then, I'll tell you a secret. Let's show commitment and trust."

"Ok," I said, "But I should get the same opportunity."

She agreed and looked out toward the light showcasing the tall building. "I want to know about your childhood. I don't know anything about your background or what your life was like before I met you."

I told her everything—about my mother and how she taught me to read, my father and his involvement with Congress, and my eventual escape from his looming presence. "I don't know what he does for Congress, but I can't imagine it's anything good," I said. "He always provided for my mother and me when I was younger, but I never knew where he got food and water and little trinkets. Now I know it was most likely his involvement with Congress."

"Do you ever miss it?" Melody asked. "Do you ever wish you could go back there?"

"It crosses my mind from time to time," I said. I told her how I initially met Sarah, and how we ran through the streets until she ditched me near the library. I explained how the library was my second home as a child—after my mother died, I felt alone, as my father and I were never close. The library filled that educational gap she instilled into my infantile mind. I relayed how I read droves of books, and spent every minute I had at the library, book in hand. Then, I told her about my first encounter with Vic, which turned into the first time she met me.

"Thank you for telling me that," she said. "The reason I asked was that I felt I was insensitive about how I assumed your life earlier today. It was stupid, and I shouldn't have said it." I nodded. She shyly smiled. "Now I want to tell you about my life before the orphanage, Mike. I haven't told anyone here about it—they only know I was a drifter for a while, which is partly true. However, it's more than that.

"I never knew my mother; she died before I was old enough to remember her. My father said she died from childbearing, but I don't know if I believe that. My father was a corrupt man. He loved himself first and gave me the scraps;

it was a hand-me-down love. He abused me when I was young. I didn't know it at the time; I thought that's just what happened, but I knew even then I didn't like it. He'd beat me, he'd scrape me... all his hatred went into me, and what little was left, he kept for later. He blamed me for my mother's passing—as if I had any choice in it.

"I left him one night after he fell asleep. He had recently joined Congress and came home drunk every night; the spoils for a day's work were fermented alcohol. He lost more teeth by the week. The abuse got harder then, and he soon started... worse things on me. I couldn't stand living in fear. I was fearful of him—his presence—what he did during the day with Congress. I was told to stay in the house, and if he caught me leaving, he promised me my death. He kept me malnourished so I wouldn't make it on my own. But screw it, I said, and I left while he was asleep in one of his drunken comas. I only wandered for a few hours before running into a group of boys—early teenagers. They could see my bones through my clothes, and the dried blood on my exposed skin. Gracious they were, as they took me in as one of their own.

"What I immediately enjoyed about these boys was that they didn't see me as just a girl. My father would use the term 'woman' and 'girl' as put-downs—it was his justification for the way he treated me—as if I was less of a person because I was attached to those pronouns. This group treated me equally. They fed me the same as everyone else. I received equal attention, equal opportunity. When I was ready, I proved myself capable, and I wasn't a ditz, nor weaker than the boys, or whatever. I felt like one of the boys.

"Besides my mother, I didn't know about any other girls. It made me feel special, in a way. I was different—mentally and physically. The boys always liked playing with my hair because it was longer than theirs. They embraced my differences instead of shunning me for them.

"I stayed with the boys for a while; my body had matured a little, and theirs too. We grew closer, and I learned more about scavenging, spotting items, and locations of interest. Late one night, though, we were raided by another group of older boys, killing everyone. I managed to escape by leaving my group behind; I snuck out while the other group finished off my friends and took our supplies. I'll never forget the ones who took me in: Biff, Zach, Chuckie, and Daniel. They took me in and raised me—like brothers. I can never thank them for all they did...

"I spent a few days on my own after the incident, but it felt like weeks. I found a few supplies lying around, but not enough to survive for long. I had just finished off my last bit of food when I came across a ranch house on the outskirts of town, near the Barren Wasteland. I snuck in and found a few shelves of canned food. I was stuffing my bag when two boys—brothers—saw me looting. They weren't mad, though, and offered me a place to stay. I thought it was odd how they lived in a house with no parents; the parentless groups lived in supermarkets and restaurants.

Nonetheless, I stayed there for a few days before I noticed them getting too friendly with me. Come to find out, they killed their parents and ate them, and aimed to eat me, too. I managed to flee, but at the cost of most of my clothes, they tried anything to keep me there, which included grasping my clothes as I ran, and they slashed open my lower stomach. They had to tear off my clothes for me to get away.

"I was bare and defenseless; no bag, no clothes, no food—nothing but the cold comforted me. The wind cut through my remaining undergarments. I was slowly bleeding out. I took my tank top off to halt the bleeding, but it dripped with blood after a few minutes. I wondered how long I had before I perished. I recall missing the comfort of my father—cruel as he was, at least it was consistent. I knew what to expect when I lived with him. Even though he beat me, I knew that was a trade-off for safety. I know it's stupid, but I was so young. I didn't know any better.

"Luck was on my side this time, and I ran into Chris and Peter. They didn't want to hurt me; instead, they asked what was wrong. I told them I'd been on my own for a while—I couldn't bear to tell them the truth. Not while it was still so fresh. They covered me in their jackets and walked me back to the orphanage. There, I began my new life—finally free from the horrors of the world. I felt like I did with Biff, Zach, Chuckie, and Daniel, a support system that cared about me and valued me. That was all I ever needed to make me feel important. It's still something I need, but on a different level."

Melody inched closer to me. She wrapped her arm around mine and placed her hand to mine, not clasping it, but resting it inside.

"I didn't know you had such a hard childhood," I said. "I feel so stupid now, assuming things about your life. I feel horrible for never trying to understand…"

"It's not your fault," she said. "I kept it hidden from everyone. I trust you, Mike. This is our secret." She smiled. "Your turn. Ask me anything."

I asked the only thing pressing on my mind then—the only thing I wanted to ask another girl. "Do you fear men?"

"What?"

"Do you fear what men are capable of? What men can do to women?"

"I'm not sure I follow…" Melody said, confused.

"I'm sorry I'm bringing her into this, but a while ago, Sarah told me a story about how she fears getting captured by men and forced to bear children with them. That's how she was born."

"Oh…" Melody looked to the floor. "I didn't know that about her… now I feel terrible for saying those things about her…"

"It's ok; you didn't know. I didn't know, either, until she told me. She says girls have their minds altered when they suffer that fate; she's afraid of the psychological pain of being

stripped of her independence. On top of that, she's killed people, Melody—people who tried to do awful things to her. Her
life is a revolving door of male predators, and she kills them to
make it stop."

"I won't tell anyone; I won't even bring it up to Sarah."

I nodded. "Nonetheless, that's stayed in my mind ever
since. I think of you a lot, and what you would do if found in
that situation. I'd be devastated to see anything bad happen
to you." Melody blushed and looked away. "After hearing Sarah's story, I felt like I didn't understand the lives or perspective of women in this world. I treated you and her as equals,
but I never thought about the awful fate that could befall
girls. I just wanted to know how you feel about it—to understand your perspective."

"While I appreciate the concern, Mike, I don't worry
about it at all. Even if that fate did befall me, a baby isn't what
would frighten me."

"Huh? How so?"

"Time for another confession—it's impossible for me. I'm
infertile."

"You're what?" I gasped. I had little knowledge of female
reproduction, despite having read so many books. It was a
vastly complicated system, so I leaned toward stories instead.

"You really don't understand women, do you?" she
laughed. "Nonetheless, remember when the two brothers
slashed my stomach? Turns out that wasn't my stomach; it
was my uterus. When Chris brought me back to the orphanage, he patched me up, but as I got older, I never had a period.
I didn't know what a uterus was at the time, but it's what al-
lows girls to make babies. Because mine was ruptured, I can
never have children." She looked at the ground. "It's fine,
though—really. I wouldn't want to give life to another person, especially not in this world..." She trailed off and looked
out into the distance. Night fell a while ago, but Melody was

still visible to me from the reflecting light in the distance. She looked at the light as if lost in thought.

"What if I told you we could change the world?" I said.

She laughed. "And what does that mean?"

"You said you wouldn't want children in the world the way it is now."

"Not with those words, but yes."

"Well, what if we changed the world to be more inhabitable; what if we created a future?"

"Oh, really?" She chuckled. "How are we going to do that?"

"This is my secret: Vic and I want to take down Congress."

"What?" she exclaimed. Her head jerked toward me.

"Hear me out: Vic and Chris are working with other groups now. What if we kept building our numbers, recruiting more members, and worked together to take down Congress? They only have, at least, eight Members. We can easily outnumber them and take them down."

She kept staring at me. A stupefied expression lay on her face. Her eyes scanned mine. They looked like a beautiful ocean—a powerful current that pulled me further into the boundless sea of her mind.

I went on: "Melody, I want to make a difference in the world outside of just a handful of people. I want a story that we can one day pass down to a new generation in a new world—a world that we helped create. And I want to do that with you. Now, please tell me: Are you with me?"

She continued staring into my eyes. They darted left to right. I could feel the essence of her entire being peering into me.

I continued: "Melody, please. This goes beyond you, or me, or us. I want to find my purpose in this world, and I think this is it. If we join forces, we can—"

She put a finger to my lips and made a shushing sound. "Please. Stop talking. I'm in."

"You're in?" I asked.

"Of course I'm in! You can't go changing the world without me." She returned her head to my shoulder. "I'm with you every step of the way."

I touched her hand. She seemed alarmed at first, but quickly released the tension from her body. It felt like she was transferring her life essence into me—the stories she told me, the hair that parted her face, the voice she held when she talked to me—all of it flowed between our grip. The world held no force higher than us. The world stood no chance while we both lived. Life paled in comparison to the smile she gave me when our eyes met.

"I have one more thing I want to say," I told her. "A secret I've been trying to tell you in a thousand different ways, with a thousand different words. Everything seemed to keep me from you, but I feel closer to you now—more than ever. I don't know what this fight will mean, or when it will end. But I'll protect you." My heart felt thinner than air. I gripped her hand tighter, to prevent floating away. My voice went into a crescendo: "Melody, I..."

She leaned in and we kissed. Our dry lips fit perfectly, warming our bodies. The cracks in our lips scraped sensationally. Her hand graced my face. She pressed her cheek to mine. Her freckles were beautiful. She held me together while my body melded with hers. The whole experience felt natural— destined to be. We were created to feel a special connection and form into one whole human—separated until found, then brought together by a relentless, unstoppable force which can't be broken by language—by difference—by belief—by rationalization. Two people made an unconditional commitment at that moment. The amour we shared flitted between the infinite words we tried to form before our lips clashed again. We went into raptures with one another—communicated by subtle movements in our lips, which quivered in their coupling. We were so young—so naïve to what these feelings could mean—we only knew it felt good. I treasured what thoughts could be going through her mind, and I idolized her compared to me. I was humbled in her eternal presence.

The crinkle in her nose enchanted my lungs. Each breath was deliberate. This moment courted our future in more ways than can be formed into prose. The magic of electricity flowed between our fingertips, as they battled for dominance in our clasped hands. My hands were cold, but my heart was blazing. The grounding and commanding nature of her kiss committed me more and more to her promises and her majesty.

Our embrace shattered. Her eyes flickered and considered mine. She brought her head in close, embraced my body, and whispered, "Me too."

Chapter 19

October 14th. Life stabilized at the orphanage for a while; Chris and Vic worked on their partnerships, while everyone else awaited instruction. Sarah and I drifted apart, mostly. While still great friends, there were fewer intimate interactions between us. She spent most of her time with Jack and taught him parkour. The two ran around the city on their lonesome. I spent my time with Melody.

Early one morning, the ground felt uneasy. The walls of the orphanage shook, and dust floated all around the building. We ducked to the floor out of instinct and waited out the shocks.

"What was that?" Billy asked, still shaking after the tremors ended.

"It felt like an earthquake," Jack said. "We haven't had one of those in years..."

"The last one was much stronger, though," Sarah said. "It felt like the whole world wouldn't stop shaking. Buildings collapsed, sidewalks raised from the ground; that was when I was a little girl, though. This was nothing like that."

"That's because this was no earthquake," Vic said. He pointed out of the window. "Look."

We crowded around to see a thick cloud of black smoke, which bellowed not far from the orphanage. It drew attention to itself—the ebony clouds mixed with the flat plateau of the gray sky, darkening the area surrounding it.

"What is that?" I asked.

"An explosion," Vic snapped. "And the clouds are a thick black, which means it's still burning."

"Should we check it out?" asked Melody.

Chris already threw on his jacket. "I think we should."

"I'm going," Myles declared.

"Same," said Sarah.

"Yup," chimed Melody.

"Of course," said Jack.

"Don't count me out, now," said Vic.

"Sure," I added.

"Actually," Billy said, "could I go this time? I never get out, and this seems exciting.

"Fine," Chris said. He slowly turned around and flicked his wrist to the crowd. "Does anyone want to volunteer to stay behind?"

We all looked, waiting for someone to take responsibility. Eventually, I raised my hand and said I would do it.

"Thank you, Mike," Chris said. "Now, let no one in, under any circumstance. I'm taking a key with me so that I can unlock the door myself. You don't leave the house, and you let no one in. If anything happens, call me on the walkie-talkie. Understood?"

"Yeah, I know."

"Ok. I trust you, I just—"

"Tensions are high, I get it. Leave before you give yourself a stroke," I said with a heckle.

Chris smirked. He turned to address the group: "Ok everyone, we stick together. We have strength in numbers. Grab everything you need, then meet me downstairs. We're wearing every mask and scarf we have in case things get hairy."

The house cleared quickly. Everyone grabbed any weapon they could get their hands on, plus food, water, and anything to cover their eyes and filter their breathing. Soon, it was just me in the house. Staying behind wasn't too bad, as it allowed me more time to listen to my music without any anxiety. I threw Fall Out Boy and PVRIS into the CD player and gave each a listen before I needed to walk around.

I walked downstairs and made sure the door was locked and checked to see if there were any masks or scarves left behind; nothing. My eyes then fixated on the heap of rubble next to the door by the back yard. I noticed a break in the debris that wasn't there before. The shifting ground must have allowed for this break, I thought, and I was able to move the rubble just enough to see past it. It was still dark, but a slight draft drifted from the newly parted rock. I climbed up the ruins, forced my body through the small opening, and slid down the other side.

A carpeted floor softened the harsh landing. I stood up and saw a long stretch of hallway, which looked to lead into a tunnelway. Light eventually dimmed to make the path seem endless. There was a room to my left, and I entered. The room contained many destroyed desks, with only a few still standing. The tables were heavily corroded and looked like they would break with any pressure applied to them.

The most exciting part of the room, though, was its center. The ceiling was decayed, and a carcass of wires and rebar hung from the exposed area. This disruption, upon investigation, led to a caged-in region behind a couple of buildings. The breach in the ceiling was covered with a screen to keep dust from entering. A small patch of light illuminated a revealed part of earth, which lay beneath broken tiles along the floor. This earth held perfectly-kept dirt and a small garden. Corn, carrots, tomatoes, potatoes, lettuce—it all bloomed from the ground. I'd never seen foliage for myself—only in picture books. The sight was beautiful. I didn't know how it got there, or how it worked, but I was entranced. A system of pipes and pulleys hung above the small garden, which looked to automatically water the plants equally when the liquid flowed into a small container next to it, which activated the device. The entire spectacle captivated me.

On the wall to my right, I found a giant whiteboard with writing on it; a basic map was displayed, which looked to be the long corridor down the hallway. The whiteboard also had some markers next to it. It looked clean, as did the markers. English was written across the board, detailing critical places of interest: "Hideout," "River," "To Surface," and "Classroom/Garden," with a bunch of red circles around it. I assumed I was in the "Classroom/Garden" area.

I left the room and rushed back through the rubble to return to the orphanage. I grabbed bags, a piece of paper, and a pen. On my way back through the wreckage, I smoothed out an area to make it easier for me to enter and exit. I only needed to move one large rock to cover the hole back up.

Once back in the room, I took the pencil and paper and copied the map. I wanted a copy so I could study it on my own time later. While copying the map, I noticed a small series of panels, also illuminated by the light next to the garden. They were solar panels, which converted light into energy. Some wires went from the panels into the walls. I noticed other outlets along the walls and wondered if they were live. I ran back to my room, grabbed the CD player, and tried it out—all the outlets were active. The solar panels provided electricity to the orphanage—they created magic out of thin air. I looked to the light and felt warm for a second.

I placed the CD player in one of my bags and plucked some carrots out from the garden. I heard a crack behind me, prompting me into a fighting position. I saw a small boy, slightly younger than me, but much shorter. He had semi-long white/blonde hair and light blue eyes. He held a bucket of water in his hands, which was now half on the floor and half on his shirt—shook from seeing me in the garden.

"Oh, you're just a kid," I said. I lowered my stature to be friendlier. "Is this your garden?" He stared directly at me—stunned. "Is this your creation?" I asked, motioning toward the self-watering system. He stayed silent. "It's rather impressive. Is that your map, too, on the wall? What's it for?" Still nothing from the boy. "How do you know English so well? Your handwriting is impressive; did you teach yourself that? Do you know about the library?"

"Leave me alone!" he screeched. "Take whatever you want, please, just don't hurt me!" He bolted out of the room, taking the bucket with him, sloshing water along his way. I followed but lost him in the thick darkness of the corridor. This mystery boy intrigued me, especially with his knowledge of English. The only people I knew that could read or write became that way through the library—he must know of it, too, but how? Many questions rushed into my head. Do more people go to the library than just Melody, Vic, and myself? Should I be concerned? What does this kid know that I don't?

While I felt terrible taking from his garden, I knew Billy would be ecstatic about having new food to cook with. Everyone at the house would be excited to eat newly grown food, so I took only half of what was in the garden and stuffed it into my bags. I wondered what lie I would need to tell Chris so he wouldn't become curious about this spot, and about my electricity. Plus, if I wanted to befriend this boy, I needed to gain his trust—not continually make things scarier for him. But did I always need to lie...

I made my way back to the orphanage through the rubble, covering up my entry hole, and I waited for the group to return. It didn't take long, and they returned just before nightfall.

"That took you all day," I said.

"Yeah, it took longer than we thought," Vic retorted. "We didn't get into any trouble, though, so it could have gone worse."

The group returned their garments to their rightful positions and made their way into the foyer. Billy was the first to take notice of my bags of vegetables.

"What's this?" Billy asked, investigating the carrots and potatoes.

"Vegetables?" Chris inquired. He soon turned scornful. "Mike, how did you get these?"

"I made a deal with someone for them," I lied.

"Mike…" he sighed. "Normally, I would be mad about you leaving the orphanage, but I'm kind of glad, actually. You better keep that deal going, ok? We'll need it soon."

"Why? What do you mean?" I hesitantly asked.

"The explosion," Chris said, solemn "was at Beringue's hideout. Everyone there is dead."

"No…" I muttered.

"It was atrocious," he continued, "but it appears the people were only collateral damage. The explosion was tied specifically to our supplies. Beringue's people just happened to be in the way."

"Who would do such a thing?" I asked.

"I have a good idea," Vic interjected. "And you should, too, Mike." He walked away. Chris raised an eyebrow at Vic's remark but soon walked away as well. After everyone else left, Melody kissed me on the cheek.

"What was that for? I asked, confused. I thought everyone was still upset over Beringue.

"As thanks for the vegetables," she said. Her expression changed to be more serious, and she whispered, "I know you didn't leave the house—your lies don't work on me."

"I can't tell you—not right now. It must be kept a secret from everyone. I'm sorry; it'll make sense later."

"Is it safe?"

"Yes, of cour—" She pressed a finger encased with a leather glove to my lips.

"Then that's good enough for me now. Just don't keep secrets too much; if you want to lead a revolution, you can't keep lying all the time." She smiled. "Billy looked happy to see the food. It'll be a good meal tonight, for sure! It'll take everyone's minds off this tragedy." She put her hand on my cheek, brushed away some of the dirt on it, and went upstairs to help Billy with his cooking. I looked out of the foyer window and noticed another cloud of black smoke further in the distance. It soon escaped into the dead of night a few minutes later.

Chapter 20

I awoke the next morning before light shined upon the ruptured Earth. The night before I had stayed awake listening to music on my CD player. Before anyone else woke up, I visited the library. I grabbed books on gardening and glanced at pictures in them. No one could know about the garden, nor the classroom, nor the underground corridors. The look of fear from the boy stayed with me; it lingered. I received that look once prior—when I killed the kid who took Peter's life. I wanted to befriend this boy, though. I needed to keep using his garden, but I didn't want that access to be exclusive only by him being fearful of me. Therefore, I needed to do my research before anyone else was awake. To keep it secret, it had to be a personal project.

On my way back from the library, I noticed the towers again. They had multiplied in number. The towers were near complete, too—the outlines of distant symbols painted on their wooden husks were on before, but they were faint enough to where I couldn't read them. Now, they were painted and clear; they bore the Congress insignia.

I returned to the orphanage right as the light began to overtake the darkness of the world. I crept inside (I left the door unlocked from earlier) and locked it behind me. I heard voices in the foyer and felt a cold sweat run down my neck.

"Who's that?" I heard Chris say. Slowly, I entered the foyer. "Oh, there you are. Everyone else was up and we wondered where you were."

"Yeah, sorry," I said. "I, uh, went out for a walk; couldn't sleep."

Vic looked at my bag, which was obviously full of books. I shifted it out of his sight, and he flashed a smirk. "We were just talking about you, Mike," he said, "Today's a big day; we're going to check on the other storage units and see what kind of damage has been done to them, if at all."

"Ok," I said. I placed my bag down against the wall, ensuring it was zipped up and the gardening books were covered with other items.

Vic kept talking: "Me, you, Melody, and Sarah are going together. Chris, Billy, Jack, and Myles are either going to stay here or talk with the other groups or something. We're not sure yet."

"I'll probably take someone to go check with Gramble Sylum," Chris said. "The other two will stay here. I don't think Congress will find the orphanage, but just in case, I want people here."

I nodded. Vic handed me some leftover beans from the night before, and I ate. We geared up for a potential fight and brought weapons with us. Vic took one of his fighting sticks and wrapped his knuckles in gauze. Melody brought two short knives in sheathes along her waist, covered with a jacket. Sarah brought nothing so that she could keep her agility. I placed a bat in my backpack. We secured goggles, masks, and scarves to keep ourselves hidden and safe from any potential smoke at the storage units. Chris and Billy waved goodbye as we walked away from the orphanage, static and focused.

We reached the closest storage unit to us and gazed upon its smoldering remains. The lock looked picked, and the contents inside had been lit aflame.

"They must have gotten the locations from Beringue's hideout," Vic said.

"Did they have information about where we live?" I asked. We started walking toward the next storage unit.

"No. We never officially mapped out where each group lived for this very reason," Vic said. "The orphanage should be safe."

"How did they find Beringue's hideout, then?"

"Who knows. They were most likely followed—hunted. Congress probably wasn't looking to kill them—not all of them, at least—but when they saw the maps of the storage units, someone must have spilled the beans. Congress owns all collateral, so having those units at all is highly illegal."

"Ok, then what would have stopped them from getting information about our hideout?" I asked.

Sarah hit me in the shoulder and mouthed, "Shut up."

Vic looked over his shoulder and said, "Nothing."

The next unit was about an hour from the orphanage. As we approached the area, we heard the chatter of deep voices.

"Hold up," Vic whispered. "Let's sneak ahead." We followed his instruction and stayed low and quiet. The voices got louder, and I could understand their conversation.

"...took apart the lock earlier! I thought you were supposed to be good at this kinda stuff, Thief!" one said.

"This isn't like the other one," another replied. "That one had an entry point. This one is internal; I can't break it without the code. And stop calling me Thief!"

"Guess we'll have to resort to the fun way," a third said. His voice was far gruffer than the others. I peeked my head around the corner to get a quick view of them; they were adults and wore thick, heavy, brown jackets. One turned around, and I caught a glimpse of a badge stitched on his right arm: Congress's symbol.

Vic tugged at my shirt and brought me back behind cover. "What are you doing?" he hissed.

"Congress," I hastily whispered. "They're Congress."

"STAND BACK!" the gruff voice yelled. We all ducked our heads in the alleyway and felt the ground beneath us rumble.

Debris flew past our heads. A shard of metal barely missed my nose. My ears rang white noise for a few seconds. Amidst the tinnitus, I heard the Congress members chat:

"...the last one, right?" one said.

"Pretty sure, if that boy we took out squealed everything," said the thief.

"They weren't lying," the gruff one said. "I saw it in his eyes; he told us everything."

"Not where their friendly groups are stationed," the first one said. "So, no, not everything."

"Bah," the gruff one spat, "If they're anything like that one, they're weak and will fall in line like everyone else. They'll all be killed, anyway, whether they give us information or not. Once we let them know—" Another explosion went off, further away. "Huh," the gruff one said, "Guess that was the last one." I heard a lighter flip open and a bottle break. Vic looked around the corner. Orange light mirrored off his sweaty face.

"That's it," Vic said. He grasped his fighting stick and ran out. We followed reluctantly. "Hey!" he yelled. "You don't get to call us weak; you killed our friends. Prepare to die."

"Oh, who are you?" the gruff man asked. He had a ballcap on and bore a thick red beard. "Part of that group we killed?"

"Something like that," Vic said.

"You kids think you can take us?" asked the thief. He was shorter than the others, with slick, black hair.

"I'd suggest running now if you want to live," the third one said. He had white hair, and a scraggly beard, though he looked younger than the other Congress members.

"Mike," Sarah whispered in my ear. Her eyes bulged. "That guy with red hair; that's my father."

"What?" I replied. I looked back at the men and saw Vic charge at the trio. We joined and took on individual battles. I ripped the bat from my backpack and swung it at the thief. He put his hand up, ending its motion. He ripped the weapon violently from my hand, tossing it into the burning storage unit. I gulped and ate a punch to the face. His fist felt like ten punches all at once. It knocked me to the floor. I got back up and took a fighting stance. He threw a few more punches, which I dodged. I kept light on my feet and focused on the man and no one else. He extended his fist, and I dodged to the left. I grabbed his arm and twisted it behind his body. He tried to shove me off, but I used the force he created to propel myself up and around his shoulders to bring my body weight down on his neck, crushing him to the ground. I threw a few punches into his head before noticing a small piece of metal attached to his ear. It had a faint purple glow to it. I stopped momentarily to observe but was pulled off by the gruff man and thrown across the road. My back scraped across the ground. My skin was raw. I landed in a puddle of gasoline, drenching my jeans.

I staggered getting up. I noticed the gruff man had made his way onto Sarah. He grabbed her by the neck and raised her in the air and began choking her. His arms held a faint purple glow to them, too. I rammed into his chest, releasing Sarah from his grip. She fell hard on the ground, knocking off her goggles and mask. The gruff man looked at her and gasped. Sarah met his eyes, then stumbled to get up.

"I'm going to see if I can get them to follow me," she told me. She started running away.

"Hey, you two," he commanded to the other Congress members. "Get her!"

"You got it, J!" the two men said and turned their attention to Sarah. She bounced from buildings and hopped over obstacles, playfully allowing the men to follow her until she inevitably scaled a building and made her getaway.

The focus now shifted to the gruff man. Vic took a swing at him, but I noticed the metal in his ear glow, and he grasped the stick from Vic's hand. He yanked it from Vic and broke it in two over his leg. He then threw a punch, which Vic dodged. He threw another punch, anticipating Vic's dodge, and it connected, knocking him to the floor. Vic's clothes tore, blood seeping through his shirt. He struggled to get up.

I was next. I ran at him with full force, which gave me a closer look at the glowing metal in his ear. The purple looked like it coursed through the metal like blood through a vein, and glowed brightly when I threw a punch. He grabbed my fist with an open hand and crushed my fingers. I screamed as he tossed me aside with a wave of his hand. I rolled on the ground but regained my stature quickly.

"Impressive," he said, as he walked toward me. "But hardly necessary." He threw another punch. I rolled out of the way and put all my weight on my hands to try a sweep, which missed the red-haired man but allowed me to get up without taking my eyes off him. He gave a few more punches, which I dodged. I tried to hit him, but he side-stepped every punch. It was like he could see what I was going to do before I acted. I backed up to give us some distance, but he continually inched forward, slowly, as if he was savoring my struggle. I ran ahead, but his earpiece glowed as I drew close. He raised his left hand and swatted me out of the way. I rolled until I hit a building.

"How does he keep doing that..." I muttered to myself. My lip had begun to bleed, and I wiped it away. Melody tried to hit the gruff man, but Vic pushed her out of the way to try and take him head-on. While the gruff man was preoccupied, I took the opportunity to jump on the man's back. He staggered, but then used my and his body weight to shove Vic out of the way violently. Vic fell backward, tumbled over himself, and bellowed in agony. He laid face-down to the concrete. He didn't move again.

The gruff man reached behind him and grabbed me by my clothes. He then swung me overtop his body, and straight to the ground. I hit the ground so hard it felt like I left an imprint.

The gruff man's eyes were the eyes of a killer. I felt power-less—useless. The shock of my impact with the ground left me immobile. I could do nothing but watch as the gruff man got ready to smash all his weight into my face. I closed my eyes and embraced for impact.

Then I heard a high-pitched yell. It was Melody; she drove her two daggers into the man's shoulder blades. He backed away from me, and I leaned forward to watch the spectacle. He hunched himself forward, writhing from pain. The daggers embedded into his back. Melody threw a few kicks into him, but he was mostly unaffected. He tried reaching for the knives but couldn't grab them. Instead, he took his arms and clasped them together and swung at Melody. I saw a faint purple glow before he hit her in the abdomen. She flew across the street and slid against the ground, holding her chest. She crashed into a wall, coughing violently.

The man looked at all of us, clutching our bodies as we laid motionless on the ground. He tried to approach, but his body seized from the knives in his shoulders. He dropped to a knee but soon got up again. He turned away and began walk-ing in the direction of Sarah. More and more blood oozed from his wounds as he continued to take steps away from us. He turned a corner, and then he was gone.

Melody landed near the fire, which now consumed most of the area around the storage unit. I crawled over to her to try and move her away from the growing flames. My jeans, still laced with gasoline, caught fire. I slapped my palm against my legs to put out the flames, which burned my hands. Mel-ody and I slowly moved away from the burning building and collapsed belly-up to the gray-cloud sky. Her arms were still cradled to her chest as she continued to cough. Blood flowed from an exposed cut on her right arm. A large shard of glass protruded from the laceration. I stuffed my hand into my jacket and ripped out the glass. She screamed and blood spurt from the gash. I lifted her shirt to look at her abs. There was a large bruise. When I touched it, Melody shrilled. I held her shirt up while I felt blood surfacing from the wounds on my body, which soon blended with Melody's. I lifted my head to look over at Vic, who still was motionless on the ground.

"Vic!" I screamed. My voice cracked from the pain. "Vic!" The wind cut through, and flames licked his hair. "Vic, get up!"

He twitched and slowly put one hand on the ground to pull himself up. "Bastards..." he muttered.

"Vic, Melody's hurt. Bad. Can you walk?"

"Let me try..." he slowly brought himself to his feet, but soon collapsed. He spat blood toward the fire. "I can crawl," he chuckled. He slowly made his way over and examined Melody. "Oh, no. Melody, are you ok? Huh? Are you ok?"

"No," she muttered. She couldn't stop coughing, transitioning into hyperventilation.

"Calm down," I said. "You'll make it worse. Here: take my hand. Squeeze it as hard as you need." I took her hand, and her grip immediately crushed my palm. My hand felt broken. Vic tried to grab the other hand, but she swatted it away and clutched it over her bruise instead. "Melody, you saved me, you know that?" I told her. "You saved my life. I want you to know that, ok?" She nodded as tears rolled down her face. Blood flowed from her elbow and down my arm. My hand twitched as it slowly brushed past hairs that stood on end. I couldn't help but let a fountain of tears leak out of my eyes. "Don't leave me," I trembled. "Please don't leave me."

Vic was on his feet by this point and looked down at us. I put my other hand in the air, and he brought me to my knees. We helped Melody up amidst her agonizing screams. I could feel her accelerated pulse through her skin. I took off the shirt under my jacket and wrapped it around her bleeding arm. We draped her arms over each of our shoulders then slowly walked away from the fire. We shuffled to my backpack, which fell off during the fight. Vic took out the walkie-talkie.

"Chris? Chris, you there?" he shouted.

A few seconds passed before we heard, "Yeah, Vic. What's up? Something wrong? Over."

"They got to the supplies. They're gone—all of them—Melody's hurt—badly. We're out by the Richard's property. Send help—now!"

"Ok, we'll meet you halfway. Over."

"Be careful; Congress members are on the loose—they chased after Sarah."

"Ok, we'll be careful. Make Melody's safety your priority. Over," Chris replied. Vic looked back at me. I already had Melody's arms wrapped around my neck. Her now-limp body weighed me down as I dragged her dangling feet across the ground. My legs burned with every step, as the scrapes, blood, dust, and dirt began to mix, agitating my open wounds. With every step, I shed another tear.

"I don't think that will be a problem," Vic muttered to himself. He turned off the walkie-talkie and threw the backpack over his shoulders.

While Vic was preoccupied, I had already begun trudging my way back to the orphanage. I followed down the path Sarah left for a few seconds before my eyes descried a faint glow. I drew closer and got a better view. It was the metal piece that Congress was using in their ear during our fight. It was triangular, with a faint purple aura given off by a thin vein that ran across its metal surface. I hastily picked it up and continued walking. Vic met up with me shortly after.

Thirty minutes had passed when we saw Chris, Billy, and Sarah run down an alleyway. They were out of breath.

"We ran all the way here," Billy said, hacking. He caught his breath. "How is she?"

"Don't talk—move," Chris told him. He took Melody from my neck, and I collapsed to the floor. I faintly felt a sharp pain in my head before my skull cracked against the pavement. I blacked out.

When I came to, we were back at the orphanage. I awoke in the foyer, my head propped with a pillow. A thin blanket rested over my body. My hand and arm were tightly wrapped in thick gauze. Vic met my eyes with a smile.

"There we go—he's ok, everyone," Vic said to his left.

"How long were you sitting there?" I mumbled.

"Since we got back. You had me worried; your head took a good hit when you passed out. But you're ok, and that's all that matters."

I gritted my teeth while I sat up. My sight was blurry. I noticed bodies in the foyer, hunched over their plates while they ate. They looked back at me and expressed their worries about how I took a hard fall. I felt a piercing pain in my brain. I grasped my head and felt more gauze. I stood up and was met with immediate criticism.

"Whoa, there, cowboy," Jack said. "You need to get some rest. It's not good for you to be—"

"Where's Melody?" I asked.

"Upstairs, but—" I was already gone before he could finish his sentence. I stumbled up the curved staircase, falling into every other one, but I dashed toward the bedroom. I walked into the upstairs foyer found Melody leaning against the windowsill. She noticed me and left the window. We collided in the middle of the room, locked in a hard embrace. I broke into tears and buried my face in her hair.

"I thought I lost you," I wept. "You saved me, and I thought I lost you. I didn't know what I would do without you. I didn't think I'd get to tell you how much you mean to me."

"Shh," she said. She pulled my head closer. Her hands hurt my bruise, but I didn't care. She brushed my hair and soothed me with her voice. "I'm here; don't worry. I just took a hard hit, that's all. I cut myself, that's all. I'm not leaving."

"I wanted to protect you, and you shielded me," I sobbed. My legs went weak and gave way.

She caught me, and our noses touched. She kissed me. "You protected me, too. You carried me until you collapsed. I was helpless, and you put my safety ahead of yours—my life ahead of yours. I just stabbed the guy," she laughed, "You're my hero." She lowered my body to the ground and I let my weight fall onto her chest. She winced at the pain and moved my head away from her bruise.

"Stay," I told her. "Don't ever change. You're so beautiful."

She brought the top of my head to her lips. Her hands rested on my shoulders. My strength ebbed, and I swooned across her breast.

Later, we walked downstairs to meet with the rest of the group. They flocked around us. Chris asked if we were alright.

"We're fine, all things considered." I glanced at my wrapped hand, still woozy from my head injury. "Tell me what happened to you, Chris; did you talk to the other groups?"

Chris sighed. "Billy and I spoke with Python of Sylum. We told him about Beringue and Dominic's demise. He wasn't too happy about it, but he didn't seem to blame me or anything— which is good. We still have an ally. Python said he'd pass along the news to Gramble, and we'll go from there. From what I understand, Python wants to stay close, but not too close. He didn't explicitly cut ties with us, but I don't get the feeling he wants to work with us for a while."

"Good," I said, readjusting my position. "I guess."

"Vic and Sarah told us about your fight," Jack said. "Pretty badass, Mike. You were doing all these flips and tricks; you had me envious just hearing the story."

"Yeah, well, it only did so much…" I trailed off. I thought about the Congress members and the metallic pieces in their ears. I straightened, remembering I found one lying on the ground. I dug around in my pocket to see if it was still there. I felt its cold, metal, diamond plating. Its grooves bumped on my skin as fingers passed over it. What were they? Why did they glow purple when we tried to hit them? And why did that only happen sometimes? Do I tell everyone about them?

A loud, distorted, crackling noise rang through the orphanage. It didn't sound like it came from inside the building, but instead was bouncing off the walls of the city. The voice projected from something—some things.

"Are they on? Are they working?" the voice said. It was the voice of a man, an adult with a not-so-deep voice. He cleared his throat. "That's a yes. Greetings, citizens of our lovely Forlorn! You may be wondering where this lovely voice is emanating from; the answer to such question is I am at home—comfy, cozy, warm—at the Capitol Building, projecting my voice across the city. Now—those towers you have likely seen around the city? They have megaphones on them. They're connected by a system which takes my voice from over here and makes it loud enough so everyone can hear the words I speak—like gospel."

The imparting voice mystified me. I was terrified by the larger-than-life presence of this person, but I focused on one aspect—electricity. My ears perked in response to this revelation. I thought of my father and felt faint.

"Who is this guy?" Jack asked, annoyed.

"That's my father," Vic replied.

The voice also answered, as if he heard Jack's question. "I am the leader of Congress: Congress Member A. I run the whole gang and keep the city safe and sound. This includes a recent cause, as of late, which seems to have been put to a halt by our scouting team. We always want to put our Citizens first and have done so by snuffing out a thieving group of individuals, colluding to take more of your stuff, and kill your families to advance their own goals."

"They're talking about us..." Sarah said.

"Bullshit, we didn't kill anyone. We loot from local stores—not from people," Vic said. I looked to the floor and grasped the Congress pin in my pocket and the purple-glowing device in the other. Vic continued, "We put up a good fight against their 'Scouters,' too. 'Course, they wouldn't mention that..."

Vic's father went on: "We will tolerate no such supply trains, as they are the downfall of what we now call a society. However, this can change—our love for protecting the city and keeping our Citizens safe used to operate from the Capitol. But we now have stations all around the city. We can offer our protection to every group, every family, every person. Today, along with the induction of our radio-towers—to broadcast news and updates from your local Congress members—we're also rolling out some new programs! Ooh, how exciting!"

"Programs?" Chris asked.

"First and foremost: to mitigate the supply-train issues, we're introducing our Outreach program. We have built specific areas devoted to holding and maintaining supplies that any citizen might have. Essentially, we will hold everyone's personal belongings, supplies, food, water—anything you want. We will be the supply holder and the supply giver. We will need a cut of the findings, of course. While you use our program, we'll guarantee that your belongings are safe and sound... but we'll take 10% of all food and water you deliver to us. This is just to make sure we can keep continuing our service and devote most of our time to keeping our citizens secure."

"Pfft," Vic exhaled.

"That's not terrible," Billy remarked. "They make sure everything you have is safe, and they only take a small cut. It sounds like a good idea."

"Yeah, sounds like a good idea," Vic retorted. "To an everyday person, it sounds like a great idea. But it's a government-mandated service for survival. All commerce goes through them, and they get to take from the poor and give to themselves—doing nothing but offer the illusion of security. They're preying on people's fears. Plus, this will contribute to more crime, which Congress benefits from, too. People will try and take from these public supply units, and if Congress finds something they want over the average citizen, they take it. They kill and pillage everyone they deem as 'criminals,' and gather more and more supplies, making them more and more powerful. They are the jury, judge, and executioner."

I tuned out of the voice speaking over the air-waves and jumped in again mid-sentence: "...also volunteer to work at said outposts. You can't miss them; they're tall, blue, and have the famous Congress symbol painted on them. As a volunteer, you report to us—any strange happenings, and we'll take care of the problem. You will be rewarded for your work in the form of free food and water. If you volunteer your time to help your community, we'll compensate you with never having to risk your life for the bare necessities of life ever again."

"They're recruiting..." Chris said. "They're offering security for work, making the Forlorn weaker as a result; no one will ever want to fight. They'll conform to the new norm. They're creating an army to spread their influence." He stood from his seat and paced the foyer.

"Also," Congress Member A continued, "we're also starting our Street Cleaning Program within the next few days. We'll send our Street Cleaners out at night to dispose of the riff-raff, thus employing a new curfew at dusk. Anyone caught out after night will be put to death. No exceptions. During the day, Street Cleaners may still be out and about, looking for suspicious activity. The idea behind the program is to make our Forlorn safer and eventually turn ourselves into a Prospect. Ah, doesn't that sound nice? 'For we must consider that we shall be as a city upon a hill. The eyes of all people are upon us so that if we shall deal falsely with our God, in this work we have undertaken... we shall be made a story and a by-word through the world.' That's John Winthrop, 1630. He knew what it was like to build a new world out of scraps. We should all follow in his model. As such, we at Congress have decided that our Forlorn will henceforth be called, "The City Upon a Hill"! Or, "The City" for short.

"To commemorate this wondrous moment, I am proud to announce that, starting soon, we will be holding Fireside Chats with our very own Congress Member K!"

"Congress Member K?" Chris and Vic exclaimed. Chris continued, "They have another?"

"A new Congress Member..." Vic said.

"Our newest Member to Congress will be providing our Citizens with a calm, cooling atmosphere for them to lay their heads down at night, coaxed with his wonderous and endless stories of a life once lived."

"So, it's propaganda, huh?" Jack snouted. "They've gotta cover all their bases, don't they?"

"Seems like it," Vic said. "But a new Member..."

"Likely means there's a new orphan, too," Chris commented. "We're now missing Congress Member I and K's children... they're out there somewhere, desperate, likely begging for a place to belong—for a place to call home."

Congress Member A continued his speech: "We're also aware that the area nearest the Barren Wasteland is heavily crime-ridden; we've heard the complaints and have decided to become much stricter with our policies and programs. Good Citizens will follow our new rules and survive. Bad Citizens will eventually get caught and eradicated. Any resistance to these new programs and laws is punishable by death.

"We hope that Congress can continue to provide a safer environment for our City. We intend to update our programs and expand our governing system to include you—the Citizens—in helping our community become the best it can be. Until next time, then! Ciao!"

A loud click ended the transmission. The air around us felt heavy. The fading light outside placed gloom into the room. Our expressions were sullen as if all our loved ones were just annihilated. In a way, they were—our fathers were effectively ending the program Vic and Chris tried to start—our source of supplies and food from the last few months evaporated and burned in just a couple of days.

Chris was the only one who didn't look broken; he was livid. He couldn't sit still. "No!" he yelled. "Our work, everything we tried to accomplish—crushed in one swift movement—gone in a single broadcast. There's no way Sylum and Gramble won't stay with us—not after that. Congress is trying to control everyone in the city. They want to run everything—have mindless, thoughtless, scared people working for them. All so they don't have to get their hands dirty anymore. I want to storm up to their 'Capitol' and scream! I want to barge through their doors and grab my father by the neck and tell him, 'How could you do this? How could you do this?'" Chris sat down and buried his head in his hands. "I... I feel helpless. I feel helpless, and that's what I'm angriest about; I can't do anything. I need to keep the group's best interest; that's what you all elected me to do. This means if I have to give in to their demands to keep you all safe and alive... I will."

"No way," Vic said. "You will not succumb to the very group we stand against!"

"I don't have much of a choice, Vic!" Chris replied. "They'll put to death those who don't comply. It seems like the only correct choice."

I spoke without thinking: "What if the correct choice isn't the right one?" My head was still toward the floor, not looking up at Chris or Vic. I listened to their fight, but thought aloud by accident, or it must have been. I wouldn't normally stand against Chris's better judgment, but something in me forced me to blurt out my thoughts before I knew exactly what I said.

"What do you mean?" Chris asked. "What's the right choice?"

"The right choice is giving in. That's what they want. The correct choice is to give them the very thing they loathe."

It took Vic a few seconds to understand what I was getting at. When he did, he scrambled over to me and tried to cover my mouth. He quickly exclaimed, "No, Mike, I don't think—"

I pushed him away. "We fight back. We give them hell. We disrupt everything they stand for and throw it right back at them."

"Mike?" Jack said. "You sure that fall didn't mess up your brain? That's inconceivable. Going up against the most powerful organization in the city? You just fought them today— you had a one-person advantage against them—and you still lost! You four have the scrapes and bruises—!"

"That's because of their devices."

"Devices—what devices?" Myles spoke up. "I'm sorry to jump in, but you guys didn't mention anything about devices," he gestured to Vic and Sarah.

"The Congress members had these chips of metal embedded in their ears. They gave off a faint purple glow, and whenever I tried to throw a punch, they'd glow brighter, then... I'd miss, or they'd dodge. It was as if they could see what I was about to do before I did it."

"Even still, they're grown adults; we're just a bunch of kids. What chance do we stand against them?" Jack said.

"Because we have this." I pulled out the ear device from my pocket and showed it to the group.

"What is that?" Myles asked, fixated on the device's perfect sheen.

"I'm not sure, but it's what Congress was using when we fought against them."

"It has a purple glow... " Sarah said. "I noticed my father's arms glowed purple a few times... "

"It likely had something to do with this," I said, holding the device out further. "They must have dropped one when they were chasing you, but we can use it to fight them!"

"You think Congress is just going to take this lying down?" Chris said, his anger boiling over me. His words seared on my skin. "If that's their big, new powerful weapon, they'll be on the lookout for it. They'll figure out it was left, and when they see it is gone, they'll anticipate someone using it against them. And now that they expect an attack coming, you still want to fight them?" Tch. Stupid boy," he said offhandedly. He crossed his arms and looked out the window.

"Hey!" I exclaimed. I slowly got up and approached Chris, who was still on the floor. "I'm more than just a stupid boy, ok? I can hold my own; I wasn't expecting them to be outmaneuvering everything I did."

"Well, get used to it, because there's a lot of things that happen in life without you expecting it," Chris retorted. He stood up and towered over me. "I lost my best friend to this world, and I'll be damned if I'm going to stand by and let anyone else I care about suffer the same fate."

"We won't!" I yelled, holding up the earpiece. "We can win!"

"How? How are we going to win against them with just a simple earring?"

"We recruit, we find people to fight against them, we... " I lost my train of thought to the sound of Chris's laughter. "We can do this! If you'd just get your head out of your ass and decided to follow through with something for a change, you'd see that too."

The room grew silent when I said that. The air felt more cumbersome than it was before. I felt light-headed. My vision began to blur once more.

"Excuse me?" he asked dumbfounded.

"I can't believe you'd stand by and contribute to their corruption and not stand up for what's right."

"I don't want you to die; that's what's right."

"I don't care if I die if it's a cause I believe in—"

"So what if you believe in it? You value an idea over your own life?" He was directly in front of me and spoke down to me from his skyscraper height.

"I'll die for what I believe in before I live my life knowing I'm a slave!" I screamed at Chris's throat. I anticipated his response—awaited some centrist answer about how it is never ok to let anyone die for any reason. I waited for him to say how death ends your fight. Instead, he looked down at me, sighed, then calmly walked away. He resigned himself to his room. I sat down next to Melody and watched Billy light a flame inside a lantern.

"For the record," Jack said, "I'm down for a fight."

"Yeah," Sarah chimed in, "I'll be dead before I do anything on my father's behalf."

"Same here," Myles said. "I'm not the best at fighting, but I'm sure I'd find my purpose."

"You know where I stand," Melody told me, nudging my shoulder.

"It was my idea, and I stand behind it," Vic said. "But Mike, that was between you and me."

"I know, and I'm sorry, Vic," I said. "I wasn't going to just sit here and let Chris decide our fate, though. If we're going to fight, it's gotta be now."

"If you wanted to fight, it should have been earlier," Billy said. "They're gonna start recruiting by the droves; it'll be harder than before to take them out. It was only 11 of them today; tomorrow it'll be an entire city against us."

"That's why we'll convince other groups to join us," I told him. "We get the city to turn against them. If we stay alert—stay vigilant—and convince everyone that they're the enemy, not us—we can beat them."

"What about the device?" Myles asked. "How are you going to get around that? We don't even know how it works or what it is."

"I'm not sure," I admitted. "But we can deal with that later. I'm in no condition to fight now; none of us are. This will be our secret; we'll play along on the surface but cause an uproar underneath."

"We can hide our identities!" Sarah said. "We can wear those goggles, and masks, or whatever downstairs and assume a new identity. A supergroup—and Congress will never know it's us."

"I like it," Vic said. "Keep that idea, Sarah." He smiled and nodded his head. "This might work."

"It will work," I said. "If it doesn't, we're dead."

"But that's the risk we take, right?" Melody asked. "If we have nothing to lose, what's stopping us from trying?"

"But guys," Billy said, "It's still our fathers we're talking about here. Are you all ok with killing what's left of our families?"

"If needed, we will," Vic replied diligently. "There is no place in this world for their type."

"My father is dead to me anyway," Sarah said. "If he were to die, it'd make me happy. He's harmed us already—he tried to kill us. He'll pay for what he's done."

I nodded. "We won't become senseless murderers. We'll help those who are being oppressed and stop the oppressors from hurting anyone else. If that's not justice, then I don't know what is."

"When you put it that way..." Billy trailed off. "Ok, I'm in. I'd rather see justice prevail in this world over fear."

We all agreed. Sarah drafted outfit ideas for our new group while threw around names. None of them stuck, and we eventually ended up parodying our own self-reliance rather than forming an actual game plan. We moved to our sleeping quarters once night crept in through the windows. Vic said he would meet with Chris in the morning and try and talk to him some more.

While everyone else slept, I couldn't calm down. Adrenaline coursed through my veins after standing up to Chris, and my bodily injuries still infuriated me. The idea that just because it's hard we stood no chance burned my soul. How would anyone stop them from taking over and running the city like a totalitarian oligarchy? Chris formed this group out of the orphans of Congress, but when given a chance to act, he wants to back out? These thoughts plagued my mind as I grew angrier with each passing minute. When I was sure Melody and Myles were fast asleep, I crept out of our room and made my way downstairs. I grabbed a small light, crawled through the rubble, and went to the classroom. I tore the whiteboard from the wall. I tunneled it back through the crawlspace, covered my tracks, and went to work. I wiped off the writing previously on the board, took markers, and wrote all over it.

Initially hesitant to share my ideas with the group, I wanted to make a difference in the world outside of the confines of the orphanage. I wanted to take back the city and reclaim it to its former glory. I wanted to create a city like the ones I read about in the library—a world where people could live without fear of their next meal, not terrified by the million ways they could die that day. Death was always so far away for people of the old world—they could plan for it. If I could create that security—real security—I felt like I would have served the world justice.

The next morning, I woke up later than usual. I walked downstairs to see everyone standing in the foyer, crowded around the wall. They gazed at the large whiteboard, now propped up against the wall.

On the board was a large-scale calendar. It was detailed with dates for the rest of the month, previous events from earlier in the month, and ideas for how to run the next few weeks. Some days said, "Gathering materials", "Practicing combat", and next to these tasks were the names of group members. The word above the calendar read, "October", and on the board, the date 16 had the word "TODAY" written in it, filling the entire square. The day before it—the 15ht—read, "The day we got our asses beat."

Next to the calendar was the word, "Fighters". Under the title were the names: Mike, Melody, Vic, Billy, Jack, Sarah, Myles. The only name missing from the list was Chris. Under the calendar was a phrase, written at an angle:

"We are the Long-Forgotten Sons", it read. The word "Sons" had numerous red underlines beneath it. Next to this phrase was a symbol:

"Who did this?" Chris barked.

"Did someone break-in? What happened?" said Vic.

"What does it mean?" Myles wondered.

Everyone stood in awe of the board; no one dared touch it. I made my way through the crowd, grabbed a marker, and added a word to the end of the phrase so it read: "We are the Long Forgotten Sons & Daughters," with more lines underneath "& Daughters." I placed the cap back on the marker and faced the crowd.

"This was you?" Chris asked.

"Yup."

"What for?"

"I was angry. I felt hopeless and useless. So, I dug this out and vented my frustrations. This is a calendar; it's a method I've been using to keep track of the days since I was little. I think we can use it as a group."

"What about the sentence?" Billy asked.

"It's art."

"And the symbol," Vic said, "Does that say... VIC?"

"I guess," I replied. "I don't know; the symbol just came to me—I needed to create art, and this was the art I created."

"Well, I like it," Sarah said. She approached the board and studied it. "I think it's a cute design!"

Jack pointed to the list that said, "Fighters" and blurted, "Ha-ha! Hey, Chris! Your name isn't on the list! Oh man, that's so petty!"

Chris investigated. "I see... " he muttered. He took a deep breath and turned to face me. He towered over me; his eyes looked red like hot lasers. "This is because of me, isn't it?"

"It is," I said, boldly, "You're too cautious sometimes. While I admire that about you, it has its faults, too. You started this group because we are all orphans of the Members of Congress. We live in an orphanage as if to remind us every day of who we are. How can you hear Vic's father proclaim Congress's plans over a speaker system and not want to take arms against them? I know you don't want to see anyone hurt, and we don't want to get hurt, either. But we all talked last night, and everyone is on my side, Chris. We all want to fight, and we want you to lead us in that fight."

Chris didn't answer immediately. He returned to the whiteboard and studied it some more. "'The Sons', huh?" he said. "I like it. We are the Long Forgotten Sons of Congress."

"Umm, and daughters!" Melody added. She jaunted over to the whiteboard and pointed to my addition, "See, it says it right there!"

We shared a laugh and formally decided to take on the fight against Congress. Vic didn't speak his excitement, but he was too giddy to ignore. He wanted this for a long time, and to see his dream realized was special.

The rest of the day was spent mostly in celebration, despite Congress's oppression. Chris wanted to go and meet with the other groups to gauge their thoughts. Melody and Sarah spent the day designing our new outfits for our new personas. Vic and Jack went to get alcohol from a place Vic came across recently, and I helped Billy prepare a grand feast for that night.

"Dinner!" I yelled when the food was ready. They came up and crowded around Billy, who passed onto everyone's plate. Soon, Melody and Sarah also went up the stairs.

"Ahem," Sarah grunted, grabbing everyone's attention. "Introducing the new and improved outfits! Featuring the lovely and beautiful: Melody Loveless!" Melody strutted into the room, purposefully showing-off her physique in a comedic manner. She wore dark glasses, where you couldn't see the eyes underneath. Her nose and mouth were covered by a black bike mask, which descended into a faded red scarf around the neck. They drew my "VIC" design onto the mask in white coloring, which made it stand out above all else. Her hair was bundled best it could into a black beret, though her frizzled hair still peeped from under the hat.

"It looks silly," Jack said, snide.

Sarah got huffy. "Hey, it was my idea!"

"Oh," he said. "Well, then it definitely looks stupid." Sarah playfully hit Jack a few times, but we all laughed it off. They joined the feast, and we decided that her design would become our new attire.

The alcohol Vic brought back was weak, though we welcomed the change in taste. We dispersed and walked around the foyer, having our own small conversations with one another. Jack and Sarah stuck near each other. Myles, Billy, and Melody talked about their endeavors in reading; Myles had started reading some of the "How-To" books Melody brought him, and he spoke about how difficult they were. My group consisted of Vic and Chris.

"How did the meetings go?" Vic asked as he shoved a forkful of cooked carrots into his mouth.

"Not great," Chris replied. "They said they're either unsure or going to use Congress's supply service. They didn't seem too concerned about the livelihoods of their day-to-day lives changing, but I expressed caution anyway. With more convincing, I'm sure we can work out a deal of some sort, though. Sylum and Gramble have no reason to attack us. I think we are in a safe place to keep pressing and pushing them on it."

"You didn't tell them about us, did you?" Vic expressed. "About our plans to fight against Congress?"

"No, I didn't. That's our secret for the time being."

"Good." Vic cleaned his plate and walked over to give his thanks to Billy for the meal.

"I have to ask," Chris said to me, "Where did you get that giant whiteboard from?"

"I can't say," I replied.

"Is it related to where the vegetables come from?" he asked. I looked away. "Mike, you have some qualities of a great leader, you know that?"

My eyes widened and I looked back at Chris. "Do you mean that?"

"I do. However, you have just as many qualities that hold you back. One of them is your constant little lies and secrets. If you want people to trust you, you can't keep every little thing hidden from people."

"I'm sorry," I said, "But this time I really can't tell you. It's for the betterment of the group, I swear."

"Mike, I have a question: Why is it that you can't reveal your secrets to anyone, but you were magnificent when blurting out Vic's secret?" I looked away again. "I'll respect this new secret if it truly must be kept hidden. However, in the future, you tell me, or Vic, or anyone else about anything on your mind. If you die, your secrets go down with you."

I nodded my head and ate more food. "I helped," I said with my mouth full.

"With Vic's idea?" he asked.

I swallowed. "Huh? Oh, no. I was talking about with dinner."

"Oh." Chris blushed.

"But, in a way, sort of with that, too," I swallowed again. "He talked with me about it, and I helped make him more confident."

"So, it was his idea, then?" Chris asked.

"Yeah. It was his idea."

"Hmm..." he readjusted his beanie.

"Is that a problem?" I asked.

"Not initially, or at least not in an orthodox manner."

"What?"

"He's smart—too smart, sometimes. I'm afraid he's hiding something..."

"Hiding something?" I chuckled. "I don't think so. You're too paranoid, Chris. You're always overthinking, considering everything more than you should. What would Vic even want out of some 'ulterior motive' or something? The only thing he was hiding from you was the idea to take down Congress, that's all—trust me."

"Alright," Chris exhaled. "I should try unwinding sometimes, huh?" He looked at his glass of nearly-empty booze. "I'll need to find some stronger stuff of this, then." We laughed. "Also, Mike, I want to apologize for last night. I was out of line to yell at you; you didn't deserve that after the day you'd had."

"It's fine," I said. "I'm sorry, too. I shouldn't have gotten so mad either. You fixed me up," I said, showing my bandaged hand and arm. "Honestly, it made me want to fight more. I didn't want to go against your orders, but I was just saying what everyone else was thinking, albeit in a much more aggressive manner. Maybe my fall did mess with my head a little..." I rubbed my bandage and laughed again.

"Nonetheless, I want to make it up to you. I'll offer you a deal; I'll let you take on a bit more responsibility around here, specifically with the fight against Congress. You've proven your worth, what, with this upstairs find, and the vegetables—even if you're keeping that information to yourself. I'll let you go out, lead some raids, and recruit new members to fight against Congress when it is right. I'll take on the duties of structuring our weeks and months if you'll teach me how to use the calendar." I agreed, and we joked around some more about my injuries.

Not too much later, and we turned in for the night. Billy stayed up to clean the dishes, but everyone else reported to their rooms to prepare for the ongoing fight for our lives.

I went up to the rooftop to look out at the city. Despite seeing Congress's corruption all around, and its expansion at an alarming rate, the city was still elegant. The lights, now turned Congress-blue, reflected off the tall tower in the distance reminded me of wandering through the city streets for the first time after I left my father. The sense of freedom to do whatever I wanted, go wherever I wanted, and be anywhere I wanted still rang true to me. A cold wind blew across the roof and flew through my course, greasy hair. The smell of stagnation stung my nostrils, but the way the lights bounced off windows and danced their way into my retinas was too much for me to care. There was a personal goal for me to reach in The Inner City, too; the goal of seeing real electricity flowing through its underbelly. The shining lights from a distance proved to me that goal was worth chasing.

The door to the rooftop opened, and Melody met my gaze. She wore a thick, purple coat and a scarf. She sat down next to me, slipped on fingerless cloth gloves, and took my hand. She smiled. "I'm proud of you, Mike."

"For what?"

"For a lot of things. For always being there for me, for carrying me back yesterday, for standing up for what you believe in."

I shook my head. "I just said what was on everyone's mind."

"Still," she pressed, "it takes some moxie to stand in the face of a leader."

"Figured I'd have to get used to it if we're going up against Congress," I remarked.

She smiled and put a tighter hold between our fingers. My hand still hurt from the day before, but her soft palms comforted my pain. The warmth of her palms covered in the gloves was fuzzy, but our fingers embraced the nighttime cold. "I was thinking," she began, "I'm getting tired of reading stories. I feel like there's nothing new to read; everything borrows from everything else. I want to write something new for myself."

I looked at her. Hair blew in her face, and she brushed it to the side. "You want to be a writer?" I asked.

"Not like that," she said, "I don't want to write made-up stories. I want to write about our story—you and me. We'll keep tabs on our lives together and all the stuff we do. Except, I don't want it just to be boring old, 'We did this, then we did this, blah blah blah blah.'" She made a mouth with her free hand, and we laughed at her silliness. "I want to create art—add our something to the library someday. I don't know; I just think we should retain some record, right? Fifty years from now, who's going to remember our story?"

I had no words. My only instinct was to match her request with my lips, pressing against hers in a remarkable show of affection. Her lips were designed for kissing, and I was their humble servant. The wind changed direction, blowing hair into my face. Her hair created a tunnel, where I could see nothing but the faint outline of her countenance locked with mine. She shielded me from the changing wind. The wool in our jackets pressed against our hot bodies and kept us warm while the temperature dropped.

We looked out at the blue-lit tower, which seemed so far away. Our arms sheltered each other. We dipped our heads in as if our minds could talk through tactility. Over the speakers we heard, "Good night, Citizens. Volunteer sign-ups start tomorrow morning. Rise and shine; we'll see you there."

A Sneak Preview from:

VICTIMS
Part 2

Chapter 1

"My family was poor; we had nothing to barter with. That was true even before The Fallout. Strangely enough, my father said that we became richer when the world ended. As the world fell into obligatory chaos, everyone else fell so hard that we had more equity by comparison. Sadly, that's still the case, but we are slightly better off now than we were then. Ever since Congress began their work program in our district, my father has been able to keep guard during the night, which keeps us fed. I don't know if I agree with Congress's motives, but hey—they feed us, so I'm complicit whether I like it or not.

"This occurred before that, though—I was nine years old then; I'm nine and a half now. It was when my family was destitute. We had maybe one night's food left for the four of us to share; my mother, father, sister, and I had one can of expired canned meat to split between us. We were so hungry and sick from the nugatory scraps we forced our infirm stomachs to digest. My parents let my sister and I split the last can, and I remember her throwing it all up later that evening. She became so ill she could barely stand. I wouldn't sit by and let her die on us.

"My mother had always told me not to wander the streets at night. My father would go out on his own, and he'd sometimes come back bleeding or hurt in other ways. He has three fingers on his right hand now. I always assumed monsters came out at night and attacked the City. I wasn't entirely wrong, but it wasn't like the monsters in fairy tales. Regardless, I thought my mother was being overprotective of my sister and me; I know it's a hard life for women, especially, and I was just a kid. What did I know about survival or caring for others?

"One night while my family slept, I snuck out. I had overheard my father talking about a settlement not too far from where we lived. He thought it might have some food we could take and some other supplies, too. I pretended I was asleep, but I heard every word. I made sure to make plenty of mental notes as he thoroughly described its location.

"I snuck out in the crepuscular hours of the night and followed every direction I could remember. I'd never set foot outside of our home before, so it was like a whole new world for me. There was different air for me to breathe. That's also when I learned we survived in a tenebrous, sunken-in furniture store. It looked uninhabitable, but my family got by.

"I wormed my way out of my home and stood in the darkened streets. I stole a flashlight from my father and turned it on. Streetlights beamed candescent lighting on the brittle roads, but it was still too dim for me to see. I crept through the streets; every frivolous noise forced my heart to shake and my every bone to stiffen. The blustering wind made it much harder to move my way through this dusty wasteland we call home.

"I had to hide when I first saw the searchlights. They were scary. Giant balls of light circled a large, wooden tower.

Some men in suits patrolled on top, guiding the lights, continually changing their positions, and looking around for some semblance of illicit activity. Some static noise came from atop the wooden titan, but I was too scared to listen. It took me ten minutes, but I maneuvered around the lights, dodging the scary men.

"It took a little while after that, but I soon found the building matching my father's description. Light shimmered off the jagged windows, and I could read a sign: "Amit's Bakery." I searched for a few minutes before finding a small crawlspace I could fit through. I don't know how my father would have ever made it in; even I barely fit! Once I was inside, it was like a dream come true. There was so much food, and water, and materials, and tools, and books! I remember I took off my shirt and forged a small bag out of the fabric and stuffed everything I could carry in it. I was cold, but my heart was beating so fast from glee that I didn't care. My extempore bag couldn't hold much more; cans fell out of my shirt-bag and rolled on the dirty ground, but I'd pick them up and struggle to stuff them in again.

"As I stuffed a bag of homemade bread in my mouth, I heard a noise. It was the sound of a can falling on the ground inside the building, but it wasn't from me. Goosebumps formed on my emaciated skin. I instinctually ran out like a mouse caught with a mouthful of decadent cheese. I wasn't sure if it was just happenstance that it fell off a shelf or if someone else was in there with me. I dropped a few cans crawling out of the building. It felt like darkness was encroaching on me. I couldn't tell a simple blanket apart from a monster's unguis or a snake's skin.

"I left the building and shined my light around. It bounced off at least five figures, all hooded and much taller than me. 'So, seems we have a little thief on our hands, huh?' one of them said. Their voice sounded harsh.

"'Yeah, you think he's the one we are looking for?' another one asked.

"'No, this one doesn't have nearly the amount of shit on him. He isn't even dressed the same. And look—he's using his shirt as a bag, for God's sake!'

"I didn't know who God was, but from the sound of it, I didn't want to mess with him.

"The figures crept closer to me, and I cowered in fear. I dropped all the food that was in my shirt and covered my head with the cloth. I remember feeling so cold, so alone, so helpless. I hoped from the bottom of my heart that it was a dream or that my father would rescue me like he always had.

"Then I heard a flurry of footsteps. It sounded like fighting. I removed the shirt from my face and gawked at the ensuing melee. Four new figures had appeared on the scene, looking more dignified than the others. While the scary people wore black hoods, they wore some beret-looking thing, bandanas, thick sunglasses or goggles, a scarf, and a flowy cape over top black clothes. They almost blended into the darkness yet shined through it with their flowy attire. I should have felt scared, but once they appeared, I knew it was alright.

"They were so cool! They were jumping around, pummeling the scary guys! One of the scary guys had their hands up trying to punch them, but then the good guy backed up and did a jump kick into him! He then landed on the scary guy, took his head, and slammed it into the concrete. I heard a crack noise, and I couldn't tell if that was the ground or his head. Another scary guy jumped on that good guy's back, and another good guy came up and stabbed the scary guy in the back, threw him into a wall, then sliced at his chest. They moved so fast I could barely keep up! This all happened within seconds. On the other end, one of the good guys was fist-fighting one of the scary guys and eventually threw a punch that made the scary guy stumble. The good guy then jammed his elbow into his back and sent him straight to the floor!

"The last good guy, oh my gosh, it was so cool! Ok, so two scary guys were on him, right? I thought he was done for. But! Then a purple, lustrous glow appeared in a sphere around him, and it was in, like, a grid fashion. I don't know what happened next because it was so fast, but he took out a small knife, and light bounced off the blade as it moved around the inside of that sphere. It was a blur to me. He then front-flipped out of the field and landed on all fours. The two scary guys fell to the floor and almost landed on top of one another. They saved me.

"I couldn't get the best view of them before the fight. It was so dark, and I was so scared—everything happened so fast. But I put my flashlight to one of their faces—I had to see them. The shaky light from my terrified fingers illuminated them—The Long Forgotten Sons! I had only heard of them before as a myth—as a legend. I didn't know they actually existed! My mother and father used them as a scare tactic so I wouldn't leave the house—once I realized monsters don't exist. They said things like they were evil, or they were murders, but they saved me! How could they be evil if they defended a nine-year-old kid?

"One of them—the one who had that purple sphere thing—he helped me pick up the food I dropped and even gave me a proper bag to carry it in. I remember that I cried. I don't know if it was from fear or happiness or what, but I sobbed, and I couldn't stop. It was the most relieving cry I'd ever had; it felt natural—like something I had to do. Like my whole life had been leading to that moment, and my spirit was so ecstatic it couldn't help but cry…"

"What? Hahaha! You cried like a little baby? That's rich, man, that's rich. And, oh, come on, Collin! I haven't known you but three months, and you're trying to tell me the Sons saved you? You tell some tall tales, but you're saying your first night out, you ran into the Sons? Even Congress has a hard time tracking them down! There's a bounty on their heads; why didn't you try and take them down?"

"Why would I do that? They saved me! They aren't bad people."

"Yeah, well, I don't care what they did. The reward for their heads is good enough for me."

"Do you really think you could take them? They wiped the floor of five guys, especially the one with that purple light. Do you really think you alone could have stopped them?"

"Hey, shut up! I'm older than you, you know!"

"Yeah, by, like, five weeks."

"That's older, ain't it?"

"Anyway, I took the food home to my family, and we ate for another week thanks to them. I wish I could run into the Sons again and properly thank them for what they did for us."

"Seriously? You sure that purple-sphere whatever didn't brainwash you?"

"Yes, I swear! You're the brainwashed one for thinking they're bad. They were super cool, and they fought with such skill! It was like a comic book character!"

"A what?"

"Never mind; you wouldn't know what that is. I feel like they could be the ones to fight against all this. I don't wanna just keep living—no, I don't wanna just keep surviving day-to-day. I want to see real progress in the world instead of seeing everyone live subservient to Congress. I don't want my father to risk his life every day, making only enough food to survive tomorrow. I'll never forget what the purple-sphere guy said to me that night: 'Cry all of your tears to-night. For tomorrow, you and I will be the ones leading the revolution.'"

"Hahaha! Seriously, Collin? Oh, come on! You're so gullible! You're so inexperienced, I swear."

"Don't laugh at me! You weren't there. You can't possibly understand. Maybe I can be like them someday. Maybe not everyone is so bad after all."

GET THE NEXT IN THE SERIES

VICTIMS

Part 2

Follow @PrestonLingle

Follow "Victims Book Series"

Join the newsletter for exclusive
info and promotions

www.ingramcontent.com/pod-product-compliance
Lightning Source LLC
Chambersburg PA
CBHW021008120726
47905CB00009B/2908

* 9 7 8 0 9 9 9 3 4 2 7 0 1 *